Mindy

Mindy

By
June Strong

Southern Publishing Association
Nashville, Tennessee

ACKNOWLEDGMENTS

My special thanks to

Members of the Writers' Workshop for listening, chapter by chapter, and for administering small doses of criticism along with generous drafts of encouragement.

Don and the children for bearing with grace and good humor a rather erratic household schedule for over two years.

Gladys Preston, who typed her way bravely into the jungle of my heavily edited third draft, bringing order out of chaos.

My young friend Stephanie, who at the beginning read the early chapters and said, "Hurry and finish. I can't wait to read it all." Sometimes that's all that kept me going.

Copyright © 1977 by
Southern Publishing Association
Library of Congress
Catalog Card No. 77-77429
SBN 8127-0139-9

This book was
Edited by Gerald Wheeler
Cover design by Brad Whitfield
Book design by Dean Tucker

Type set 11/12 Souvenir
Printed in U.S.A.

FOREWORD

Nearly every event in this story really happened to a young woman long ago. In this sense it is a *true* book.

Her reactions to these events, her emotions, her thoughts, her seeking after God, are all so intermingled with my own that I can scarce tell where hers leave off and mine begin. In this sense it is *a book of truth,* or perhaps I should say *a search for truth;* for Mindy sought to know all that is proper and possible for humanity to know of God, and so do I.

The book bears other messages as well, but I shall not spell them out for you, choosing rather that you stumble upon them for yourself.

It is also my hope that you find this story of one woman's ordinary, yet not-so-ordinary, life a pleasant reading experience.

The Author

For obvious reasons the names of all characters in this book have been altered.

PREFACE

Calvin Coolidge—nicknamed "Silent Cal" by his associates—typified Vermonters. According to Foster Dulles, "There was no joy of living in his makeup." Hardworking, virtuous, solemn, frugal, and closemouthed, Calvin Coolidge shortly after his marriage returned home from work with a bag stuffed with fifty-two pairs of hole-ridden socks. When his bride asked if he had married her to mend his clothes, he soberly replied, "No, but I find it mighty handy."

The American stereotype of individuality, sternness, and determination has traditionally focused to the point of greatest intensity in Vermont. Their wresting a living from the stubborn land produced strong bodies and equally strong wills. There the Puritan work ethic became the chief virtue, and emotionalism the supreme vice. There one showed devotion to God in stern worship and devotion to family through material support, not by giving vent to feelings. There solidity of behavior—not ease of expressing oneself—characterized the individual.

Against this setting, *Mindy—Tintype of a Marriage* unfolds its story of the drama and trauma of the alternating attraction and revulsion that mark and mar the marriage of disparate personalities who have fallen deeply in love.

What contributed to the tension between Mindy's relationship to God as she understood Him and her relationship to Carl as she understood him? It was, in part, a conflict based on her Adventist scruples, which first antagonized and then alienated the man she loved, and typical Vermont reticence, which bred austere individualists not always prone to verbalize their true feelings.

June Strong's gripping but solemnizing account of Mindy's poignant marriage will leave the reader with bittersweet emotions that undoubtedly parallel those Mindy knew so well. *Mindy—Tintype of a Marriage* creates a mood that no one will soon forget.

The Editors

PART
I

Chapter 1

Fuzzily, through the snowy wind-whipped world of which she was the core, Mindy took her bearings from the fence posts lining the road. This Vermont blizzard was attacking her like a monster. It did not take her seriously but aimed to lift her frail body, long brown coat and all, and drive it about at will.

"Well, think again, Storm. I am human, built to cope, created to survive." She stood tall and straight against the wind, her dark hair whipping in little wisps from under her hood.

"I can do more than survive. I can enjoy." She set the words, cool and silvery, to a tune and let them escape her lips into the wind. She imagined them tinkling into ice notes, catching on twigs and hanging in some new musical form upon the hedgerows. Ice notes tinged with blood. This was not her usual pleasure walk, though often she'd struggled down this same narrow road against some fitful antic of the elements for sheer joy. She walked now as her thrust against the enemy, the disease which had driven her, coughing tiny flecks of blood, to Dr. Wells.

"Tuberculosis," he had said, frowning at her as though she'd contracted the disease out of pure perversity. "You will have to go to the sanatorium."

On the spot she'd determined never to imprison herself behind those frightening brick walls with the chronically ill. "I shall recover at home."

"You are an optimist to use the word *recover,* my dear, though it's quite possible you'll do as well at home as anywhere. There's the fresh-air cure, which is about as hopeless as all the others. You'll be no worse for trying it."

And so she had walked through the hazy autumn afternoons with silly excited leaves cavorting about her high-laced shoes. Through bleak November and on into December's pale buttermilk sunshine and fierce storms.

"Enough. You cannot endure this weather," her mother said. "You will die." But still she walked, as if in defying nature she might defy disease itself.

"Pray," her father urged. "Pray as you walk that God will heal you." Sometimes she did, though she wasn't exactly sure about God. Was He really concerned with seventeen-year-old Mindy Wheeler, Greensboro, Vermont? It was possible to believe Him a personal friend of her father. Her dad was as comfortable with God as with his next-door neighbor. Even her thin, hardworking mother seemed cupped protectively in His hand, but Mindy felt strangely apart from these relationships. Often she saw her father kneeling by his bed praying earnestly, with no concern for eavesdroppers. She had become accustomed to hearing her own name, along with those of her brothers and sister, upon his lips at these moments. It was fitting and good, but she could not picture herself fraternizing with Deity in this way, though she did kneel nightly and offer Him some sort of awkward recognition.

Through the storm she listened for an oncoming horse and sleigh. She had grown to let her days pivot in anticipation about the possibility of its arrival during her walk. Carl Matthews drove a high-spirited black mare and was usually past her before she had time to wonder why it even mattered, but it had become a part of her routine. On the days he did not approach, in a flurry of snow, she felt an unaccustomed bleakness.

Today she didn't really expect him. Wherever he went at this hour, surely it would not be necessary in such weather. It didn't matter much. She loved the feeling of isolation and strength a blizzard birthed in her. So when he whirled out of nowhere into her little white world, she was not prepared. She was still singing that silly ditty into the wind and wondering how she could possibly be so cheerful, yet dying at the same time.

He reined the dancing mare to a stop, and they faced each other in their swirling, white room. She looked a long, appraising moment at this man who had never before done more than raise his hand in greeting as he flashed past. She saw blue eyes, a brilliant October-sky blue, that she'd never seen on a man before. High cheekbones. A straight good nose, and a smile which she had the feeling he did not bestow upon just anyone. His heavy eyebrows had collected little drifts of snow, which made her laugh.

"I'm not sure what's amusing you," he said, still smiling, "but it's nice to find someone who's not afraid of all this weather. Let me drive you home. It's twice as exciting behind Belle." The horse moved about impatiently at mention of her name. Mindy took his mittened hand, and he swung her easily up beside him.

"I don't even know where you live. You're just the mystery girl who walks this valley road in the late afternoon. Sometimes I wonder if I dreamed you, but next day you're always there. How come you're never at the dances in town on Saturday night?"

So soon. Must she grapple with this now? "I'm supposed to be ill," she told him cautiously. It was half the truth anyhow.

It was his turn to laugh. "I'd have sworn you were the hardiest little character in the valley. Who says you're ill?"

13

"Dr. Wells. I have tuberculosis, and I'm taking the fresh air cure."

He sobered. She felt him scrutinizing her carefully, though she did not turn her head to look at him. "So that's why you walk so faithfully. Now, which way is home?"

"Straight ahead and turn right at West Hill Road. It's the big white house beyond the sawmill."

He rearranged the lap robe to cover her knees, gave a little snap to the reins, and they flew, in a spray of snow, back along the road she had just walked. She wondered how he could find the road. Perhaps he depended upon the horse. Pulling scarves across their faces and fighting for breath, they made no attempt to talk. It was a strange way to meet, Mindy decided. Much better than an awkward introduction at some stuffy social occasion, however. She'd probably never spend any time with him again, but this had been a special, exhilarating moment to which they both responded. She glanced at him, and the cool blue eyes lighted and warmed for her above the wool muffler.

She had heard about Carl Matthews from Nell. Lovely Nell of the creamy skin and dancing eyes. Mindy and Nell had been friends from first grade. They had gone together through the whispering, note-writing, arms-entwined stage. Nell dropped in often now with tales of her adventures at the Saturday night square dance. Mindy didn't dance, nor did the rest of her household or the members of her church. Sometimes she asked herself why she conformed. Was she afraid of her father? She knew better. He was mild in all his relationships. She did not want to hurt him, perhaps? Did she have any strong convictions of her own about these trappings of religion? She wasn't sure. But she *had* heard about Carl. "Sometimes he's fun, sometimes he's stern, and *every* girl in town wants him," Nell dimpled in a most betraying manner.

"You, too?" Mindy had asked, a little surprised, for

14

Nell usually enjoyed the variety of her many admirers. "Me most of all," Nell laughed, twirling about in a swirl of long skirts at Mindy's bedside.

It was because he was new, Mindy felt sure. The local boys were all too reminiscent of school days, but this slightly older man from downstate brought with him some mystery of unknown past, however ordinary it may have been. At least now she could report to Nell that she'd not only met him but gone riding with him.

As they spun into her own dooryard and came to a breathtaking stop, she turned to this prize of the Saturday night square dance and said, "That was fun. Now tell me where *you* go every afternoon so promptly at four."

"My father is building a barn a few miles away, and I drive over to pick him up in time for supper. Why don't you start your walk a little earlier tomorrow, and I'll bring you home. I don't want to cut down on your walking time. You must get well." He stopped and looked at her curiously once more. "You don't *look* sick, you know. It's hard to believe."

She was glad he couldn't see her minus the color with which the wind and cold had endowed her. And no need that he know how her legs shook even now as he helped her from the sleigh.

"You *will* start early tomorrow? Try to get at least as far as Mill Creek Bridge before I come along. That will give you your usual walking time, and you'll have the ride to look forward to."

"He's just being nice to a poor dying girl," Mindy thought, annoyed, and raised her dark eyes impatiently to tell him thank you just the same, but something in the sober blue ones regarding her left the words piling up on her tongue.

"It will also give *me* something to look forward to," he added, as though reading her thoughts.

In spite of herself she smiled.

"Hey, you're pretty when you do that," and before she could blush, he was gone.

15

Walking into her mother's cozy, lamplit kitchen, she felt strangely new and alive. For the first time in many months she had cause to anticipate a new day.

*   *   *   *   *

When Mindy left home the next afternoon, she did not walk along the road toward Mill Creek Bridge but took a less traveled side path instead. It had not been plowed, and she had to pick her way clumsily among the rough tracks of teams and sleighs. The exhilaration of the evening before had fled, leaving her more depressed than she had been since Dr. Wells first diagnosed her illness. She didn't intend to stagger into Carl Matthews' life with her fits of coughing and all her unexplainable, "No thanks, I don't dance, don't play cards, don't do this or that."

These last months she had been nourished by the shadows shifting and changing across her mountains, by the Oriental loveliness of brown weeds against snow. She had seen in her walking a wild and delicate art she'd never known existed. Sometimes she'd carried a dusty black-eyed Susan half a mile, looking with wonder at its simplicity. It had been a rebirth. Something she could not share with Nell or even her mother.

Once she had found her father sitting on a cliff above the valley road while his waiting team fed idly below. She sat down at his feet, and he put his large rough hand gently upon her brown head. They did not speak at first—just close in a rare and tender silence.

"What do you see, Father?" she asked at last.

His hand stroked her soft hair lovingly. "The footprints of God, Mindy. He has moved across our land with color and imagination. Beauty was supposed to die when sin came along, but God isn't much good at making things ugly, girlie. Even a bare, dead tree has grace, and if it happens to stand against a pink sky, well, the Almighty Himself must be startled at what He's come

16

up with. What do *you* see, Mindy?"

"Our shadows on that boulder to the left. See how the sun glistens on the pine bough over them. Those red leaves caught on the rock are just enough color. It's like a painting."

He moved his hand, and the shadow waved at her. She raised hers in an answering salute.

"Lord, thank You for Mindy. Don't take her away from me unless You have to." Her father's voice caught and was still. Mindy almost expected to see God sitting on the next boulder, smiling at them benignly.

That had been in October. Now it was January. More and more she had been sustained by her inner self, a self grown strong from something she found in the land about her. But today she saw only the churned, soiled snow and her own long shadow lying across it.

Dr. Wells was puzzled that she was still walking. He didn't say so, but his penetrating look had told her he'd not expected her to be up and about. Yet there was the cough, so hard at times it tore at her young body cruelly, and only this morning her handkerchief had come away tinged with blood. Was she winning the battle or losing it? Was the walking only a silly exercise in stubbornness?

"God," she said aloud, "are You there? Do You know that yesterday I was confident and sure, and today I have no courage for the battle? I want my youth. I want to finish school. To teach. Would I make a good teacher, Lord?" For a moment she saw God through her father's eyes, striding across the earth, His garments touching barren trees into pale-green bud, His footsteps blossoming into small patches of wild flowers behind Him. If His eyes fell upon her, she would be well. No death could exist in His presence. She knew that. But He wasn't here. He was remote and far away. A year ago she wasn't even sure He existed, but she no longer questioned that.

She walked a long time. Slowly the despair passed from her. Returning home through the violet shadows of early evening, she saw her younger sister coming to meet

17

her. Pearl was light and laughter, a sunbeam dancing ever at one's fingertips. Mindy smiled at sight of her.

"I'm the bearer of news," Pearl called, gathering her long skirts and running between rows of pines.

Mindy straightened her thin shoulders and stood taller. She had disciplined herself to show her family only strength. What Carl had said was true. Outdoors she didn't look ill. There was something close to beauty in her glowing ivory skin and dark, intense eyes. When she smiled, the sober, almost severe, lines of her face broke into startling radiance for which one was never quite prepared.

"Tell me, little one," she said, "what brings you leaping through the drifts?"

"Three times he drove past the house, Mindy. Three times," Pearl announced, breathless, "looking for you."

"Who?" Mindy asked, outwardly confused, inwardly sure. "Who, Pearl?"

"Why, that boy who brought you home, silly. Finally he stopped and asked Mother if you were sick, and when she said no, that you had probably walked in some other direction, he was angry."

"How do you know?"

"Because he didn't whistle anymore, and he walked right by me on the drive and didn't even see me." Pearl bit her underlip and made her dark eyes big. "You know, Mindy, boys don't walk past *me* in a fog unless something's wrong." Mindy, looking at her saucy, pretty face, had to agree.

Chapter 2

The kitchen, mellow with the last rays of a February sunset, awaited the Sabbath, fresh-baked bread rounding on the shelf between baked beans and berry pies. The pine floor, newly scrubbed, glowed white beneath bands of sunlight. Emma Wheeler removed her apron and sighed softly. Mindy, glancing at her, smiled. "It's the best hour of the week, Mother, but we certainly earn it."

The house was clean, even in its far corners, and food for the Sabbath prepared to require only heating. Through the afternoon each family member had carried pails of hot water to his room to bathe. "We're scrubbed—every inch," Mindy thought—"except inside. Strange we can never wash away the flaws inside even for the Sabbath." She had mentioned this to her father once, and he'd replied that God would help with that, but it took a lifetime.

She heard him now in the back hall removing his heavy outer clothing and talking to her brother Wright. It amazed her that their hardworking household could, on Friday at sundown, come to a complete standstill.

The living room smelled pleasantly of furniture polish and burning apple logs. Emma's thin, chapped hands lay strangely quiet in her lap. Gray hair drawn severely back emphasized her straight features. Mindy wondered how her mother had looked as a girl. It was difficult to imagine her teasing, laughing, carefree, beguiling. Her conversation was now as sparse as her frame.

Hiram, washed and combed, settled into his rocker, sons Nathan and Wright flanking him on either side. Low sun, fingering through starchy curtains, fell across his bronzed face and the open Bible on his knees. "A patriarch, a pilgrim," Mindy thought. A Seventh-day Adventist was indeed a pilgrim. A stranger in the land. Eight or ten families in the area gathered in their homes now at the sunset hour. Everyone else was milking, preparing meals, pitching hay from summer-scented mows.

Hiram looked fondly at his wife for a few moments. "It's good to see you sitting still, Em. You move so fast taking care of us all, I seldom get a real look at you.

"Mindy, I have not heard you cough this day. Am I imagining you look better? Let's thank God for this sign of hope.

"Pearl"—there was a bubble of delight in his throat when he spoke her name—"welcome to the Sabbath, my little one."

He turned to his sons with, "God's blessing on you both." They were there out of respect, having already forsaken his vision in favor of more earthly conquests.

" 'Remember the sabbath day, to keep it holy.' " There was something about this moment of the week which knit all Mindy's raveled emotions into a lovely reasonableness. She caught glimpses of her father's God, sometimes high and lifted up, sometimes tender and very near.

Their voices followed Hiram's. " 'Six days shalt thou labour, and do all thy work: but the seventh day is the sabbath of the Lord thy God: in it thou shalt not do any work, thou, nor thy son, nor thy daughter, thy manservant, nor thy maidservant, nor thy cattle, nor thy stranger that is within thy gates: for in six days the Lord

20

made heaven and earth, the sea, and all that in them is, and rested the seventh day: wherefore the Lord blessed the sabbath day, and hallowed it.' "

"Always remember," Hiram added, "*that* commandment was important enough for God to place it right in the midst of the basic moral laws of His universe."

Pearl squirmed in her chair.

Hiram had barely launched into Matthew 6 when there came a knock at the door. A good firm, businesslike knock. Wright, small-boned and dark, rose to answer it.

With a start, Mindy recognized Carl Matthews' voice intruding upon their sacred circle as though from another planet. Always she had recognized the chasm which yawned between their God-centered home and the outside, but never had it seemed so vast as at this moment. Surely Wright would send him away, telling him to come back another time, but her brother had not been raised to turn anyone from the door, and he brought Carl rather hesitantly into the parlor.

"You have a visitor, Mindy," he announced, regarding his sister with a droll expression.

Hiram filled the gap with his natural hospitality. "Sit down, Carl. We are opening the Sabbath with a few verses of Scripture. It is a privilege to share our time of worship with a guest."

Mindy bit her lip in an attempt not to smile, for this confident young man had been reduced in seconds to an awkward school boy. She felt sure he longed to flee back into a world where God kept His distance and did not require any friendship of man. He managed, however, a courteous thanks and settled down upon the settee beside Wright, looking so uncomfortable that Mindy felt a stirring of pity.

"We are Seventh-day Adventists, Carl," she told him, knowing how strangely the words rattled against his ears. "We believe the Sabbath Christ kept still to be the right day of worship, and we observe it from sunset to sunset." He said nothing, waiting for her father to take up his reading,

21

but those unrevealing blue eyes settled upon Mindy so intently that it was her turn to squirm.

She didn't hear much of Matthew 6, and when they knelt to pray, she could create only silent, disconnected pleas. "Lord, don't let him feel uncomfortable. Don't let Father talk religion to him. Show me how to handle all this."

As they rose from their knees Hiram went to Carl and shook his hand warmly. "We haven't met, my friend, but Mindy told us of the lively ride you gave her. You are welcome in our home. These are my sons, Nathan and Wright; my wife, Emma; and our youngest, Pearl. Now supper is all but on the table, and we insist you stay."

Carl relaxed under Hiram's simple welcome, but not enough to eat with them. "Thanks, but Mother will expect me. Father's working on a barn down near Barre this week; so she's alone with my two younger sisters." He turned to Mindy, coming at last to the purpose of his call. "If the weather favors, I'd like to come and take you riding tomorrow night. There's a speaking contest at the schoolhouse, if you feel up to it. If not, we could just ride. Belle loves a good spin under the stars."

"Oh, do take me to the contest," Mindy responded, so quickly that she startled even herself. She'd not realized her hunger for contact with the normal world beyond her illness till this man shouldered his way boldly through the walls of her loneliness.

When he had gone, the doubts began to trickle in. "Whatever got into me, Mother? I had no intentions of going anywhere with Carl Matthews and have been so careful to avoid him."

"Why?" her mother asked, flat voiced.

"Oh, lots of reasons. I'm germy; I could worsen and die any minute; and I have a strange religion which has already been an embarrassment to him." She could have added that if she ever married, she wanted a deeply spiritual person like her father, but there was a perversity about her this night. She could not give him the

22

satisfaction of such an admission.

"Well, since you've promised him one evening, make it a pleasant one. You've had little enough joy these past months." Her mother added a pan of beans to the island of lamplight on the kitchen table. "Pearl, please slice the bread. Mindy, call the boys."

One evening. Of course it was nothing. She was running ahead, tumbling over obstacles of her own making.

Hiram, she noted, wasn't reading as he usually did while waiting for his Sabbath evening meal, but he sat instead in a rare troubled silence.

*   *   *   *   *

Before the mirror the next night, Mindy examined herself more carefully than she had in a long time. Pearl had combed Mindy's long brown hair back into a bun and curled her bangs till they waved soft and shining on her forehead. Why were her cheeks so pink? From excitement? Surely not from the walk she'd taken hours ago. Perhaps only a reflection from the dark red dress Pearl had chosen for her.

"That V-neckline with the ruffle is just right for you," Pearl concluded, stepping back to survey her creation. "No one's ever going to believe you're fighting a terrible illness, Mindy. Somehow tonight you look like your old self."

"I don't even dare to hope, Pearl, but lately I've *not* been coughing so much—only in the mornings when I get up. I'm so afraid if there's any smoking in the schoolhouse, it will send me into a spasm. I should have been sensible and stayed home."

"And let some other girl have him?" Pearl gazed at her sister, wide-eyed.

"I don't have the faintest idea what I'd do with him if *I* had him. He's all wrong for me, you know."

"Not if you get well."

23

"There's more to it than that, Pearl. I have the feeling he's a good man but not a religious one. There's a difference, you know. I'd always have to be two Mindys, his kind and a private me."

"Well, I certainly don't intend to limit myself to the handful of Adventist boys around here, if *that's* what you're saying."

"I don't really know what I'm saying. Perhaps just that if I had a choice, I'd choose a home like the one I've grown up in."

"You're too serious. Come on. I want to show you off to Mother before he comes."

For Pearl, Mindy twirled about before her family, making the long skirt spray out into a rainbow of reds.

"You look like my old Mindy," her mother said, a tiny, glad smile curving the corners of her mouth.

Wright, about to leave, chuckled from the doorway. "I'm glad I'll be there ahead of you. There's a lot of feudin' goin' on over old Carl in town, and I want to see the girls' faces when he walks in with the only female they've never thought to worry about. To them you're as good as buried, Mindy. Maybe you ought to know that when you make your entrance."

As the door closed upon that little speech Hiram dropped his newspaper and, rising to his feet, took Mindy's hands in his. "I feel God has heard our prayers in your behalf. I'll admit I'd feared we'd never see you again as you look tonight. If He does indeed spare your life, you must be careful not to waste the precious gift."

She said nothing, only kissed him lightly on the cheek. What was there to say? That tonight she felt carefree, almost reckless, not inclined to be one of God's loners. Maybe tomorrow she would feel different.

*   *   *   *   *

Later, tucked snugly into the sleigh beside Carl, she looked up at the far-off sky, flung with shattered crystal,

24

and wondered who she really was, this girl spinning along beneath snowy pines with a man she had only begun to know. The night was crackling cold so that the runners made a squeaking noise against the hard-packed snow.

"Aren't you glad you didn't die after all?" There was something lightly mocking in Carl's question. Always this arrogance about him. Yet before she could retort, he added, "It would have been a shame to have missed tonight," with a quick shift to gentleness which disarmed her.

"This *is* a special night for me, Carl. Sort of a celebration of hope."

The scarves which protected their faces weren't conducive to conversation, but they didn't hamper thought, and Mindy would have given a great deal to have peeped into Carl's mind.

As he helped her out of the sleigh at the schoolhouse, she felt an unaccustomed reluctance to make an entrance. This was her schoolhouse. Her people. Her childhood. But she felt no kin to the pig-tailed little girl who had run in and out of this very door through all the chalk and lunch-box years. In walking, fear, loneliness, isolation, there had evolved a new Mindy whom she hardly understood.

She followed Carl through the crowded room, head high, heart fluttering, until her eyes fell upon Wright seated with his girl along a side wall. There was such a look of satisfaction upon his face that she could barely keep the laughter in. *So,* for him she'd play the game. She nodded, smiled, spoke softly to each familiar face, and found it came naturally. Somewhere along the miles of pain and introspection she'd left the unsure schoolgirl behind.

Soon after Carl found seats near the back, Nell appeared beside them. "Mindy, I can't believe my eyes. You're absolutely glowing. What happened to my invalid pal?" She dimpled at Carl, "I know you're endowed with a lot of charm, but I wouldn't have believed you are up to this miracle, Carl."

"I'm afraid I can't take the credit," Carl answered,

not matching her lightness. "I only hope she's as well as she looks."

"I'm still here," Mindy reminded them. "Let's stop discussing me like some medical specimen. I *do* feel better and have hopes of outliving you both."

Carl could not have chosen anything which would have pleased Mindy more than the speaking contest, for it was the sort of thing in which she herself would have enjoyed competing. Words, written or spoken, brought her great pleasure. At its close she found herself surrounded with friends—the curious, the envious, the well-wishers—until at last Carl said gently, "You're going to be awfully tired when you get home, Mindy. I think we should leave."

It was the first time she'd heard him say her name, and it birthed an unexplainable delight in her, akin to finding a patch of rare arbutus in the deep woods.

At her door, after the cold, quiet ride under the stars, he asked her, in his serious way, "Why did you walk another way after I offered to drive you home each day? I almost decided to pretend I'd never met you."

"Why didn't you? It would have been better."

"I found you weren't easy to put out of mind. Every time I thought of you walking, walking, stubbornly, day after day, in your own private war against all the odds, I wanted to help you."

"That's what I was afraid of. I don't want your pity."

"Wrong word, my dear. Admiration."

"You're just being clever with words, Carl. It all means the same thing."

"All right, little miss," he said, cupping her chin in his hand until her eyes lifted to meet his, "after that first half hour with you, every other girl in town seemed like a silly waste of time. Is that what you wanted to hear?"

She had driven the words from him—reluctant, almost angry words. So *he* knew it was all wrong too.

To herself she thought, "Maybe I'll die and solve your problem," but with her hand upon the latch she smiled and said lightly, "When the sun comes up in the morning, you'll find I'm quite dispensable. These stars are the problem."

He ignored her frivolity. "You go straight to bed and sleep late in the morning." Her heart pirouetted about the concern in his voice, concern still tinged with anger.

Through the kitchen window she watched him circle the drive and melt into the darkness. He did not wave or even look back.

Chapter 3

Mud boiled deep along the rutted road over which Mindy and her father jostled toward home behind a team. A brisk April breeze spun Mindy's hair into soft brown fans about her face. Everywhere the sun teased the earth back to life, touching even the thin girl with its healing warmth. Small streams raced their unruly courses along both sides of the road, gnawing at forbidden boundaries with flighty indifference.

They had driven into town for Mindy's monthly checkup, and now she broke the silence. "Aren't you even going to ask me what the doctor said?"

Hiram worked worn leather reins between his calloused hands a moment before answering. "I'm afraid to, girlie. Heartache's harder to bear in the spring than in the winter. I fear we've all built up too much hope."

"I've kept it a secret, Father, but I've not coughed once in three weeks—not even in the mornings—and Dr. Wells with all his listenings couldn't find a single thing to complain about. He said, 'Young lady, either your father's God has smiled on you, or you've outwalked a hopeless disease. Go home and consider yourself cured.' So what do you think of that?"

Hiram's head dropped onto his chest, lips moving in

prayer, dark stains of his tears dotting the wool of his mackinaw.

Mindy slipped her hand into his. "Papa"—she reverted to her little-girl name for him—"tell God a thank-you for me too. I really don't think it was the walking."

Hiram lifted his head and hugged her thin shoulders. "Mindy, I've been so afraid of losing you. I've told God over and over that I would accept His will in this, but the heart knows nothing of such decisions. Now I can feel the sun and hear the birds. That's a redwing blackbird singing right now. Hear it? Your life's been given to you all over new. What are you going to do with it?"

"I've been thinking a lot about that lately. First I must finish high school. Then I'd like to teach. Are those dreams too big for a scrawny farm girl?"

Her father did not answer her question. In fact she doubted if he even heard it. His mind was already ahead. "What about Carl?"

Strange that he should ask that, though the question had not been far from her own mind. Carl had taken her to a box-lunch social, and she'd experienced ridiculous pleasure in being seen with him. Nell, who was now seriously caught up in a romance of her own, repeated the village gossip. Imagine Carl's choosing, of all people, little straitlaced Mindy Wheeler, who couldn't even hope to live long enough to marry.

Then again he'd come on a Sunday afternoon and had asked if he could join her on a walk. He was not a man who walked for pleasure; she knew that. Yet he had stabled Belle in their barn and set out beside her along the bleak March roads.

"Tell me about your family, Carl. You've met all mine, but I know so little about yours—only that you have two sisters."

"They're just little girls," he began. "Carrie's twelve and Sally's ten. She's a pretty one, Sally is. Someday I want you to come and meet my mother. Would you like that?"

"I'd love it." Mindy sensed this woman was special to Carl, the tie between them warm and strong.

Almost as if he read her thoughts, he said, "My father's always been away a lot, working in logging camps or building barns. He's an expert shingle maker. It was always my job to take care of mother and the stock, to see that wood was cut and ready for the stoves. Mother and I've weathered out some pretty rough times through the years, but she's not a complainer, and we've always managed."

Surprising glimpses into the past. She felt a tenderness for the boy who'd carried man-size tasks on shoulders too young. She wondered if he'd minded when the baby girls came along to share his mother's love, but she was too shy to ask.

"Your father, what is he like?"

Carl did not answer at once, and when he did, he chose his words carefully. "Just the opposite of yours. A stern, hard-driving man who drinks too much and has little patience with weakness of any kind. But he's an honest man and a hardworking one."

"He'll frighten me when we meet," Mindy admitted. "I don't know any stern men, except you."

Blue eyes fastened upon her sharply. "Do I frighten you?"

"Sometimes a bit. You're not like my father or my brothers."

"Then why waste your time with me?"

She gave him that quick, startling smile which lighted up her thin face like candlelight. "Because I *like* being a little bit scared of you."

He had stopped her then and held her away from him, looking at her. Shyly she met his gaze and found in his eyes an amused tenderness. Finally, letting her go, he said, "Mindy, what if I'd never found you blowing about in that January blizzard?"

Once, later, he'd taken a village girl to the Saturday dance. Mindy pretended, even to herself, that it didn't matter. The next Saturday night he'd whirled into the dooryard, Belle all ajingle, insisting she go for a drive. Afterward, over cocoa in the kitchen, she asked him why he hadn't taken someone to the dance instead. He'd reached out and taken her hands almost protectively in his. "I've tried, Mindy, to free us both. I'm not what your family planned for you at all. You're young; you need more time to grow and expose yourself to others. I hadn't planned on coming here tonight, but somehow Belle refused to take any other direction. I'm trying to be practical, but you make it difficult."

Mindy looked at him, startled. "I don't mean to. I don't even know how to flirt."

He laughed out loud, a spontaneous, unguarded sound that delighted her. "I know. That's why I love you."

She would always remember that she first heard those words mingled with laughter and spoken lightly, too lightly perhaps to mean anything.

"What about your religion, Mindy?" he went on. "Is it terribly important to you or just something you go along with for your father's sake?"

So there it was, lying like a wounded bird on the table between them—her religion. Was it important enough to raise this constant barrier between them? Could she, even if she tried, cast it aside? Taking her hands from his, she stacked their cups and saucers neatly, organizing what could be organized.

"For some time, Carl, I've tried to decide this for myself. Since before I met you—even before my sickness. The last year has brought me closer to conclusions. I've tried to read the Bible for myself, not through my father's eyes, and found it difficult. This morning in church I looked about at the others and wondered at their courage. It isn't easy to be different all your life. Several were there alone because their husbands or wives are indifferent or scornful."

"Are there young men suitable for husbands?"

She laughed at his sober, stilted question. "Well, there

31

are some young men, but I have no way of knowing about their marital qualifications. How does one tell?"

"Don't be silly," he blurted out. "You still haven't answered my original question, or don't you know the answer?"

That mocking challenge irritated her. Her head came up, and she met his eyes squarely. "Yes, I do know the answer. Perhaps only now, this moment, have I had the courage to acknowledge it. I have searched the Bible through and through. I cannot find even the slightest hint that God changed His original day of worship from Saturday to Sunday. History makes plain it was man's doing. I don't want to believe this, Carl. I have no desire to be a trailblazer, but truth is a tough companion." There. She had said it. He would leave politely, and she'd never see him again. A high price, but not too high.

He rose, took his coat from a chair, and moved toward the door. Hand upon the knob, he turned to face her. "Well spoken, little friend. The Lord is lucky to have you on His team. Good night."

* * * * *

The earth struggled out of the last grips of March, thrashing between blizzards and melting winds. Mindy, too, knew highs and lows. She worshiped with her fellow believers, at last one with them, no longer wary and searching. She stood, telling them timidly of her convictions, and after the service was enfolded in a warmth of fellowship she'd never known before. Hiram, standing beside her, said nothing, but there was such gladness on his face that she could hardly bear to look.

Riding home in the back seat of the buggy beside her mother, she asked a question that had long bothered her. "Mother, did you feel it was very solemn, almost frightening, when you joined the church?"

"Your father and I made the decision together," Emma replied, as though that were an answer.

32

To herself Mindy thought it wasn't something you decided *with* someone. She tried again. "Does it still seem important to you today?"

Emma Wheeler looked down, uncomfortable. "I'm not much at putting things into words, Mindy, but it's like a candle inside me that burns with a steady flame. Nothing from the outside can ever touch it, and if it were to go out, there'd be nothing left to live for."

Hiram and Pearl in the front seat stopped their chatting to listen, moved by her rare eloquence.

"You mean it burns all the while you're mending and scrubbing and trying to make five dollars do the work of ten?" Pearl asked a bit scornfully.

"It's why I don't really mind scrubbing," Emma said.

Hiram looked back at his wife and smiled. "You girls keep your eyes on your mother. I've learned a heap from her over the years."

She didn't know her mother at all, Mindy decided. She hadn't before and still didn't, but she glimpsed something worth pursuing.

The fitfulness of March with its hints of spring made her walking a pleasure. Carl no longer drove along her road, and sometimes she forgot him for days at a time. Nell, soon to marry, reported that he often brought girls to various activities in town but left early. She thought he looked miserable. Mindy smiled. "You see what you want to see, Nell."

Her strength returned, and with it came old hopes. High school presented problems. She had completed two years at an expense her father could ill afford. It was necessary that she board in Canton some distance away. They had previously managed somehow. She had ironed after school for the village women and thus provided her own food. Now in the fall she hoped to go again if Dr. Wells approved.

*   *   *   *   *

What of Carl? Why had her father asked it? It was hardly an issue since she hadn't seen him in over six weeks. She had almost convinced herself that sunshine on tall tamaracks and daffodils against stone walls were enough in a girl's life. Who needed fierce, blue-eyed young men?

Chapter 4

It never seemed to stop raining all that summer. Crops, too wet to harvest, rotted in fields. Families tightened their belts against the winter. It didn't seem to hurt the garden much. Emma and the girls canned until the cellar groaned with their efforts. Hiram's potato crop, on a high, well-drained spot of land, survived, and he filled the large basement bin to overflowing before putting the remainder on the market. Watching Nathan prod them, pale and thin skinned, off the wagon toward the chute which funneled them into the basement, Hiram said, "Well, Em, there's wood cut for the stoves and food to see us through till spring. The good Lord has kept His word."

"And what about the stock?" she asked. "There's not hay enough to last the winter."

"We'll cross that bridge later. We've a bit of money put aside if it comes to that."

Hiram refused to let Mindy work in the fields, and her mother insisted she rest in the afternoons. Obviously there wasn't going to be any money for high school. She did not even mention it. The winter would be a struggle at best. The thought of spending it hovering about the house like a frail, pampered ghost seemed intolerable, yet there appeared to be no alternative. Thus, in late August when

Hiram said he'd written Mrs. Anders in Canton to reserve a room, she looked at him with unbelieving eyes.

"Father, you can't afford it. I know there's barely money to meet the regular expenses this year. You don't really think I'd make the whole family go without just so I could finish school, do you?"

"No, nor would I. But for what do you think we'll lack? The house is stocked with food, and we do have the milk money every month. If necessary the boys and I can do a bit of lumbering. I've left that wood lot standing a good many years for an emergency. Maybe the time has come."

Mindy flung herself into his arms. "I'll work so hard, Father. I've already decided to do the two years in one."

Her mother, mending at the kitchen table, brought her back to earth. "It wouldn't be good for your health to carry such a work load. Better not to race ahead. Your father failed to mention there's not a penny to buy any clothing for you, or for any of the rest of us for that matter. You can't wear these threadbare cottons to school."

Mindy did not care a great deal about clothes. It was Pearl who loved bright colors and rich fabrics. Nevertheless, her mother had a point. There were a few essentials one must have. Her father had bought her a warm walking coat the year before. Otherwise, most of her scanty wardrobe had been passed down to Pearl, for with returning health, Mindy had filled out and grown taller.

Emma, having robbed the impractical ones of their dreams, now proceeded to return them. "There's an old coat of your father's in the attic. We could probably get a skirt out of it if we were to figure carefully. With the last egg money I bought enough material for a couple of shirtwaists. You'd have the red dress for best. All depends on how bad you want the schoolin'."

"That would do fine, Mother," Mindy agreed. "You know I don't put much stock in clothes." She didn't even want to think of the red dress, much less wear it. There must still be upon it a dusting of snow and starlight and the touch of Carl.

36

Pearl would not let her help with the shirtwaists. "You'll make them just alike and deadly plain. I know you. This beige material will be pretty with the brown skirt from Papa's old coat. I'm going to put some tiny pleats into the front so even though it's tailored, it will have a touch of elegance. I'm still thinking about the pink. If it were for me, I'd trim it with lace, but lace is not for you."

Sun, so rare at this summer ending, shimmered across the crisp new material. "Mindy, leave Pearl and me to this business of making something out of nothing and get out of doors," her mother urged. "Soon enough you'll be cooped up in a classroom."

"I feel guilty. Pearl has nothing new for school, and here she sits sewing away for me. It's not very fair."

"I have your hand-me-downs," Pearl said cheerfully, "and I intend to doctor them up a bit."

"You know Pearl is never happier than when she's creating a new fashion; so run along and enjoy the sun." Her mother made a shooing motion toward the door.

Once outside, Mindy let herself blend into the late August afternoon. On impulse she unlaced her shoes and left them sitting under the spirea bush at the corner of the house. As she walked she unpinned her long hair, letting it tumble over her shoulders. She decided to climb the back hill and indulge herself in a last look at the valley. Sort of a farewell to summer, for when she returned at Thanksgiving, snow would secrete the land.

The grass felt good to her bare feet. She noted with satisfaction that in spite of the steep climb she neither coughed nor found breathing difficult. At the top she stretched out on a sun-warmed ledge where her eyes could traverse the long sweep of valley with its infinite shadings of green. The ribbon of dusty road below tied neighbors comfortingly together across this forested land.

Under the sun's hypnotic spell she must have dozed, for the steady drumming of a horse's hooves eased rhythmically into her consciousness. Lifting her head, she spotted the horse and rider not too far down the road. It was a rare sight in this era of buggies and wagons, but she noted that the man rode bareback with the easy grace of an Indian. There was something heart-tuggingly familiar about the rider as he came closer. Set of shoulders. Tilt of head.

Impulsively she picked up a small rock, and as he rode beneath her she curved it neatly over the treetops and down the cliff which towered at his left. It rattled over rock and rolled into the road in front of him, just as she had planned. Impatiently his eyes arched up and over the cliff, though he did not slacken pace. Already she was on her feet and running toward him, the pink gingham of her long dress gathered in one hand. He reined Belle to a stop, then guided her quickly around the edge of the cliff and up through the long grasses toward Mindy.

She stopped, suddenly aware of her own boldness. The terrible loneliness she had known for him moved over her, washing away pride and reserve. Slipping from the horse, he held out his arms, and she ran into them. In afteryears she often thought that it was there among the goldenrod and purple asters that they were truly wed, for she gave him her heart without so much as his asking. He held her for a long time, not saying a word, only stroking her long hair. Finally, hand in hand, they walked back to the ledge and sat down together.

"I don't know what got into me," Mindy sighed, trying to sound ashamed.

Carl chuckled. "You were the sweetest sight I've seen in all these long months, coming down that hillside with your hair and your skirts flying in the wind. It's been a miserable summer. I've tried to work so hard there'd be no time to think, but it didn't do much good." He was quiet then, waiting, she knew, for her to commit herself. Hadn't she said it all in that immodest flight down the hillside?

Silence grew about them, but she felt no need to talk. Sitting there beside him with the late afternoon sun tossing their long shadows down the granite ledge, she knew only that she was truly happy.

"I'm going back to school next week," she told him finally.

"We're going to be a long ways apart, Mindy. That's one reason I came down your road on my way from town, hoping for a glimpse of you at least, for I, too, am leaving. Father and I are going to be working in a logging camp in the southwestern part of the state all winter." Abruptly he turned to her with excitement. "Does that mean you're well?"

She laughed at his delayed reaction. "As good as new. Can't you tell?"

He looked at her then, so long and thoroughly that her eyes fell before his scrutiny. He tilted her chin and made her look at him. "Sometimes I've awakened in the night," he said, "filled with terror that you'd die, never knowing how I felt about you. Now you are here before me, rosy and stronger, and I shall not be such a fool again. I love you, Mindy, too much to be sensible. I'm sorry. I've tried."

Behind them bees droned lazily in a patch of milkweed. She turned her cheek into his palm, not wanting him to see her tears. She'd had no idea she'd been so hungry for those words.

They talked then of the winter. "I'm going to do my last two years in one," Mindy said. "But I'm not telling my parents, for they still fuss over me. Father won't let me work at all; so I'll have plenty of time to study."

"And time to write to me?"

"Of course. Will you be far back in the mountains cooped up with a bunch of men all winter?"

"That's about it."

"At least I won't have to wonder what you're up to on Saturday nights." She leaned her head against his arm and was comforted by the hard muscular warmth of it. "What about your mother and sisters?"

"Father has hired a neighbor boy to do the chores. Mother can hitch up Belle whenever she needs to go into town."

The horse picked up her head at mention of her name.

"I have to go now," Mindy said. "I've played lady long enough. Mother and Pearl will be getting supper, and I should be helping."

Carl spoke to Belle, and she came toward him with a mincing, playful step that made Mindy laugh. "I'm almost jealous of her. She's so beautiful and knows you so much better than I do."

"Come," Carl invited, helping her up and lifting her onto Belle's back before she had time to protest. "Let's see how you two girls get on together." Pink skirts fluttered about Belle's head, and she sidestepped nervously, but Mindy spoke to her gently until she calmed. Walking before them, Carl guided the horse toward the less-steep southerly descent.

The sun-drenched valley with its bleached late-summer grasses cupped them in peace. There would never be anyone else, Mindy knew, as he walked before her, tall and broad-shouldered, down the hillside.

"Carl," she said softly, "don't turn around or come back. Just listen and keep walking. Look all about you at the river shining below us and the dusty goldenrod along the roadside. At the little cemetery where people, once alive and young as we are now, sleep. Memorize it, and then you will always be able to carry it like a good-luck piece to take out and comfort you when we're apart. Are you still listening?"

He nodded.

"Be sure, because I'm too shy to say it when you're looking at me. I love you."

He started to turn back to her then, but she stopped him sternly. "No, Carl. Please stay there, for you're part of my memory to carry through the winter."

At her doorstep he helped her down, and she felt suddenly very aware of her bare feet and tousled hair.

"This is really good-bye," Carl said. "Father and I leave tomorrow. We are part of the crew who will ready the camp and mark the trees for cutting later on. We go in

40

ahead of the others. I shall think of my little student every day, and when spring comes, then I will tell you everything that's in my heart. Will you wait?"

She nodded, not trusting herself to speak. He kissed the top of her head, sprang onto Belle, and all that was left in the drive was a hazy curtain of dust which wavered and glistened through her tears.

Chapter 5

Three outfits rattled about forlornly in the deep closet of the bedroom to which she'd been assigned in Mrs. Anders' rooming house. Mindy wondered if ever before a girl had gone out to meet the world with such a scanty wardrobe. It had not taken long to put her few belongings into the drawers, and now the remainder of the afternoon stretched before her. She had watched Hiram out of sight with a lump in her throat, but then she'd taken herself sternly to task. "Mindy Wheeler, you are lucky to be able to finish school, and Carl loves you. How dare you cry!"

Throwing on a brown lacy shawl her mother had crocheted for her, she wandered about the town, looking in the shop windows with a country girl's delight.

Later, as dusk softened the angles of day, and lamplight gathered families home, she went back to the rooming house and climbed the stairs to her third-floor room. Upon a little tray she laid out the sandwich and cookies which her mother had packed. Then seating herself at the desk in the corner, she wrote as she ate.

Dear Carl,
Already it seems so long since
we sat together out on the hillside. Our

*separation didn't seem unbearable then, but
. . . When school starts I shall be all right, but
this afternoon has surely had two or three
extra hours. If only Pearl might have come
with me. It's impossible to be lonely with her
around. . . .*

She would write him a bit each day until his first letter arrived. What if he never wrote? She put aside the discomforting thought. She would go to bed early, hurrying morning.

"Dear God," she prayed, kneeling at her bedside, "help me to use well the mind You have given me and not to waste Father's money. Thank You for health and for teaching me never to take it for granted. Bless the dear ones at home and keep them safe." Attempts to pray for Carl left her uneasy. In his strong young manhood he seemed to defy any need of God. When she said lamely, at the last, "Please take care of Carl," she could almost feel amused blue eyes upon her nightgowned back.

Mindy read a chapter from her Bible, and then she lay a few moments looking about the room. The lamp threw a wavering circle of light upon the ceiling. From the open window beside her bed she heard a man's voice and a child's answering laugh as they passed upon the quiet street below. Already she liked this small hideaway. She was no longer Hiram's little girl or yet a wife. Just Mindy Wheeler, eighteen, and eager for tomorrow.

The high school always gave her a feeling of pride. One must climb the long tree-lined street toward the imposing spot from which it overlooked the town. It wasn't dingy and scarred, as some high schools she'd seen, but stately in red brick. Inside, it was filled with hushed chatter, youth, and the smell of chalk like any school.

There were courses to choose, books to buy, and old friends to greet, each of whom asked, "What happened to you last year?" Everything was the same, yet there was a difference. Something vague upon which Mindy could not put her finger.

It took some special arrangements and some pleading with the principal to carry the two-year load in one, but this was finally accomplished.

Upon dismissal, she wandered home through the tingly September afternoon, a pile of books under each arm. She had declined an invitation to join a group going to the drugstore for ice cream. There was neither time nor money for such activities. Depositing her books in her room, she walked briskly three times around the block to fulfill a promise to her mother, then settled in for an evening of study, broken only by a brief supper hour in Mrs. Anders' dining room. It was to be the pattern of her days throughout the school year. She soon realized that it was not the school which had changed, but she.

Girl chatter no longer interested her, and the boys seemed shallow. Somewhere in that sobering seventeenth year she'd left them behind. The revelation was a bit saddening. Girlhood was brief and precious at best.

The first letter from Carl, lying under her door on the third day, delighted her with its neat, elegant script. This was no farm boy's scrawl. There was so much about him that she didn't know.

Friday evening

Dear Mindy:
I've just finished looking at my memory. Are you sure it's such a good idea? It left me lonely. As I worked about the camp today, getting things into shape for the crews to arrive, I thought of you. You would have exclaimed over everything, for even I am awed by this forest now in September when it's overrun with sunlight and ferns, but I expect, come January, it will be bleak enough. Hiked above the timberline yesterday and could see for miles, the Green Mountains on one side and the Adirondacks on the other. I

*felt very small up there, with the wind about
to whip me right off into the next valley and
no other human in sight. It's really wilderness
out here.*

*You must work hard and learn for both of
us, my Mindy, for I had to quit school after
eighth grade and go to work. Father felt it was
time I helped bear my share of the family
expenses. It was not an easy decision to
accept, for I had hoped to go on to high
school.*

*The boss will be in tomorrow, and he'll
take this letter out for me. Once a week is
about all the mail service we can expect.*

Yours,
Carl

Each afternoon she laundered one blouse and ironed
the other. Carefully she sponged the dark brown skirt, top
to bottom, and hung it to air, switching next day to a black
one. The monotony of her wardrobe mattered little, for
she felt strongly her good fortune in simply being alive.
Her studies stimulated and challenged. Often her light
burned late as she read on or struggled with a difficult math
assignment. Her mother would not have approved, but
she'd never felt stronger or happier. Perhaps the year of
looking inward had prepared her for learning in great
gulps.

Twice in the fall her brother Nathan made the long trip
to bring her home for a weekend, and both times she
found the visits revealing. The little room on Maple Street
had become home and the farmhouse only a pleasant
place to visit. The shady streets of the small town framed a
new era of her life which she recognized as an interlude
between childhood and something waiting.

Two days before Christmas she busied herself with
unnecessary dusting and straightening of her small room.
She expected one of her brothers to come for her for the

holidays and was in no mood for serious studying. When the knock upon the door finally came, she called out, "Come on in." Slipping into her coat and gathering up a pile of books, she turned to find Carl's tall frame filling the doorway. For a moment she thought she'd taken leave of her senses. Dropping the books, she flew into his arms and wondered, too late, why she was always so impulsive around him. She was conscious of his cold face against hers, the bulky roughness of his coat, and the wonder of finding him, unexpected, in her doorway.

He laughed at her eagerness. "That's the Mindy I love."

"The one who flies at you instead of being proper?" She wrinkled her nose in surprise. "What *are* you doing here? Why didn't you tell me you were coming so I could daydream about it?"

"I wanted to surprise you," he said, "and besides I wasn't sure it would work out until the last minute. I daydreamed for both of us."

Mindy, gathering up her books and small items, sneaked a glimpse into the mirror, and she was glad her hair shone from last night's washing. In fact, she wondered if the glowing face looking back at her could possibly be the sober student who had inhabited this little room only moments before.

Skimming over the snowy roads behind Belle's steady hoofbeats, they talked as they never had before, eagerly, without care for their words. She felt sure he had never shared himself with anyone like this before. She had crept behind his aloofness, and he liked her there. He told her of the lonely world of the lumber camp, new to him but so familiar to his father. Her shy revelation that she'd made the honor roll caused him to whoop with delight and sent Belle skittering, the sleigh whipping about wildly.

At her door they discussed how they'd spend the three precious days before Carl had to go back. "You *will* go to church with me tomorrow, won't you?" Mindy asked matter-of-factly, feeling sure he could refuse her nothing.

46

She was not prepared for the coolness that fell between them or the detached iciness in eyes which had just been filled with warmth and laughter.

"If you choose to go to church," he said stiffly, "I will see you tomorrow night."

"Carl, we'll lose a whole day together!" The words hung like a child's thin wail on the frosty air.

"It seems we will," he agreed. Setting her books and bag inside the door, he left her without another word.

Neither the affection of her family nor the warmth of a familiar hearth could heal the hurt. She only sampled her mother's lovingly prepared dishes and rudely ignored Pearl's eager chatter.

The next day in church she struggled with an unaccustomed emptiness within. Hiram, tall and sure at the end of the pew, represented something stable and good, something she understood. Sunlight streamed through rosy glass and lay in blocks of brightness across the polished floor. Everyone about her seemed serene, even joyous, upon this holiday Sabbath. Yet some, she knew, had left heartache on the doorstep at home. Or had they brought it with them?

Young Ned Billings tasted his father's scorn every Saturday morning when he walked away from the duties of a busy farm to attend church. Lucy Mott and her little ones sat alone, Ralph never at her side. Jake Crandall worshiped without his wife, his children not allowed to attend his church.

She longed to cry out to them, "Is it worth it? Can one bear it for a lifetime? Is your heart able to worship under such a burden?" Slowly a peace came over her, and she found herself singing Silent Night with the others. The little Mott girl, hardly more than a baby, stretched out her arms to be taken, and Mindy lifted her over the back of the pew, comforted by the trusting softness of the small body. There was something of the Child of Christmas in the curly head tucked under her chin. She was glad she had given Him the gift of loyalty. Perhaps it was better than frankincense

47

and myrrh. A desperate, frightened part of her cried out from deep within, "Whatever lies ahead, stay with me, Holy Child." The babe on her lap and the Christ in her heart jumbled and turned until there was no separating them, and she relaxed into their love.

*　　*　　*　　*　　*

When Carl arrived on Christmas Eve, he showed no sign of irritation. Mindy, refreshed from a day of worship and relaxation with her family, decided to ignore his rudeness of the night before.

"Could you spare Mindy for the evening?" he asked her mother. "I know it's Christmas Eve, but my mother has teased me to bring her home so long that I promised I'd try tonight."

"Don't blame her a bit," Em answered quietly. "It's time she had a look at Mindy. Give her my greetings. In fact," she said, rising, "I'm going to send her a jar of my raspberry jell. Get a scrap of Christmas paper, Pearl, and wrap it pretty."

As they neared the lighted farmhouse with its surrounding barns, Mindy put her arm through Carl's and shivered. "This scares me—I'll probably say all the wrong things. I want them to like me, especially your mother."

"You can't do any worse than I did, stumbling into your family's evening worship hour that first time," he laughed. "They'll love you, though Father may be careful not to let you know it."

Mindy's first thought as she met Martha was that perhaps all middle-aged Vermont women were honed by poverty into a type. There was about Martha the same tight, contained spareness she saw in her own mother. A crucifixion of self into a nonperson, no longer the victim of emotion. Martha was taller than her mother, and when she smiled, there was a fleeting glimpse of Carl which reminded Mindy sharply that he was not hers yet, or never would be fully. This woman loved him too. What was it

48

Carl had said? Something about their having weathered a lot together.

The little girls, Sally and Carrie, took Mindy's outstretched hand shyly, but she was well aware they hadn't missed a thing from her boots to her bangs. From an old sheet dyed pale blue, Pearl had created Mindy's Christmas gift, a softly ruffled blouse which rounded the lines of her thinness, setting off her fine neck and thick, glossy hair.

"Your blouse is so pretty," Sally said, touching the full sleeve lingeringly.

"It was my sister's Christmas present to me," Mindy answered, smiling at the pretty child. "I think she planned it to match Carl's eyes, don't you?"

They all looked at Carl and smiled, and there was an easing in the room. She noted that Sally's eyes were the same blue as Carl's—only tender instead of fierce.

"Father, this is Mindy," Carl said, leading her by the hand to a rocker in the parlor.

Seth Matthews took his time looking up from the paper he was reading, and when his eyes at last met hers, Mindy knew she would have to reckon with this man as long as she loved his son. There was no welcome in his eyes. Even his courtesy was paper-thin. "Good evening, young lady," he acknowledged, and there was in his voice and smile the same mocking arrogance she'd noted on occasion in Carl.

He was a handsome man, with the smooth, strong-boned face of one much younger. Even while she struggled with her mute tongue, she was thinking that Carl's mother must have been quite a girl in her day to have won him.

"Carl has been telling me about the lumber camp," Mindy said, grasping at anything which might interest him. "I guess it's an old story for you, but he finds it lonely."

It was the wrong thing, and she knew it even as the words tumbled out. Carl's hand tightened on hers, and she sensed in that instant that he feared his father.

49

"There is no room in this world for loneliness," Seth declared. "It's a sickness."

"What is important then?" Mindy asked, looking him straight in the eye. "Do you discount love? It's the mother of loneliness, you know."

"Don't give me pretty talk," he chided. "Work! that is what's important. It must be, or you die in this part of the country. Would you know anything about work?"

He was making her angry, and she must not let it show; yet she would not allow him to reduce her to stammering and scraping. "Work is not unrelated to love, Mr. Matthews. You spend these long winters away from home because you love your family and want their lives to be comfortable."

"Perhaps I do it to get away from them," he said, chuckling. "Ever think of that?"

"I don't believe it, Father," Sally told him, slipping her arms about his neck from where she'd been listening behind his chair. He ignored her, but Mindy noted a softening about his mouth and chalked up a point for Sally. She'd been foolish to take him so seriously.

"If I didn't know before, I'm learning a bit about work this winter," Mindy said. "I'm taking eight subjects and never dreamed there were so many things in the world to be learned."

"Might better be home helping your mother," Seth remarked, returning to his paper.

Carrie brought a bowl of popcorn, and Martha followed with a pot of cocoa. They sat around the tree and made uneasy conversation until at last Martha took the girls off to bed. As she opened the stair door, she turned and came back to Mindy. "Thank you for coming, my dear. You have made Carl very happy. I see the change in him. I'm proud you're doing so well in school."

Tears stung Mindy's eyes. She knew the words had not come easily to this reserved woman, nor had the sharing of her son. It was love that had enabled her to do this, whatever Seth might think. Love for the little boy who'd fought out the long, lonely winters with her through the years.

"And thank *you* for sharing Carl with *me.*" It was all she could manage without crying. She shuddered at what Seth would think of any such display of weakness.

Later she and Carl sat alone with only the snapping of the wood fire to break the silence. Taking a tiny package from under the tree, Carl said, "This is your Christmas present, Mindy. Will you open it now?"

Shyly she tore away the green tissue and lifted the lid of the small white box. Inside lay an oval gold locket, ringed about with delicately engraved flowers.

"Open it," he urged.

When she released the catch, before her, under the glass, lay one perfect violet pressed against a background of cotton. "Oh, it's lovely," Mindy whispered. "It surprised me. I expected a picture of you."

"*That* you're supposed to carry in your head," he replied with something of the abruptness of his father. "Let me tell you about the violet. I found it last fall in a little sunny nook on the south side of a rock. There was a great patch of plants, all the leaves thriving and deep green, storing up their energies for spring, but this was the only blossom. It stood alone on a tall stem, defying every rule. For all the world, it reminded me of you last winter, fighting off a fatal sickness against all the odds. Plucky and pretty."

Seth had said work was king. Carl was much like him, Mindy thought. She had won him, not with feminine wiles, but with courage. "It's a beautiful thought," she said softly, "and all my life this flower will challenge me to live to the full—to blossom even in the fall. And now, Carl, here comes again one of the stumbling blocks to our happiness if we choose to let it be. I do not wear jewelry. It's not easy to explain to *you,* who think so differently than I, but it has to do with my own unworthiness in the light of the high price which had to be paid for my sins. Or more simply, who am I to deck myself in gold, when Christ wore a crown of thorns?"

He said not a word, but the hurt was there in that face she loved, and she could not bear it. "Carl, I shall wear this locket often, probably always when we're apart, under my blouse. There, close to my heart, it will be to me a symbol of your love and a thousand times more meaningful than if I wore it for show. It's the sweetest gift I have ever received."

He smiled then and took her hand. "Mindy, sometimes I am jealous of your Christ. He asks so many strange things of you, and you follow Him so willingly. Do you think there is room in your life for both of us?"

Why had he put it that way? Couldn't he have just said, "Will you marry me?" like anyone else? *Was there* room in her life for this man she loved and the Jesus she was only beginning to know? How could she answer that, sitting here in the firelight with Carl's dearness only a touch away and God far off on His throne?

"Christ is not mine, Carl," she said, sorting words. "He is yours too. Ours. Everyone's. Didn't your mother teach you these things? Have you never been to church?"

"My mother is a good woman without attending church," he replied testily. "I am aware of God sometimes in the woods. I acknowledge His existence but question how much He meddles in the affairs of men. Don't ask me to believe as you do." There was controlled impatience in his voice, but it softened, and he said, "I'm asking you to marry me, Mindy, in the full knowledge that we'll face our life together under a handicap. I'm asking you, not because of a sensible, thought-out decision, but in spite of one. Because I can't find any happiness without you anymore."

"And I'm saying yes, in spite of such a proposal. It's not a very good way to start a marriage, is it?"

He cupped her face in his hands and kissed her gently. "I don't know, Mindy. Only the years will tell. Maybe our love will be enough."

*　　*　　*　　*　　*

52

Sunday afternoon before Carl's departure they sat with Em and Hiram in the big, beamed living room on the Wheeler farm. Carl planned to speak to Hiram, and Mindy had chosen to stay with him.

"If he says no, I want to hear his reasons," she'd said more lightly than she felt.

"Hiram"—Carl's voice was calm, and Mindy realized with a little inner handspring of delight that he had no fear of *her* father—"I have asked Mindy to marry me in the spring. I will do all in my power to make her happy and provide her with the comforts of life as I have health and strength to do so. Do we have your blessing?"

Mindy watched her mother's face, but there was not a flicker of emotion, only downcast eyes over the knitting in her hands.

Hiram was quiet a long time, and in his face she saw a sadness that frightened her. Could he see ahead toward some dark, awful thing in the future? Did he think they had no ability to live together, each with his own opinions? Had he so little confidence in her?

"Mindy is not an ordinary girl, Carl," he began finally.

"I'm aware of that," Carl answered, a little smile twitching at one corner of his mouth. "That's why I have chosen her."

"I am not talking about superficial things like personality or looks or even courage, though she has all these." He reached out and took Mindy's hand fondly. "I am telling you, Carl, she is sensitive and conscientious, and her heart is very tender toward God. She will be easily hurt, and to remove her religion would be to destroy her. I am going to ask you a hard thing, but I know you to be a man of your word. I am asking you to promise me you will never trouble Mindy about her religion or ask her to forsake it—that she will be free to practice it according to her conscience as long as she so desires."

Again Mindy saw Hiram as a patriarch, strong and unrelenting in matters of the soul. "He has the courage to say what I should have said," she thought.

Carl surprised her. He waited only for Hiram to finish and then said quietly, "I had no intention of asking Mindy, now or ever, to give up her beliefs. The things you and her mother have taught her have undoubtedly made her the woman I love."

He had called her a woman, and she wore it like a crown.

"Come sit here on the sofa by Mindy," Hiram suggested, motioning to Carl. Then standing, he placed his workworn hands on their young heads and asked God's blessing on their lives. As Hiram's gentle words fell over them, for no reason she could understand Mindy thought of Seth, and little tongues of doubt flickered through her happiness.

*   *   *   *   *

When springtime danced over the land, teasing wild flowers up from the forest floor, Mindy became both graduate and bride. She tucked the diploma away on her closet shelf and gave herself up to Pearl's patterns and everlasting fittings, protesting all the way. "The dress I wore for graduation is fine. It's white and washable and quite sensible."

"Very pretty also," Pearl muttered, her mouth full of pins, "but you are not going to be married in a little cotton dress. Father told me to get the best of material." She ran her hand fondly over the stiff ivory moiré billowing about her. "Never have I had the pleasure of working with such elegance. This suit will be my crowning creation. The skirt will swirl about your ankles, and I shall make the jacket short and trim to show off your tiny waist."

"Carl has promised to bring a huge bunch of violets for me to carry. He knows a place where they grow thick on a hillside."

"It's too bad you aren't marching down a long aisle," Pearl said dreamily. "You could at least have been married in our little church."

Mindy, making tiny bastings in a long seam, did not reply. She wished Pearl had not mentioned the little church. It was part of the price she must pay for marrying out of her faith. Oh, she could have been married there, but it would have been but a mockery, for the Adventist preacher could not perform the ceremony, could not unite her with an unbeliever. So she had decided on a simple home wedding.

After a long time she spoke, so softly that Pearl had to turn her head to hear. "I hope I am not making a mistake."

"Nonsense, Mindy. You are the envy of the countryside."

"But I'm going against the counsel of my father, the church, and the Word of God."

"You just have last-minute jitters. Besides, Carl will probably come around to your thinking once you're married."

"I don't think Carl is one to tag along in important matters, nor would I have him to be. But if only he'd study the Bible for himself, he'd see it all so clearly. He's a logical man."

"It's too late for 'if onlys,' Mindy. I think you are a lucky girl and should stop fretting. He's such a reserved man, but when you walk into a room, he can hardly take his eyes away from you."

"I feel that way about him, too," Mindy said, blushing. "Just the sound of his voice fills me with joy."

When she and Carl stood, two weeks later, in her parents' living room before the Baptist minister and a handful of family and friends, Mindy knew she would remember every detail of the moment forever. Sunlight spilled over her mother's collection of plants in the bay window and across the old blue carpet. She could feel its warmth on one side of her face. Nell and her husband stood beside them, and Mindy heard Carl repeating the vows as in a dream. Was it really happening? Was he promising to love and cherish, to care for her in sickness and in health? She felt the rough cloth of his suit under her

55

fingertips, and beneath that the muscular hardness of his arm.

She thought of that first day in the snowstorm and knew she'd loved him even then.

When she began her own vows in a clear, steady voice, he looked down at her with such tenderness that she faltered and could barely finish. As they turned to face the guests her eyes were wet with tears, and she marveled that such a wondrous thing could happen to an ordinary mountain girl. Surely no shadow could fall across such blinding joy.

Chapter 6

"I want to talk to you," Carl said, tipping his chair back against the kitchen wall.

Mindy, clearing away the supper dishes, stopped and gave him her full attention, something in his voice alerting her. Her eyes rested with delight upon his high cheekbones, generous mouth, clearly defined lips. She loved the flash of white teeth on those rare occasions when she enticed him to laughter, but tonight he was sober. In fact, recognizing two lines of concern upon his forehead, she would guess he was going to speak to her of money. "Don't be so serious," she admonished lightly. "I haven't spent our nest egg on a fur muff or anything."

He barely heard her. "Mindy, how would you like a house, a whole house all your own?" He didn't smile, but there was pleasure dancing on and off in his eyes.

Mindy looked about the tiny apartment they were renting and realized she'd never know more happiness anywhere, yet she sensed he awaited her enthusiasm.

"I would feel very grown up," she told him, hands on hips, saucy faced. "Now tell me, where would two poor newlyweds like us find a house we could afford, dreamer?"

"Well, I've found the house, but you are right, we can't afford it."

"If only you had let me take a school this year, Carl, maybe we could have managed." She still chafed under Carl's decision that she was not to teach, even though she'd attended the local college during the summer to obtain her credentials.

"The money would have helped," he agreed, "but I don't want you working. My mother has never had to leave her home. Why should you?"

It was an old argument, and she refrained from repeating that she longed to get into a classroom and exercise her new skills. That it had nothing to do with his mother, or her own for that matter. She shouldn't have brought it up at all. "Where is the house? Whatever made you think of a house anyway?"

"Only because this one has some special memories for me, or at least the land about it. As a boy I lived on the same farm, though farther south on the property. Our place burned, but this particular house has been right there for a good many years, and for some reason it holds a special place in my heart."

It must, Mindy thought, to inspire even a moment's consideration, for they had only Carl's small salary from a feed and grain store, plus a tiny savings account. She could not imagine practical Carl daydreaming about a house at this point, but there he sat with an unfamiliar gleam in his eye, and she wasn't surprised when he announced they'd drive out to look at the property the next Sunday.

He would not tell her where it was, but as Belle trotted along dusty roads through September's gilt-leafed splendor, Mindy noted with pleasure they were heading toward the hills of her birth. It was well after two when they turned out of a small village onto a narrow road leading gently upward and away from civilization. Only an occasional farm brought cleared land to the road's edge. Belle, tiring, moved more slowly. After a year of town life Mindy reveled in the aroma of spruce and pine, the clean, clear tang of autumn.

"When we round this bend," Carl promised, "there she sits."

Later Mindy wondered what she had expected. A little white house close to the road, perhaps. Certainly not what she saw. To her right across a stream laughing its way around boulders, across a meadow, across a low rise, sitting on its own higher hill, a weathered old house settled so completely into the landscape that one could almost believe it had grown there with the balm of Gileads which dropped great golden leaves on its front doorstep.

She gasped, and Carl, seeing it suddenly through her eyes, apologized, "Hasn't seen a coat of paint in years, but that's nothing. She's sound as a rock. That's what counts."

Mindy knew that the house had been awaiting her always, but she hugged this knowledge to herself, not wishing to share it yet, even with Carl. They rode silently along beside the exuberant stream, looking, each thinking his own thoughts.

When the house was out of sight, a ragged excuse for a drive broke away from the main road and wound in an offhand manner back toward the farm. They stood in the front yard, looking down the valley through which they had just traveled. The stream followed the road in and out through low scrub.

"The land needs care. Everything's badly run down. I itch to scythe that riverbank right down to the water's edge. No way to let a place go."

Mindy looked at Carl in surprise. She had never thought of him as a farmer, never seen in him this love for the land.

His thoughts suddenly came back to her. "Here we stand talking about the haying, and I suppose all a woman wants to see is the kitchen sink and the size of the bedrooms. I guess I should warn you. The inside is pretty bad, and you know as well as I do there's no money to do much prettying up. If it's all too much, we'll just forget about it and go home to our apartment where we belong anyway. It's just something about the way the valley looks

59

early in the morning with the fog hanging low over the meadows . . ." He shook his head impatiently, not understanding this unfamiliar weakness in himself.

Everything was so still. They pushed open an unlocked door and found themselves tiptoeing through empty rooms. Plaster hung loose from damp ceilings. Worn linoleum, dingy with age, covered the floors. Water dripped a welcome into a rusty sink. When Mindy tried the windows out for views, Carl's laughter bounced off the barren walls. "You'll wish you'd looked at something besides the scenery if we're ever foolish enough to move in here," he said.

"Plaster is cheap," Mindy reminded him. "We could fix the ceilings. A good wood fire would soon remove the dampness." Mindy wrinkled her nose in distaste at the drab walls and floors, wondering if there would ever be money enough for new wallpaper and linoleum.

"You are not going to believe your eyes, Min. The former residents used the second floor for a chicken coop, and they didn't make any effort to hide the fact when they left." Following him up the narrow dark stairway, Mindy found he had not exaggerated. There, in rich abundance, lay the dried droppings of several generations of chickens.

Carl eyed her with a glint of amusement. Inwardly appalled, Mindy said lightly, "If you'd haul up some topsoil, it ought to make a delightful indoor garden."

Carl chuckled. "Seriously, I could shovel the whole mess right out the window in less than an hour."

"And it shouldn't take me more than a couple of years to get it scrubbed and disinfected," Mindy answered wryly.

"I want to check the cellar and the water pipes." Carl headed down the stairs. "Then let's eat."

Outside, Mindy took the lunch basket from the wagon and seated herself on the great flat stone at the front door. Sun-splattered shade from three old trees fell over the front of the house. She leaned back against the weathered sill and watched cloud shadows move slowly and stately across the valley. On the other side of the brook and the road an evergreen-studded hill rose abruptly. She had always known long views with blue mountains scalloping the horizon. This was different, a little world all one's own. Now gilded with sunshine. Tomorrow, perhaps, softened with mists, as Carl remembered it. Carl sat down beside her, and they ate hard-boiled eggs and cold beef sandwiches, not saying much.

Finally, gathering up the leavings, Mindy asked, "Do you suppose the house knows we belong to it?"

Carl, who had stretched out on the grass, eyes closed, sat up with a start. "Are you serious, Mindy? We have to be practical. The price tag is $800, which is cheap enough, but we simply don't have even a down payment."

"Well, you'll have to think of something," Mindy said airily, "for I intend to be here when that apple tree at the back door blossoms next spring."

He pulled her down beside him, and she watched the tight lines soften across his face, his mouth relax. "I'll work on it tomorrow. If there's any way, you shall have your apple blossoms."

A month later they moved in, and Mindy pretended to be horrified that she'd married a gambler. It had meant leaving the security of Carl's job, plus going deeply into debt. They stood in the shabby kitchen, their meager belongings in boxes about them. "Where am I going to get $150 before the first of March?" Carl wondered.

"*We*, Carl, not *I*. If God prompted that banker to let us move in without a penny of down payment, surely He will provide."

Carl patted her hair absently, and she knew already he was plotting and planning, that he'd be tense and edgy until the six-month deadline had been met. "I'm going to have another look at the barn," he said. "If we could get a cow cheap, it would cut down on our grocery bill."

When he had gone, Mindy knelt among the boxes. For the first time she felt a tiny twinge of some nameless hurt. It *was* frightening, just the two of them pitted against that

61

impossible amount of money, but God was still on His throne. She wanted Carl to share the security of that knowledge with her. She prayed, "O God, be with us in this home. You know we have nothing but our youth and our determination, but we will work hard to raise the money. Will You go before us? Bless this house, and may it be filled with love—our love for You and each other and Your love for us."

Pearl helped her make ruffled curtains for the windows out of feed bags. The oatmeal-hued, rough-textured cloth perfectly framed the pink geraniums her mother had given her in abundance for the sills. Wright had built her an oval kitchen table, which gleamed under her polishing. Disgusted with the faded linoleum, she'd torn it up and scoured the pine floor beneath to a color that matched the curtains. She kept the black range oiled and glowing that Carl had bought her during the first week of marriage. Coming in at night from helping one farmer or another in the area, Carl would smile at the cheeriness of her kitchen. She knew the smell of good food, his own table neatly laid, and her steady confidence were healing to the fear twisting within him; so she timed the kettle to sing at his arrival and tied a starched bright apron over her thin and faded dresses. They sat within the circle of lamplight many nights, going over and over their expenses, trying to estimate a most indefinite income; and always spring hung over them like doom. They put in a supply of staples—flour, sugar, oatmeal, potatoes—bought a cow for their milk and butter, and Mindy determined to buy nothing but eggs until spring. She had canned bright shelves of vegetables from their summer garden, little knowing it would mean the fine edge between hunger and plenty, come winter.

When the harvesting jobs ran out, Carl turned to the forest. He had had it in the back of his mind all along, but it was like him not to have mentioned it. One day in November he simply remarked, "There's money in those woods, Mindy. It was one reason I went ahead and bought this place. Father agreed to let me use his team all winter while he's away. I'm going to haul out enough wood by spring to get us over the hump."

"You can't do it alone, Carl. Lumbering's hard enough when you've got help."

"It can be done," he said sharply, and she knew it was hopeless to pursue it. He was strong and driven and scared. Probably it *could* be done, and fatigue was easier to bear than fear.

The winter days settled into a pattern. After an early breakfast Carl milked the cow and set off for the woods. Mindy cleaned and did her baking or churning for the day. Slowly she was restoring the second floor to normalcy, though there was no money to furnish, decorate, or even heat it. At noon she packed sandwiches, hot soup, and homemade cookies into a basket, donned some of Carl's heavy outer clothing, and set off through the drifts toward the sound of his ax. In that still white world she could not be afraid.

Trudging between the towering pines which bordered her path, she marveled that 563 acres of this untouched wilderness belonged to them. The stream gurgling beneath its coating of ice, the gray cliffs, snow-dusted in their winter bleakness—all theirs. Each time she placed her foot upon the well-packed pathway, she rejoiced that this land had awaited them through the years. They were winning with the bend of their backs, the tightening of their belts, and the blessing of God.

She'd build a little fire, and sitting beside it, they'd eat and allow themselves to dream a bit about the future. Carl was more himself with an ax in hand and pungent chips at his feet than any other way. Mindy loved to watch the tireless rhythm with which he teased a tree to the ground. At her insistence he taught her how to snake the logs down to the road after he had chained them behind the horses. Crude, slow lumbering. No proper tools. Just vigor and the threat of losing this land they loved to prod them on. But the pile was growing, and when the logging teams came later there would be money. Enough money? That was the question that dogged their days and flitted in and out of dreams.

Church was quite some distance away on the other end of the valley. On good Sabbaths Belle carried Mindy briskly over the miles, but during the winter months there were often days when she knew better than start out. In the chilly, sparse living room, with sleet pelting the windows, she'd sing the familiar hymns of her girlhood, read her Bible, and then spend long periods upon her knees. It was more meaningful somehow than worship had ever been before. She was there at her appointment with God spontaneously, without the urging of her elders. Choice—the sweet gift of God to His children. Slowly she was beginning to comprehend its possibilities.

On Saturdays she did not haul logs for Carl, only took him his lunch and chatted while they ate. Nor did he ask her to. Sitting at the edge of the dark forest, with fire crackling at their feet, she longed to speak to him of new concepts sprouting in her own mind, but she could not. There was an independence about him that denied all need of anything beyond his own muscular young body. He did not mention her religion, acknowledging it only in the placing of a quarter beside her purse on the Saturdays she attended church. She would thank him shyly, awkward in her awareness of their poverty.

Mid-March Carl sold their logs and came home whistling, about him once more the cocky arrogance which had first attracted her. Handing over a grocery bag, he grinned at her delight in oranges, bananas, and a small sack of chocolates—luxuries they'd long done without. Using a hoarded jar of her mother's home-canned chicken, she prepared it with dumplings, serving it with baked squash and cabbage salad. She was grateful for the cold, spooky cellar which had held their vegetables crisp over the winter. They ate the fruit for dessert and dared to believe at last the home would be really theirs.

"There's still a mighty hunk left to pay," Carl worried,

carving an orange skin into a heart shape with his paring knife.

"But it's only a little each month, silly. If you've managed this first terrible hurdle, the rest will be as nothing." Mindy took the orange heart from him and cut their initials into it. "God has been with us this far. We can trust Him for the future."

She raised her eyes to his, wanting him to agree, but he only said gruffly, "God's got more on His mind than where you and I are going to spend our days."

Mindy wrote the check for the bank that night in her round, neat script, and they gloated over the $15 balance.

Spring came, endowing them with a wealth all unrelated to savings accounts. When tiny chartreuse leaves uncurled over the valley and Carl scythed the riverbank down to its gurgling edges, they knew they had purchased paradise for a song. After breakfast one morning Carl led her to the back door where her apple tree had exploded into fragrant knots of deep-pink buds. "All for you," he said, breaking off a sprig and tucking it into her dark hair. Mindy looked at the tree in wonder. A great bouquet of love he had promised and won for her. She wanted, like Miriam after crossing the Red Sea, to dance and sing before the Lord with joy, but instead she hugged Carl fiercely with laughter and kisses.

"All this," he exulted, smiling and pleased, "for one old crab apple tree?"

Chapter 7

Mindy turned from the blackboard on the last day of school and surveyed her classroom with a tinge of wistfulness. Those heads—each one so familiar, so dear—bent over books. From the tousled curls of tiny Ruth to the well-groomed head of Ralph, her oldest and most dependable student, she loved them all. Even Edward, who taunted and mocked his way through life. Over her two-year teaching stint she'd gentled him a bit. She liked boys, understood their awkwardness, channeled their energies. Her pay had helped buy a team of horses, a few cows, a minimum of secondhand farm equipment. Carl still chafed at her absence from the home, but had to admit things would have gone much more slowly without her help.

Now it was over, for she was expecting a baby. Today she would give the last few tests, the children would clear out their desks, then they'd picnic together in the grassy yard behind the school.

They brought her their papers, lined dog-eared books along shelves, and raced outside to start the food preparations. They were protective of her these days, not allowing her to lift or carry.

Later, in the sunshine, she told them how happy

she'd been as their teacher. They sat about her in a circle, all eighteen of them, and she talked to each one, telling him of her hopes for his particular talents. Even in the slowest and dullest she found something to praise.

When the salads and sandwiches were gone and the great chocolate cake consumed, the boys harnessed Belle to the buggy, and they gathered round to tell her good-bye. Little Ruth cried, and one of the older girls had to comfort her. For a strange, unreal moment Mindy had the feeling they were *her* children, as surely as the child within her. Their eager, responsive young faces, sun-kissed and smiling, nodded below her perch on the buggy seat like a collection of rare flowers. How would they survive without her? Who else would ever understand that Johnny Buckman couldn't do arithmetic, no matter how hard he tried; that Joe Davis must clean the schoolroom because he couldn't learn, and he needed to excel at something; that Win Billings' sharp, probing mind thirsted for a challenge?

She clucked at Belle, and they broke ranks to let her through, but even as she waved and smiled, she read something in the eyes of the little group that matched her own sadness. She had learned within that simple one-room school that she was a teacher by more than training, that she could make plain facts sparkle and glow for wriggling children. She had never found a way to share this awareness with Carl. She longed to tell him of the excitement that rose within her as a little one learned to read or an older student did outside research on a subject far removed from his mountain world. It sounded silly when she tried to explain it; so when she came home at night, she left the classroom behind, and they talked about the hay crop and where she would have the baby.

All summer she puttered about the house or hovered over the garden, snatching each new vegetable, as it ripened, for her glass jars. In August she rode home from the fields in the fragrant, misty dusk on the hay wagon with Carl. She felt, in her awkward earthiness, one with the haze-touched land. It had produced generously. So would she. A boy, she hoped, for Carl. For herself too. She wanted a son. Sometimes she stretched flat out on the soft, jostling mountain of hay until she could see nothing but the bowl of stars upturned above her. Then God seemed very near, and she prayed wordlessly for the unborn child.

Not long after school bells summoned the village children back to the classroom in September, she awoke early one morning with sharp, unfamiliar sensations heralding a new adventure. With a blending of terror and excitement she let the pain move over her, exulting in her womanhood. What could a man ever know of this act of creation? Placing her hands over the mound in the covers, she marveled at the strong contractions. Tears slid down the sides of her face onto the pillow, partly from fear, partly from wonder.

She waited a long time before waking Carl, wanting to be alone with birth, but there came an hour at dawn when she knew she could not delay much longer. She wanted to catch and hold the moment. Their bedroom had only one window, laid lengthwise along the slant of the roof line. She called it *her* window and had often watched the moon's bright path across it as she lay in wide-eyed peace beside Carl in the darkness. Now she heard the stirring of birds in the eaves outside and watched a soft pinkness lighten the window's black squares.

When she spoke his name, Carl looked at her in sleepy confusion. "This is your son's birthday, Carl. Maybe you should get Dr. Wells for the celebration—the sooner the better, in fact." She curled into a ball of misery, and Carl was out of bed in an instant.

"Why didn't you wake me sooner, Mindy? We were fools to think you could go through this at home."

"I don't need a hospital, just a doctor and my mother. Go quickly."

She heard Belle's hooves following the river down the valley and knew Carl rode in a lithe, bareback oneness with the horse. By the time Nathan drove in with her mother over an hour later, she wanted only to bury her head on that familiar shoulder and cry. She had had no idea of the intensity of the pain. It left her nauseated and frightened.

"Just relax," Emma soothed, massaging her back with cool, efficient fingers. "You may have a long spell ahead of you yet. Don't fight it."

She cried out in sharp little yelps of pain, ashamed that she could not keep them back, and begged for Carl, knowing he was riding Belle beyond all reason to return to her. All her plans for calm good sense were lost in this sea of torment. "How did you ever have four?" she gasped to her mother between spasms.

"The first is the hardest." Emma's stoicism was a rock to which Mindy clung. "After that, 'tain't much."

"Pray, Mother. I can't. Ask God to help me."

Em's eyes flickered away from Mindy's, and she said nothing at first. Then slowly, the words coming hard— "I've *been* praying right along, but I can't do it out loud. Never had no occasion. Your father's always done the praying."

"That's good enough for me," Mindy told her, taking her mother's rough hands in her own. "Just let me hold onto you."

Carl came then with the doctor, and everything after that seemed an eternal blur of pain, with only Carl's hands holding her to reality, while some voice faint and far away cried out and begged him to help her. Her window filled with sunlight, then darkened and grew black once more before she felt the final strong forces within her driving the child before them into life. The new mother cried out in agony, yet in joy, that she had done this wonderful thing, and she heard Carl saying, "Take it easy. It's all over." She saw tears on her mother's face, where she had never seen tears before.

69

Later she looked at the boy and recognized instantly the strong facial bone structure of Carl's family. A soft dusting of auburn curls gave him a maturity, strange in a baby. And there was a tiny cleft in his chin, gift of no ancestor.

"Well?" Mindy lifted her eyes to Carl's. "Do you approve?"

"He'll do. Might even make it on the other end of a saw, give him a few years."

"It was harder than I expected—having a baby."

"Where was your God through all that?"

"Right here, Carl, as concerned as you were, I believe."

"Do you think I would have let you suffer like that if I had had power to help you?"

Mindy did not answer quickly. It was an old question. Carl was not the first to ask it, and she didn't have any pat answer.

"Sin and suffering are tied together somehow," she said, taking his hand. "Not necessarily my specific sins, but sin in general. If God removed every handicap from His followers, all the world would flock to Him, but for what motive? And He *did* help me, Carl. I felt a kind of inner strength in spite of all the noise I made.

"I was sure I'd be the brave, pale type with little drops of sweat on my brow but never a word of complaint." She grinned up at him, mischief lighting her dark eyes. His own stern blue ones softened, and he lifted her hand to his lips.

Ned made a difference in their home. Carl grew more serious, more driven to outrun poverty. Mindy, expecting to miss the schoolroom, found that this small creature filled her world with joy. She marveled that Carl could refrain from handling the child, kissing him, talking to him. Yet she saw pride in his eyes as the baby grew strong and active. She didn't doubt his love for his son.

From the beginning this baby was special to Seth. All

his grandparents doted on him, but Seth claimed him very personally as his own. He would carry the child about, talking to him in his own tart, no-nonsense way. Ned's eyes never left the haughty, handsome face, as though he already understood his crusty ancestor.

"It's a wonder your father's breath doesn't kill him," Mindy declared sharply after the Matthewses had gone one evening, for Seth drank with a steadily increasing fervor over the years.

"It does my heart good to see Father thaw a bit. The boy doesn't have any notions about a whiskey breath yet, Mindy. He'll learn to be critical soon enough."

She caught the reprimand, and tears stung her eyes. She felt, for no good reason, that Seth's shadow hung ominously over them, but brushed the thought aside. It was heartwarming to watch the baby transform his grandfather, and Martha beamed with joy at the relationship.

Hiram and Em took a quiet pride in the child and showed him off at church till Mindy grew embarrassed. She and Pearl, when they were alone, played doll with him sometimes, dressing him in his best outfits and wheeling him in the sun.

But it was the hours alone with him that Mindy enjoyed most. Watching him reach for patches of sunlight on the wall above his basket, turning to find his eyes following her about the room, warming herself at his quick, eager smile. She realized sometimes, watching him, that the rest were all too sober—Hiram's household, Seth's, and their own. It came of poverty and hard work, no doubt. Ned seemed of some other substance, freer, unencumbered with their fears. It could have been just his babyhood, but Mindy fancied she saw in him some bent toward laughter, alien to his heritage.

She wondered about his future. Could she fasten him so securely to God that his father's indifference and his grandfather's scorn would fall harmless upon him? Her dark head bent often above his basket in concern.

71

She understood for the first time Hiram's sorrow at her decision to marry Carl.

Once, gathering her courage, she said to Carl, "I hope that Ned will always walk closely with God. I don't feel equal to teaching him alone. Couldn't we do it together?"

"I shall teach him to work hard and live an honest life. That's all I know of God, Mindy."

Thinking of his integrity, Mindy reached out and touched his cheek lightly. "Ned is lucky to have such a father. It is true he will learn much, simply from being with you, but I want him to experience the joy of prayer, to really know God as a friend, not just as some vague far-off being. I'm not sure I can teach him all that alone."

Carl opened his mouth to answer, changed his mind, and remained silent. After that they never talked of the matter again.

*   *   *   *   *

Two years later Stephen Wayne was born, Mindy barely escaping with her life. Carl, grim and worried at her bedside, insisted, "No more children," and she knew he meant it. He had changed over the two years, Mindy thought, as he rested, head back, eyes closed, in a rocker beside her. His laughter, always rare, seemed nearly stilled. There was a sternness in the set of his mouth and a weariness already in the young face. Pearl said he was getting more like Seth every year, and in some ways he was. The same sharp sting to his words when he was irritated, the obsession with work.

Yet there was a basic kindness and a strength of character in Carl which Seth lacked. Mindy did not fear her husband, but she felt him growing away from her. She could seldom get through the haze of worry and fatigue. She could not understand his fears. They lived frugally, but so did their neighbors. It was not a prosperous era or locale. They had learned they could not

72

make a living from their own farm, but Carl had no trouble finding work among his neighbors. It meant, of course, doing his own farming nights and weekends. Small wonder he was weary.

This new child, what would he be like? Two sons. No daughter ever. She didn't really mind. She preferred boys. She ran her finger over the baby's cheek, and he opened startlingly dark eyes. Their intensity was Carl's, the color hers. "Will you be fierce as an eagle like your daddy?" she asked, looking long into his unfocused gaze.

Em pushed open the door and stuck her head into the room. "Ned wants to see the baby. Can he come in?"

Carl opened his eyes and beckoned to his older son.

Ned walked slowly, shyly, toward his mother, unused to seeing her in bed. Mindy reached out to him and moved the blankets aside that he might better see the baby. He grinned, and her heart turned over at the dimples which twinkled on and off. He brought joy with him, this boy, whenever he entered a room. He touched the baby's curled fist and then scrambled onto Carl's lap hastily, not knowing quite what to make of the newcomer.

"His name is Stephen, Ned, and when he grows a bit he'll be company for you. Daddy and I are very lucky to have two healthy sons."

"Can I take him on the hay wagon?" Ned asked in the clear, ungarbled speech which always amazed her.

"Soon's he gets big enough to hold a pitchfork," Carl said, chuckling.

They stayed that way, the four of them, till dusk moved into the room, Carl's rocker beating a dull, comfortable rhythm, Ned relaxed into the unaccustomed luxury of his father's idleness, Mindy dozing and worn but excited by the man-child in the crook of her arm.

Chapter 8

"What's wrong with you, Grandpa?" Ned asked, climbing onto Hiram's bed and patting the big idle hand.

"My old ticker is getting tired, Ned. Sometimes it just says to get into bed for a few weeks and rest."

"Do you hurt?" the small boy persisted, peering closely into his grandfather's face.

Hiram smiled and pulled Ned down beside him. "Not so long's I mind your grandmother and don't wiggle even my big toe. What story shall we have today, young man?"

As Mindy tidied the room and listened to her father launch into the old tale of Samuel and Eli, she willed him to live. What male voice would speak of God to her sons when he was gone?

When Ned scampered off, having had his fill of patriarchs, Mindy sat down by her father's bed. Lying, eyes closed, his breathing short and raspy, he seemed but a shadow of the strong personality who had towered over her childhood; yet when he opened his eyes and smiled, there was within the same man. The urge to talk to him now, while that wisdom lingered, fell strong upon her.

As if he knew, he reached for her hand. "How is it with you, Mindy?"

Suddenly she wanted to cry, to put her head down on that familiar old shoulder and be patted and comforted like a child, but she didn't. It was not the nature or the custom of her people.

"Some days, Pa, I think I'm doing everything wrong."

"If Ned and Stephen are any indication, it can't be quite that bad. I'm proud of those two boys. Just what is it you're not doing well?"

Mindy knotted her dustcloth at one end and did not look up. "I'm not keeping my home a happy place."

"Who's unhappy?"

"Some of the time I am, and I'm afraid Carl is too. So far the boys are pretty unaware of our problems, but in time they'll sense the tensions between us."

"Carl is good to you, Mindy. He leaves you free to worship as you please and provides for your needs. What fault can you find in the boy?"

She felt reprimanded but had to go on. "He is all you say, Father, and I find no real fault with him. It's just that the joy in our marriage is all slipping away. Sometimes we seem like two strangers struggling together up a rocky mountain."

"Marriage isn't a game, Mindy. Sometimes it is more struggle than anything else, especially in our area where money is so hard to come by. Do you still love Carl?"

It was an odd question. The people of her world did not speak of love, the word being a bit too frothy for their taste. There was, however, a tenderness about her father, foreign to his kin. It bubbled easily to the surface in his relationship with Em, who handled it awkwardly but prized it. Now she must answer his question, and she found a bit of her mother's reticence weighing upon her tongue.

"When he sits at the table at night reading in the lamplight"—she hesitated—"I want to put my arms around him and beg him to make things as they used to be—the way they were that first year."

75

"Why don't you do it then?" Hiram asked mildly.

"That's the problem, I guess. We aren't open with each other anymore. We're guarded and careful, not sharing much of ourselves."

"Why?"

Suddenly an anger in Mindy surfaced and tumbled out. "I can't forgive him for leaving all the spiritual training of the boys to me. Already Ned asks why Daddy doesn't pray and why he doesn't go to church. First thing you know he'll be right out in the fields with Carl on Sabbath."

Hiram said nothing for a moment. Out in the kitchen the cadence of Em's rocker mingled with Stephen's baby laughter and Ned's chatter. The words Mindy had spoken hung about the room, smoldering. The answer had suddenly become obvious to her. She had wanted Carl at any cost. This was the cost.

"You must remember, Mindy, it is a burden Carl carries too. He sees no sense in your times of prayer with the boys, yet he does not interfere. Perhaps he even fears it will make them unmanly or expose them to ridicule later on. As head of the house he has the right to forbid your teaching the boys your beliefs. He does not exercise it. You must give him credit."

This was not what she had expected from Hiram. The justice of his words stung her like sleet. She had come for pity and found none. But she could not stop. "I am lonely for someone who thinks as I do, who will look out at the morning and be thrilled at what God has done with the earth. All Carl ever sees is how much hay is left to cut. I want someone to talk with about the boys' future. Someone to help me save so they can go to Adventist schools someday. All this I must keep locked up inside—the important things I must never mention."

"That is right. You must do the best you can to help your sons find God, but you must do it alone. Do not ask of Carl what he cannot give and never promised you. Share your religion with him in the only way you can, by

76

your unselfish love and your cheerfulness about the home. As a follower of Jesus Christ, you must be willing to give more to this marriage than you ask from it."

"It was a mistake to have married him, wasn't it?" Mindy asked, so softly that Hiram strained to hear.

"Do not say or even think those words, Mindy. Carl is a good man. You owe him your loyalty. We may not talk to each other again in this way. I trust you to walk beside Carl without self-pity and to sustain him in every way."

Mindy knelt beside Hiram's bed, tears falling upon the patchwork quilt. He stroked her brown head lovingly. There were no more words between them.

Three weeks later they stood about his grave in a quiet cemetery just down the road from his home. Nathan and Wright with their young wives, Pearl with her older husband.

"Who would have thought my giddy Pearl would have chosen an old man," Mindy had said to Carl on the wedding day.

"Thirty-six isn't exactly over the hill, you know," Carl had whispered back.

Well, maybe not, but here in the lush stillness of August by the open grave she looked like his little girl. Em stood apart, looking pinched and lost without Hiram's tall figure beside her. Nathan and his wife would be living with her, but it would not be the same. They were all empty shells without him, Mindy thought. They would have to learn a new way to exist. She would have, at least, Hiram's God. She hoped the rest had as much.

That night when Carl folded his paper and wound the clock, he turned toward Mindy. "Already I miss your father, Min. I wish the boys might have known him longer."

Remembering Hiram's counsel, she smiled. "They have a good father of their own to guide them."

She caught his fleeting look of pleased surprise before they climbed the stairs in a path of lamplight.

* * * * *

October scuttled about outside the old white farm-house, scrappy little gusts of wind hurtling dry leaves against the darkened windows. Beyond the mountain-tops a high, cold platinum moon rode the sky with serene indifference. Inside, flames flickered cheerily behind yellow squares of isinglass in the living-room stove. Ned already slept in his chilly room on the second floor, but Stephen curled contentedly into Mindy's shoulder as she rocked him, loathe to lay his sweetness in the crib. Carl, sitting across the room, pretended to read, but moved restlessly in his chair.

"I won't have a baby to rock much longer," Mindy said. "Already Stephen has to be sleepy to put up with me. Ever since he learned to walk, he wants to be on the move. He's different than Ned was."

"Spunkier," Carl added. "I feel it when I hold him. He's like a coiled spring."

"And harder to discipline. When I tell him no, he just looks at me with those bold, dark eyes. He's not easily discouraged even by spankings."

"Mindy"—Carl laid his book aside—"I think I'm going to buy the little Barker house down the road. It's pretty run down, and they're selling it cheap."

Mindy looked at him in disbelief. "For what?"

"Since Hiram died I've been thinking. Father's getting too old to go off lumbering every winter, and I don't like Mother being left alone either. Now that the girls are gone, if the folks had a small place of their own, they could get along on whatever odd jobs Father might pick up in the neighborhood."

The old fear of Seth rose strong in Mindy, and a nasty resentment joined it. They went without so many things. She practiced every frugality known to the New England housewife, and what made Carl think he had a right to take on additional expenses for his family?

She said nothing, groping for calm words.

78

"If Father had ever been able to get a place of his own, they could have managed without us, but as it is, the rent always hangs over him and must be met," Carl began, trying to explain.

Mindy fought down her anger. "You mean we can pull our belts a little tighter and the boys can go without so Seth can go on drinking. No wonder he never owned a home." She did not say the words, but as if he read her thoughts Carl answered sharply, "He's always provided adequately for his family. He's a hard worker."

"Will it take all our savings?"

"Yes, and some besides, but I think I can haul out enough lumber this winter to finish it off. Father will be here to help me."

"Whatever you wish, Carl." The words were docile, but the set of her shoulders as she carried Stephen to his bed told the young husband much.

The next morning Carl took Ned with him when he drove into town to see the real estate agent. Mindy put the house to rights, bundled Stephen against the chill wind, and climbed the hill behind the farm. From its crest she could see the length of the valley, its barren trees still carpeted with red and gold. Through the stripped-clean countryside, the river glittered cold and blue beside the road. She turned her face up to the sky. Stephen, rolling in a pile of leaves, sat up puzzled as she spoke.

"O God, there is nothing in me but anger and fear. I don't want Seth just down the road to scorn my religion and influence my sons. Maybe I don't even want to share Carl with him. I'm too selfish to pour our scanty savings all out for him. I can't find one good thing inside myself. Forgive me and help me."

Stephen stood by her feet, clinging to her skirt. She picked him up, holding his cold, soft cheek tightly against her own. "My son," she said, "I wish I could hide you from all that lies ahead, but never mind; look down the valley. It is your heritage. We are both alive and together on such a morning. Perhaps that is enough."

On a gray November afternoon Mindy hitched Belle to the buggy, tucked the lap robe snugly about the boys, and set out the half mile between their farm and the little house. She had promised to help Martha paint the kitchen cupboards. As she drove into the front yard Seth lifted a hand in greeting, but went on with his roofing job. She noted new front steps, a mended railing on the porch. Inside, Martha had made a home already. Starched white curtains framed the shining windows. The wood stove gave off a welcome warmth. When Mindy laid a pound of her fresh butter with its tiny flower print on the shelf, Martha admired its pale gold perfection and took it to her cold cupboard on the back porch. Then together they attacked the rough old cupboards, sanding and painting.

"I feel bad about Carl buying us this place, Mindy," Martha told her after a while. "I know money's scarce with you, same as us"—she smiled then, a shy, disarming smile —"but it *is* right nice to fix it up cozy and know we won't be movin' in a year or so. Seth's handy with his tools, and he'll have us snug in no time. When we're gone, the place'll be worth more, so perhaps you won't lose in the end."

"It's giving Carl a lot of satisfaction," Mindy admitted, "having you close by and knowing you won't be alone all winter. He's never forgotten those winters the two of you struggled through when he was a boy."

Martha held her paintbrush in midair, thinking. "He was always so good to me. Seth expected a lot of him— too much sometimes, I thought. But he never complained. I hope he's good to you like that."

"He is," Mindy said, her paintbrush flicking with a steady rhythm over the wood. "He works his fingers to the bone for all of us."

When she left later, she stopped to say a word to Seth. He was placing handmade shingles with speed and skill. There was about his movements the grace of a craftsman. Ned sat at the top of the ladder, handing him nails and a running conversation.

"Tell Carl I'll be up in a couple days to do some patching on his barn roof with my leftover shingles. Noticed he had some bad spots. Made these shingles myself, and he won't find none better."

"Are you learning how to roof a house, Ned?" his mother asked as she helped him down the ladder.

"I intend he should know a lot of things, for he's of age," Seth said through a mouthful of nails.

Riding home, Stephen turned his face into Mindy's coat to escape the wind, but Ned knelt backward on the seat shouting good-byes to the figure on the rooftop. Seth's faint answering shout filtered down to them through the fog which had settled over the valley. When they could no longer hear each other, Ned turned about and snuggled close to Mindy. "Grandpa Seth is my best person," he confided, "next to you and Daddy."

Chapter 9

Mindy kept one eye on the valley road as she put the finishing touches on the house. She had warned Ned not to loiter, but there were so many things for a seven-year-old to see along the way. She *did* want him from school by sundown.

The house was still sparsely furnished, but there was a snugness about it this Friday afternoon. She had scrubbed and polished every corner. Brown bread cooled on the shelf. The rich sweet aroma of baking beans filled the kitchen. In the center of the table sat Carl's favorite cake heaped with mounds of ground-raisin frosting.

"It's nearly sundown, Stephen. Put your toys away. When Ned comes, we'll have worship. Maybe while we're waiting, you could set the table."

She saw a small figure round the cliff at the spot where the road curved out of sight and called, "He's coming now. Hurry, Stephen!"

By the time Ned opened the kitchen door, supper preparations were complete. A last thin layer of winter sun gilded the treetops and upper portions of the mountains. Mindy helped Ned out of his outer clothing and put a chair close to the living-room stove for him.

They took a worn hymnal from the closet and sang together, "Day is dying in the west; Heav'n is touching earth with rest . . ."

As they knelt to pray Carl came into the kitchen, milk pails rattling noisily. Ned hesitated in his prayer. "Go on," Mindy said quietly. "Daddy will wait for us to finish." Before Stephen added his simple petition, he rose from his knees and headed toward the kitchen. Mindy caught her breath and reached out for him, too late. She saw the tension in Ned's sturdy frame as he huddled into the unnatural quiet of the situation.

"Please, Daddy, come and have sundown worship with us. It would make Jesus happy, and Mamma too."

Mindy reached out and took Ned's hand as they waited. She longed to fortify him against the words he would hear. She could see in her mind's eye the little scene in the next room. Stephen's intense, dark-eyed, trusting face tipped upward toward his father's height. She knew well the trapped, annoyed look of Carl at such a moment.

"I'm not much good at praying, Stephen. That's your mother's department. Run along. They are waiting for you."

"I could teach you to pray, Daddy. It's easy."

Mindy smiled in spite of herself. There was a stubbornness in her youngest from which one did not easily escape.

"Go to your mother at once," Carl said sharply.

Stephen's voice trembled and his words were disconnected as he knelt beside his mother, but he did not cry.

There was an uncomfortable moment as they gathered about the supper table, but Ned broke it by sticking his finger in the frosting and carrying the gooey treat to his father for sampling.

Friday evenings were pleasant in the old kitchen. Mindy laid the table with a white cloth and used her good dishes. There were special foods, and usually even Carl

83

seemed to relax into the weekly celebration of the Sabbath. Tonight, however, he did not respond to the boys' chatter or to Mindy's attempts at conversation. Stephen had rippled some quiet anger within him.

When he said later that he was going to drive into town for the evening, the boys followed his jacketed figure with wondering eyes. He seldom left home without them, and evenings were not a time for going to town.

"Why are you going, Carl?" Mindy asked, swallowing her pride.

"I need a change of scene." He neither looked back nor offered any word of farewell.

The boys helped her straighten the kitchen, but something had gone out of the room with Carl's leaving. In quietness they washed the dishes and brushed the crumbs from the table. The raisin cake was a mockery as she carried the remainder to the pantry. Only when the boys were tucked into bed and she sat beside them telling Bible stories did the strangeness recede. Lamplight glistened on Ned's copper-colored hair. He looked so much like Carl, but that was all. No fierce independence burned within him. He wanted laughter and peace on earth. She was sorry. She could not offer him that. Stephen cared not so much for peace. He wanted solutions and pursued them with tenacity. He asked her now, "Was Daddy angry when he left?"

"No, Stephen," she answered, pulling the covers up under his chin. "Maybe God was speaking to his heart, and he was trying to run away from that. We must show him by our love that God's way isn't something to be afraid of."

"I shouldn't have asked him to worship with us tonight. It spoiled everything," Stephen blurted out.

"It sure did," Ned said from his side of the feather bed.

"I don't think it was a mistake," Mindy told him. "Jesus has no other way of inviting him than through

84

your lips and mine. Someday perhaps he will say yes."

Kneeling beside her own bed later, she fought a new loneliness. Carl had never walked out like this before, deliberately choosing the company of others over her own.

"How do I handle it, God?" she prayed. "Carl is hurt, I'm hurt, and the boys are caught in the middle. I have brought sorrow into our home with all my good intentions."

She cried a long time there upon her knees until at last the promised Sabbath blessing surrounded her and she climbed wearily into bed. Out her lengthwise window, stars glittered far away in a black sky, speaking of another world beyond her splintering one. She lay sleepless, ears awaiting the beat of hooves along the narrow dirt road. When Carl lay down beside her hours later, she reached out and touched his face hesitantly.

He said, "Good night, Mindy," and there was in his voice the same loneliness she herself knew.

*　　*　　*　　*　　*

"Let's have a big Christmas, Carl," Mindy said, as the holidays approached. "I'd like to invite my mother and Pearl and her husband. Nathan and Wright are going to their wives' homes. I've already asked Seth and Martha and both of your sisters if they'd like to come."

"It's up to you, Min," Carl told her. "It sounds like a lot of work."

"The boys can help me, and our mothers will bring food." Mindy danced Stephen around the kitchen table, singing "Jingle Bells" until finally she had to stop, laughing and out of breath. Carl looked at her strangely, and she realized she hadn't felt giddy and girlish like this in a long time. "We've become grim," she thought, "and not yet thirty."

In the weeks that followed she taxed her ingenuity for ways in which to add to the meager pile of gifts beneath the tree. Pearl came for a day, and together they sewed for their mother a lovely dark brown dress with a creamy lace collar. Mindy knit mittens in every size and design. For a year she had worked in her free moments on a patchwork quilt for Pearl. Now, down in one corner she appliquéd a red heart on which she had embroidered "To Pearl from Mindy—1913."

With the boys she strung popcorn and cranberries for the tall spruce which Carl brought home one night from his lumbering.

The house was fragrant and gay with evergreen boughs and fat red candles when the family began to arrive on Christmas Day. Carl's parents came first, bearing a great tray of Martha's deep-fried apple tarts. Carl's eyes met his mother's warmly as he took the tray from her hands. Mindy did not even attempt to make those apple tarts. They were something between Martha and her son, some ritual from holidays of the past.

"Might better have et around our own tables," Seth said, setting a bowl of squash down with a thump on the kitchen shelf. "All this fussin' and fixin's a waste of time and money."

"Now, Seth, you know you wouldn't miss it for the world," Mindy said, giving him a quick hug and noting with dismay the strong odor of alcohol about him. She would not let him ruin this day. He went outside to where Ned was trying out new skis, and Mindy watched with a stab of uneasiness. How defenseless the child, with his dimpled grin and copper curls, was against the influence of his beloved grandparent! She wanted to scoop him up in her arms and run far away with him, but she turned back to her biscuit dough, wiping her eyes with a floury hand and leaving a dusting of white across one cheek. Carl, passing by, brushed it off in a gesture so tender and so unlike him that she wanted only to fling herself into his arms and beg him to be once more the Carl of long ago.

Pearl and James came then, bringing Em. Carl's

sister Sally and her husband arrived just as they were sitting down to eat. As Mindy looked about for someone to ask the blessing upon the food a great loneliness rose in her for her father. She knew now what the day lacked. Somehow it seemed appropriate for a man to praise God at this special occasion, but there was no man at the table who even knew God. They waited, all of them, in deference to Mindy's custom. She could not pray. She was too close to tears; so she turned to Ned. He did not refuse, but his eyes told her no. She saw the amused triumph on Seth's flushed features. In desperation she steadied her voice and said, "Stephen will offer grace." Stephen looked at her surprised, shy, but bowed his head and prayed, "Dear Jesus, thank You for all these grandpas and grandmas and aunts and uncles and that we are all together. Thank You for this good food, and happy birthday to You. Amen."

From his seat beside the boy Carl placed his big hand over Stephen's small one. "Well done, Son," he said. "Your Grandpa Hiram would have been proud of you." For the second time that day, Mindy's heart reached out to Carl, but when she looked at him, his eyes held her at a distance.

Later, when they had eaten beyond comfort and the gifts had all been opened, they sat among the wrappings and chatted. Pearl, six months with child, sat quietly beside her husband, who was discussing the scarcity of hay with Carl. Over Pearl's lap lay the bright quilt, a garden of color beneath her pretty face and dark hair. By the stove Em read to Stephen softly from a new book.

Chatting with Sally, Martha stroked a lacy white shawl Mindy had crocheted for her. Sally's husband had gone with Seth to teach Ned how to handle the small rifle Seth had bought him. Mindy had gasped in disappointment when he'd unwrapped it, and even Carl— hating killing and never hunting, though it was a common sport in the area—had spoken sharply to his father,

"Don't you think he's a bit young for that?"

"You spent too many years alone with your mother, Carl," Seth said. "I'm around to bring this one up right. The quicker he learns to hunt, the better."

She had been furious, trembling with anger. "Raise him right, indeed! Whose son was Ned, anyway?" She felt her mother's eyes upon her, and something in them said, "Be still." Now the sharp crack of rifle shot echoed down the valley, and a little boy's excited laughter mingled with men's voices beyond the window.

Martha turned from her daughter and remarked simply, "I'm sorry. I tried to talk him out of it."

"It won't hurt him any to learn to shoot, I suppose," Carl said, "though there's something in the eyes of a trapped or injured animal I can't stand."

"Just one more little skirmish lost," Mindy thought.

When they were all leaving, Em put into Mindy's hand a small package. "This is sort of a gift from your father," she said. "It's something he valued and would have wanted you to have. I'm not much of a reader myself."

Mindy put it aside until the sleighs had all disappeared into the snowy dusk and the cluttered house had been put to rights. While Carl and the boys ate cold turkey sandwiches and leftover fruit cup in the kitchen, she sat down by the living room stove and opened the book.

As she thumbed through the worn pages she found them filled with her father's underlinings and notes. *The Desire of Ages*—how often she'd seen him on Friday evening with the book in his hands or found him during the noon hour under a tree with a sandwich in one hand, the book in the other. Sitting beside him, sharing the lemonade or cold milk she'd brought, she'd listen as he read her a bit here or there. She opened the book and began at chapter one. The words that had meant little to her as a child, though she'd loved the sound of her father's voice, now moved her deeply.

"Carl," she called impulsively, "when you're finished, bring the boys. I want to share something with you."

Ned and Stephen stretched out upon the floor beside the shorn tree. Carl sat across the room, but he did not take up a magazine as he usually did when she read from the Bible to the boys.

"This book was Grandpa Hiram's," Mindy explained. "Mother gave it to me today. It is written by a woman whom we believe to have direction from God in her writing. My father told me she passes all the Biblical tests of a prophet but that he did not read her books only for that reason. He read them because they made the Word of God so plain and beautiful and because whenever he put one down, he longed to be a better man. He said for him that was the true test of a prophet."

"Chapter one is entitled 'God With Us,' and it tells why Jesus chose to come and live with us upon this planet and finally to die upon a cross. It seems a fitting way to close our Christmas celebration."

The boys would not understand, as she had not understood so long ago, but perhaps they would find a blessing in the beauty of the words. It was to Carl that she read, willing him to hear and believe, to be moved by that Life given for him. Snow mounded softly about the old farmhouse, the fire snapped and glowed behind the stove's small-paned windows. Mindy's voice fell over her husband in an intensity of love and longing, but he sat silent, impassive, and there was no way to tell whether or not the seeking Christ had found, or ever would find, a welcome in his heart.

PART
II
THE YEAR
1921

Chapter 10

Thunder rolled down the valley on the heels of the last slits of sunlight trying to escape blackening skies. August had tortured the land with searing heat. The brook shrank from its boundaries. Dusty black-eyed Susans drooped at the roadside edge. Everything waited, it seemed, for the relief of rain.

Carl had cut the lower meadow two days before. With Ned's and Stephen's help the hay had been dried, raked into windrows, and finally stacked for loading onto the wagon. Now, on Saturday, Carl raced to get it under cover. He had not stopped for dinner but had only grabbed a sandwich on one of his trips between field and barn. From the kitchen window Ned, a tall, well-built fifteen-year-old, watched his father pitch hay onto the wagon, then jump on it himself to arrange the forkfuls into a proper loading pattern. It was a three-man job. Carl's single-handed attempts had cleared only one small corner of the long field. Ned paced restlessly between living room and kitchen. Mindy, her dark hair slightly gray at the temples, her face a bit fuller, sat reading quietly in her favorite chair by the window. Or at least she pretended to read, but the tension in the room was such that it was impossible to concentrate.

Stephen, thirteen and slight of frame, sprawled on the floor, dark eyes troubled. "I never felt so uncomfortable in my life, Mother," he said. "Read me the commandment. I can't take this another minute."

Mindy took her Bible from the table beside her chair and opened to Exodus 20. "Ned, perhaps it will help you to hear this, too," she suggested, smiling up at her eldest. "Stop pacing and sit down a moment."

He obeyed, but his mother feared he was beyond listening.

Slowly she read the words, so familiar to all three of them. " 'Remember the sabbath day, to keep it holy. Six days shalt thou labour, and do all thy work: but the seventh day is the sabbath of the Lord thy God: in it thou shalt not do any work, thou, nor thy son, nor thy daughter, thy manservant, nor thy maidservant, nor thy cattle, nor thy stranger that is within thy gates. For in six days the Lord made heaven and earth, the sea, and all that in them is, and rested the seventh day: wherefore the Lord blessed the sabbath day, and hallowed it.' "

"What about the next one which says, 'Honour thy father and thy mother'?" Ned asked, his voice angry.

"Obedience to God comes first, Ned, and perhaps it does not honor a parent anyway to join him in wrongdoing."

Mindy turned again in her Bible and read from Matthew 10:37, " 'He that loveth father or mother more than me is not worthy of me.' We must consider both of these texts in the situation we face today, my sons. It is not a pleasant choice to make, between one's earthly father and his heavenly Father, but if it is any comfort, I believe your earthly father understands your decision and will not hold it against you."

Rain touched the windows in small uncertain splatters. With a driven desperation, Ned rose. "Maybe you can sit here juggling texts and watch Dad struggle with that hay alone, but I can't." The screen door banged behind him.

94

From her spot at the window Mindy watched them work together, Carl and his son, one loading, the other placing on the wagon, in an urgent rhythm as they raced the storm. Her eyes filled with tears. Stephen, standing beside her, placed a hand upon her shoulder. "You cannot lead Ned by the hand into the kingdom of heaven, Mother. He is impulsive and tenderhearted. It is you yourself who has taught us compassion, so don't be too disappointed in him." She could not speak but gave the hand on her shoulder an affectionate squeeze.

That night, half the hay under cover, the other half soggy beneath steady, drenching rains, they gathered about the supper table. Carl's face was haggard in his weariness, but he seemed relaxed, almost happy. Had Ned's coming meant so much to him? Mindy watched for some sign of his displeasure with Stephen, but there was none. When the meal was finished, Stephen said in his direct, clear-eyed way, "Staying in the house this afternoon was the hardest thing I ever did, Dad. I am sorry I could not help you."

"If you were lazy, Stephen, I couldn't accept your actions, but you are a hard worker and have a strong conscience. I know what it cost you to stay inside, and you don't need to ask my forgiveness. But you might tell me, while we're discussing it, just what your fussy God would do with a field of dry hay on the Sabbath with a storm rolling in."

"He would leave it there, or perhaps He would not have cut it till after the Sabbath. Grandfather Hiram farmed for many years without doing more than caring for the needs of his animals on the Sabbath. I believe God helps and protects in special ways when we are obedient to His commands."

"Hiram and God had a partnership," Carl replied good-naturedly. "It's not fair to drag him into this."

Stephen did not pursue the discussion, and Mindy was glad he knew when to be still. She looked at Ned, wondering what thoughts were his, but he ate the Satur-

95

day night brown bread and warmed-over beans, avoiding all part in the conversation.

That night in bed, she said to Carl, "Thanks for understanding Stephen."

"Have you ever thought, Min," he questioned, his voice controlled and without emotion, "what you do to us as a family—what you ask of the boys?"

"If we believed alike, Carl, there would be no controversy. We are simply heading down different roads. When we decided to marry, I thought only of you and me. I never considered the hurt to our children. I was so young"—she hesitated—"and so in love. It was hard to be sensible and foresee all the problems."

"And now you are neither so young nor so in love," he went on wryly, "and there are only the problems left."

"No, Carl, that is not true. Tonight when you were talking with Stephen, my heart was full of love for you. Father once said you were a good man, and he was right. You will never know how much I want you to share the joys of following Christ with the boys and me."

"And at the supper table tonight I too had a wish," he said, "that we might be done with our differences forever and put this religion which drives us apart out of our home."

She turned into his arms weeping, and he held her until at last she slept.

*   *   *   *   *

The day would be hot, but here on the porch in the early morning it was cool, and before Mindy's eyes the valley lay serene and dew-spangled, as though fresh from the thoughts of God. She'd made a habit of coming out here in good weather at the beginning of her day. She spoke now in a kind of one-sided chat with her Maker. "Everything is perfect in Your creation, God, just like the day Carl and I first looked down this valley.

96

The land hasn't changed, but we have. We've learned some hard lessons, and some I just can't learn. Help me to love Seth, or at least to have respect for his humanity. Care for the boys and give us wisdom to train them. Let me be a blessing to Carl to show him Your love."

She had looked up into the clear blue early morning sky with its wisps of white clouds at the fringes as she spoke. Now she brought her eyes back to the forest-clad hills bounding the farm and spread out her arms in a joyous, encompassing gesture. "And thank You for all this. No matter how much I hurt or stumble, there is this beauty which heals and feeds me for every new day."

She went in then to start the breakfast preparations. Ned was building a fire in the stove. August or not, they must cook. Carl wanted a hot breakfast the year around. He and Stephen had gone to the barn, milk pails clanking, even before she'd left the bed.

Ned lagged in the morning, and his father had assigned him the task of preparing the fire for Mindy.

"I'll be glad when I never have to set foot in a barn again," Ned exploded, dropping an armful of kindling into the woodbox.

"There are worse ways to keep the wolf from the door than farming," his mother replied over her clattering of pots and pans.

"If so, they haven't occurred to me," he said grimly.

"Well, you can't ski and hunt and drive a car forever, Ned." Mindy felt a vague impatience with this son sometimes. Since they'd purchased the Essex he had resented his duties about the farm even more than usual.

"Skiing and hunting, if one has the basic equipment, are pretty inexpensive pastimes," he replied good-naturedly, "but I'll have to admit a car is a greedy toy. You don't really expect me to be a farmer, do you, Mother? You know I hate the sight of a cow."

"With your mind, Ned, you can pick your career, but right now, off to the barn with you. You know it irritates your father when you dally."

97

Mindy poured chopped potatoes into sizzling butter and broke eggs into a bowl for scrambling later. And she thought about Ned with his straight A's and his peculiar lack of motivation. He spent as much time with Seth as possible. The two of them knew every inch of the surrounding mountains and brought home a steady supply of meat for the table. The older man, a wizard with his tools, had attempted to pass on his skills to the boy, but he had found Ned an indifferent apprentice.

She loved this hour of quiet—the breakfast preparations, the unblemished possibilities of a new day. After setting the table, she made a quick dash for the garden and a bouquet of nasturtiums. In an old white soup tureen on the blue-checked tablecloth they were lovely. There was a lot of satisfaction in flowers. You could arrange them, and once you got them just right, they stayed that way.

The screen door banged behind Stephen, and he set a jar of cream on the table.

"Have you looked at the morning, Mother?" he asked, smiling.

"Not only looked at it, Stephen, but thanked God for it. And you?"

"I stood so long in the pasture just soaking it all up that Father roared at me from the barn door."

"What did he say?" Mindy chuckled. Poor Carl! One son who hated cows and another who soaked up the morning during chores.

"He said if I were praying the cows in, he doubted it would work, but when I did bring them down, he came out and stood beside me in the barnyard and told me it wasn't a bad idea to stop a moment on a morning like this and be glad for life." He was quiet, pouring the cream from the jar into the breakfast pitcher. "I love Father. He's a rare, good man. How would you ever teach anyone so practical the magic of Jesus Christ?"

"What's more practical than coming to a lost planet and giving His life for a lot of ungrateful humans?

That's not magic. It's decision and work and action. The only magic is the change in us when we come to Him."

"It *all* seems like magic to me," Stephen marveled, his dark eyes glowing. "Imagine the Son of God walking this earth like a common man!"

"In some strange way He took on our humanity for all time." Mindy picked up a book from a reading table by the window. "Listen, Stephen, I found this yesterday:

" ' "*God so loved the world, that He gave His only-begotten Son.*" *He gave Him not only to live among men, to bear their sins, and die their sacrifice. He gave Him to the fallen race. Christ was to identify Himself with the interests and needs of humanity. He who was one with God has linked Himself with the children of men by ties that are never to be broken.* . . . *He is our Sacrifice, our Advocate, our Brother, bearing our human form before the Father's throne, and through eternal ages one with the race He has redeemed—the Son of man.*'

"It was a new idea to me that He had identified Himself with us for eternity. It makes me love Him all the more."

"That's what I mean, Mother. There is a quality of love about the whole thing beyond our understanding. It's exciting to me, and I want to relate to Him in some special way by working for Him."

"In what way?" Mindy asked, looking at her youngest and seeing his intensity through appraising and delighted eyes.

"I want to be a doctor," he said simply, as if he had known it always. "Do you think it's an impossible dream?"

Before she could answer, Ned and Carl came, setting milk pails under the sink and pouring hot water into a basin for washing.

By the time they finished, Mindy had brought the crusty browned potatoes and scrambled eggs to the table, buttered a stack of toast, and dished up the oatmeal. Sitting down, she asked, "Carl, if you'd had opportunity and money to choose any occupation, what would you have done with your life?"

"Only fools play the 'if' game," he replied, pouring cream over his oatmeal. "You live with today like it is if you're smart. Why do you ask such a question?" There was a coldness in his voice, an impatience, almost as though he begrudged her the words.

She refused to turn the breakfast table into a cheap drama, so she said steadily, "Well, the boys both happened to mention something of their own futures this morning, and as I looked at you just now I wondered, had you been as free to plan your life as they are, what your dreams might have been. It seemed strange that after all these years I really didn't know."

"Nothing strange about that. No one was allowed any dreams when I was young. And what are yours?" he asked testily, turning to his sons.

"Mine's to be a chauffeur for Rockefeller," Ned said, laughing. "Imagine getting paid for driving."

How often that laughter had broken a tense situation as it did now.

"You're sending him away to school for *that?*" Carl said, looking at Mindy, but he was smiling. He turned to Stephen. "And you, my young sun-worshiper, what are your dreams?"

Stephen flushed, but he answered quietly, "I'd like to be a doctor. Maybe I'm not smart enough, but I'd like to try."

"Not smart enough? What kind of nonsense is that? You're a good student." Carl's eyes flashed almost in anger at his son.

"Only an average one, Father. Ned is the student in this family. I have to work twice as hard as he does to learn half as much."

"Poor fellow," Ned said, dimples flashing. "It's too bad all your ambition and my brains didn't get together."

"It *would have been* a more practical arrangement, but like Father said, wise men take today like it is and do the best they can with it."

"And these three wise men have more work lined up for the day than six could handle; so let's be about it." Carl pushed away from the table, and the boys followed.

Mindy washed dishes, swept floors, and scoured the milk pails, taking them to a wagon wheel mounted on a stake in the backyard for drying. She stood there a moment, letting the breeze move over her, watching Carl scythe the riverbank. Scything was a beautiful activity, like ballet, and Carl did it as he did everything, with grace. He kept the farm like a garden, she thought. Who else in this demanding land worried about riverbanks?

She could hear the boys sawing up stovewood in the near pasture, their voices coming to her on the wind.

Mindy knew the task which awaited her, and she shrank from it. In three days Ned would be leaving for academy. It was a victory she had won, but she could not bear the loss of him. She had shopped and sewed and mended but had not been able to bring herself to put the things in his trunk. Now she could delay no longer. In his room she took the new sheets and towels from his closet and laid them at the bottom of the trunk. A light blanket. A heavy homemade quilt. She folded shirts with loving care. More and better clothes than he'd ever had before.

"Be sure he doesn't go shabby," Carl had said in a fierce family pride which overrode his normal frugality. She took a jacket from its hook, decided it needed laundering, and proceeded to empty the pockets methodically before tossing it into the pile of soiled clothes at her feet.

From the breast pocket she removed a small package and gasped in dismay at its contents. Cigarettes. She held them dumbly, looking at them, not believing. However frivolously Ned lived, he had no reason to smoke.

Even Carl did not smoke. He would not last a week at Pine Valley Academy smoking. All her long struggle to win Carl's permission in vain! She stood there, making no sound, holding the crumpled package, tears streaming down her cheeks, when Ned walked in, having returned for his watch, which he'd forgotten.

She held them out to him without a word.

"I'm sorry, Mother," he said, his eyes not meeting hers. "I didn't mean for you to ever know."

"*Why*, Ned? Why do you feel the need to smoke? You know we have no right to destroy the body God has given us. It's such a cheap, dirty habit. Oh, Ned!"

At the sorrow in his mother's voice, the boy only looked more uncomfortable and twisted one sturdy boot against the other.

"How did you start?" Mindy asked, feeling suddenly sure she knew the answer.

"Grandfather," the boy told her, miserably. "He said Father had always been too straitlaced. He made it sound pretty foolish to be so stuffy. It's not the end of the world, Mother." Ned looked up then, the familiar sweet, teasing smile lighting his eyes. "I promise not to smoke at academy. . . . At least I promise not to get caught."

She finished the packing, and the days slipped by, but the joy had gone out of them. She had thought to send her eldest away clean in body and soul. True, he didn't always go to church with her and Stephen, but he wasn't rebellious. He had respect for his church and his God. He had not resisted going to the academy, even though he had had a year of public high school. She suspected that his release from farm duties played a part in his willingness, but she hadn't really cared. She understood his abhorrence of haying and milking. But to send him away like this—to sneak and break rules and be a stumbling block to other boys. She could not bear it.

Seth came into her kitchen on the morning before

102

Ned was to leave, bringing a sack of sweet corn, a new white variety he had raised.

"Thank you, Seth," she said, trying to be courteous but hearing the words fall brittle and broken from her lips.

"What's eatin' *you?*" The old man looked at her sharply. "My corn ain't good enough for you?"

"I've been hoping you'd bring us some," Mindy answered levelly. "I've never tasted white corn before. But, Seth, there really is a question I want to ask you. Why did you urge Ned to smoke, when you knew how Carl and I feel about it?"

" 'Cause I don't want him raised no sissy, that's why. A smoke's a lot of comfort to a man sometimes. Carl wouldn't be so tight-mouthed himself if he'd relax with a smoke now and then. Ned's a fun-lovin' boy. You can't keep him wrapped up in a lace doily the rest of his life. You may stuff Stephen with all that religious hocus-pocus, but Ned's not made that way. Martha made a goody-goody out of Carl, and you're doing the same with Stephen, but things will be different with Ned."

"Seth Matthews, you have no right to destroy him. He's our son, not yours!" Mindy heard her own voice edged with tears, and she knew what Seth thought of tears.

"We'll see," Seth declared calmly, his eyes stubborn.

Chapter 11

Carl was late coming home from town meeting. Stephen had the cows all milked, and supper had waited long on the back of the stove. When he did arrive, he was filled with rare exuberance. It had been an exciting day, filled with the heated arguments and stern business of small-town America exercising government by the people. He described each action in witty detail, even remembering to pass on the compliments Mindy's cake had collected at the noon meal. Stephen laughed aloud, delighted at his father's levity. Mindy, sharing eagerly in the news of her neighbors and their doings, nevertheless looked at her husband shrewdly. Here was an old Carl, almost forgotten. What had happened on this muddy March day to surface his laughter?

She rose, cut a piece of custard pie from the pans on the broad shelf, and brought it to his place. As she leaned over his shoulder he caught her hand and did not let her go. It had been a long time since he had touched her in eager, open affection, and she found herself shy, especially under Stephen's appraising eye.

"Mindy," he said, laughing and foxy, "they not only liked your cake, but they voted your husband into the best job he's ever had. For the first time in our married lives we'll have an income we can depend on."

"What are you talking about, Carl?" Mindy traced with the index finger of her free hand the strong, high cheekbone of his face and thought how easy he was to love when he moved out of the shadows of his bitterness.

"Meet the new town road commissioner," he announced, with an embarrassed little bow.

"What's that?" Stephen asked.

"Well, it'll be my job to see that all town roads are in good condition in the summer and free of snow in the winter. I'll have a crew of men working for me. I'm looking forward to it already."

"That means no more hunting for jobs every summer and lumbering all winter. I can't believe it. Will we still farm?"

"Snow removal won't keep me busy all winter. I'll still probably do some lumbering. And you know, Min, I'll always farm. I didn't buy this place to let it grow up to bushes. I'll just have to go on fitting the farming in around my other work as I've always done."

So Carl would continue to live with weariness and overwork after all, but since he was happy and they should live more comfortably, she hugged him and said, "You've earned it, and this town will have the best roads it's ever seen. With my teaching money we'll be positively rich."

"Well, not quite," Carl told her, sobering. "By the time you pay Ned's school bills, you won't have much left." That had been the bargain when Ned went away to school, that Mindy must be responsible for his tuition. It had meant for her a return to the classroom, but she enjoyed every moment of teaching, and this time Carl had not opposed her.

Stephen and his father sat at the table chatting as Mindy rose to clear away the dishes. "Wait till Ned hears this news!" Stephen said. "He'll want to drive truck for you."

"Too young. Maybe in a couple of years."

Mention of Ned brought a stab of loneliness to Mindy. She had never really grown accustomed to his absence or the loss of his dimpled grin. His letters were brief and sporadic, telling her little beyond his need for pocket money.

Over his Christmas holiday she had watched him closely. What had this new experience done for her first-born? He had been the same, yet not the same. Laughing, charming, teasing, warmhearted, generous. The Ned she'd always known. But there was a subtle new independence—a loss of childhood, perhaps. It had made Mindy long to reach out and place her hand on the auburn head, but at the same time she knew she must not. The faint stale odor of cigarettes clung to his jackets. She wondered how he managed at the academy and if she should take him out. She felt a deep responsibility for his influence on others.

She brushed aside her thoughts and tackled the dishes. There were papers to correct, lessons to prepare, lunches to pack, and later on she'd show Carl her pride and pleasure in his achievements. She smiled a little, thinking about it.

After Stephen had gone to bed, they stood together a moment on the long front porch, taking a breath of fresh air before retiring. A damp mist hung over the valley which lay mottled with patches of snow and dead grass. The sharp chill of winter persisted, and Mindy shivered. Carl, standing behind her, placed his arms around her, sheltering her from the wind.

"You know, Min, what hit me today, coming home from town meeting?"

"What?"

"That I was never going to accomplish anything great. That I'm forty years old, and it's too late to be a success. I'll just go on working and barely making ends meet. The boys will soon be gone, and we'll have a little more to fix up the place, but we'll still be just poor hill people. I guess I always thought if I worked hard enough

106

and ran fast enough, I could leave poverty behind and do something worthwhile."

Mindy turned in his arms and took his face in her hands. "I wouldn't love you a whit more if you were president of Ford Motor Company. But you *have* failed in one thing."

"And what is that?" he asked, almost fearfully, in the darkness.

"You've failed to kiss me in many a week," she said softly.

With a harsh, half-sad little laugh, he tilted her mouth to meet his own.

Two days later Nathan called to say that Em had pneumonia and they were taking her to the hospital. That evening when Carl and Mindy visited her, Mindy knew with a sharp certainty that her mother would never go home again. Though they spoke her name over and over again, Em could not break through the barrier of shallow breathing and deep lassitude which shut her away from her son and daughters.

Seated at the funeral a week later, Mindy avoided looking at her mother. As the minister spoke of her life of toil and her faithfulness to God, Mindy barely listened. She looked at her brother and sister and their offspring. Childhood seemed far away, with Em the last link to it. Wright had died some years before in a hunting accident. Already Nathan bore the stoop-shouldered mien of all men who wrestled with New England's rocky farms. His wife, small and dark, was a blessing to him. She did not whine about her lot in life or grow quiet and bitter as did some women. Their three children sat beside them, sturdy, sober young people, already honed by responsibility and hard work.

Childbearing and poverty could not touch Pearl. Mindy looked long at her sister sitting among her graying husband and their four children. They were a handsome couple despite their age difference. It seemed to Mindy that Pearl grew lovelier with the years. She had a

107

funny urge to reach out and touch the glossy black hair, the glowing skin, and to say in some tangible way, "I love you," to hold the past a bit longer. She sensed their beginnings had become endings here in this room where they had gathered to mourn the loss of their mother.

While the preacher spoke comfort and the assurance of resurrection, her thoughts wandered. Carl's hands caught her attention. How strange they looked folded and still in his lap. Stephen sat beyond Carl, erect and handsome in his Sabbath suit. He *really was* handsome, she thought proudly. There was an openness about him. Something more too. Purpose, perhaps. They hadn't brought Ned home from school, preferring to let him remember his grandmother as she had been.

She realized suddenly that she couldn't face her mother's death. She did not want to look at the loved familiar face and be reminded that the years slip away and life could be nothing more than a repetition of a thousand lives before. Maybe that's what Carl had been talking about that other night on the porch. When her children were babies, she had felt sure that with perseverance and training she could mold them into men of God who would break out of the family mold and do something grand with their lives. Now she was not so sure. She had watched Ned's progress in school with wonder over the years. Learning came so easily, perhaps too easily. She had taken such pride in him. But along with his astonishing report cards had come the small warning evidences of a nature too undisciplined to use the gifts with which it was endowed.

Stephen was another story. She tried hard not to pin too many hopes on him, but he had never disappointed her. How could she help but hope?

Her marriage. Was it like any mature union, safe and sure—and dull? Instantly she dismissed the word *dull*. Something *had* gone out of their relationship, but marriage to Carl would never be dull. He seldom gave himself fully. One always felt there was more to know, more to be had, and she loved that about him. But often in the past years a coldness in him shut her out and left her lonely.

No, marriage hadn't been the fairy tale she'd hoped for, and she would not attempt to place the blame. She knew her own deepening relationship with God often left Carl lonely and confused. It was a pathway in her life that he chose not to walk.

So what was life, after all? Just individuals stumbling and hoping and dreaming. Watching the dreams pop one by one like the soap bubbles in her dishpan. Finding out in the end you were really all alone, no matter who or how many had blundered along with you. Only there was God. He'd walk with you any time you invited Him, but you had to care—to really want Him. Sometimes she was too weary to care, or too proud, or just too indifferent.

But there had been some rare, wonderful moments when she had understood that He was everything, that life could be very bland—or even tragic—but it didn't really matter, because God was an experience above all these earth happenings. She caught glimpses of Him often in the out-of-doors or upon her knees—or sometimes a verse in her Bible would come into focus, and it was like seeing through the ordinary to something splendid and mystic and waiting. Only you really didn't have to wait if you could find it now.

Everyone was leaving. She stood beside the casket and cried at last, the tears falling on the brown dress she and Pearl had made Em years ago. The tears made tiny spots which spread into dark stains as she watched. Pearl, at her side, said, "Come, Mindy. Carl is waiting. And Mother wouldn't have you sorrowing."

On their way home they stopped off at the mailbox, where Carl handed her a letter addressed in Ned's hasty, left-handed scrawl. Her heart lifted, and she tore it open carelessly.

109

Dear Mother and Father:
I will be home Friday on the three o'clock
train. Someone advised the faculty of my
secret smoking spot, and I was asked to leave.
I am sorry to disappoint you, Mother.
Tell Grandfather to get the guns oiled.
Love,
Ned

Mindy did not need to read the accompanying letter from the school in its official white envelope. She placed her lips tightly together and disciplined her already frazzled emotions. Carl, reading over her shoulder, spoke quietly, "He wouldn't have hurt you for the world, Min. He's just very young and very unwise. Don't judge him too harshly."

"It's my own fault," she said, her voice careful and resigned. "I should never have sent him, knowing he had the habit. When he promised he wouldn't smoke, I wanted to believe him. I wasn't being realistic."

She suddenly thought of Stephen, sitting in the back seat, and handed him the letter.

"He'll be home in time for sugaring." It was all Stephen said, but Mindy heard the gladness in his voice. So he had been lonely. Seth too would rejoice. She could already hear his amused chuckle. How far the fingers of his influence had reached into Ned's young life! The tears would no longer obey her, and for the second time that day she watched them fall and spread into dark little blobs. Such useless things—tears.

She glanced at Carl, but he maneuvered the car about the curves of their winding driveway without a word, even his face telling her nothing.

When Ned arrived the next afternoon, they did not scold or discipline him. She had prepared a special meal with all his favorite foods and invited Seth and Martha to eat with them. After the first awkward moments he was light and laughing, but he did not tease his mother

110

in the usual way or even look at her, for that matter.

When the dishes were washed and the kitchen straightened, they still lingered about the table, bringing Ned up to date on the local news. Mindy watched a bar of sun recede along the blue linen tablecloth and knew the sundown hour was approaching. She needed to meet this Sabbath with God, company or no company. They would never miss her. She slipped away and headed for her bedroom. As she placed her foot on the first stair she heard Seth's voice, smug with approval, "Guess you showed them straitlaced teachers what you thought of their silly rules, hey, Ned?"

Ned's answer came quickly, almost angrily. "It's not much to be proud of, Grandfather."

She ran then and threw herself, sobbing, to her knees beside her bed. When, moments later, she heard someone enter the room, she did not get up or lift her head. She did not want anyone to witness her sorrow. She had thought to hide. "Go away," her mind said. "This is nothing you would understand, Carl. What do you care for the boy's soul? Not even enough to stand up against your father."

But it was not Carl.

"Mother?" There was sorrow in the voice, akin to her own. She got up then, ashamed of her red eyes and her weakness.

"It has been a hard week, Ned, with Grandma's death and . . ." Her voice trailed off, not willing to make him bear the burden of her tears.

"And my failure," he finished.

"Oh, Ned, you haven't failed." She reached out to him in a gesture so reassuring that he could not have doubted her love. "Failure is only when we have dismissed God from our lives and no longer desire to please Him. You have not come even close to that. I made a mistake to let you go away to school, knowing you were smoking. I had my heart set on your going and refused to give up my pretty dream. Now I am paying the price.

111

Perhaps I'm the one who should say, 'I'm sorry, Ned.' I put you in a hard place."

The boy looked at her then and smiled, something of childhood lighting his sober face for a moment. "You will never know how sorry I am to cause you one moment of heartache. I did a lot of thinking on my way home on the train. I'm going back in the fall, and I'll do it the right way this time. I won't try to outwit anyone, and I'll study hard. That's my gift to you, Mother. But you have to accept the fact that I hate school, and I'm not going on to college. You must not ask it of me."

She started to speak, but he held up his hand and went on. "I'm not sure I can live your kind of life." There was a break in his voice like a sob, forbidden to be born. "It doesn't come as naturally to me as it does to Stephen. I believe all you've taught me. I know every defense for the Sabbath. I can quote you the texts for the Second Coming. I even understand the principles by which Jesus Christ lived." He hesitated. "But I'm not at all sure I can live them."

"Ned, who of us can? We all fall again and again. That's what salvation is all about, forgiveness for our failures. You know that."

"There's something in me that doesn't care," the boy continued sadly. "That's different from what you're talking about. I'm bitterly sorry that I've disappointed you, but I want to live life with all the stops out—without God breathing down my neck—even though I know it's a dead-end street."

"That is partly youth, Ned. We've all had rebellious feelings. That is the time to get down on our knees. He was young once, too, you know, and probably tempted to live life with all the stops out. His victory is ours, Ned. Stephen is an unusually disciplined boy. You must not always compare yourself with him. You are a very special person in your own right—to your father, to me, and to God."

"Let's welcome the Sabbath together, Mother."

112

Chapter 12

On the seventh day of September Mindy started early for the school house in the village. She drove a smart little black mare as much her own as Belle had once been Carl's. As the buggy rattled along the dry, rutted road, she thanked God all over again that Carl had dared to believe this valley might be theirs. She knew each turn of the road, each fitful foaming of the brook alongside, each ledge which humped its back against the thin New England soil. Young spruce trees marched up the banks in graduated heights, lifting their glossy needles to the sun. Her whole being exulted at the simple wonder of the earth. She was on her way toward a work she loved, and she was eager for the challenge. This morning she could not stoop beneath a single burden. She felt tall and free and filled with joy.

Two days before, they had placed Stephen and Ned on a train headed for boarding academy in Maine. Stephen had been eager, excited, his black eyes snapping in anticipation; Ned, quiet and resigned. His soft, "Don't worry about me, Mother" as he hugged her good-bye had broken her heart. She well understood what such resolve had cost him, and for whom he had mustered it.

It had been a good summer. Just as she had predicted, Carl had thrown himself into his new work with an enthusiasm which ensured his position for years to come. Mindy and the boys had done most of the haying themselves, singing and laughing in the fields as they worked. Carl would not let her attempt any part of the loading, so they brought the hay to the barn in the coolness of the early evenings after the chores, the boys pitching the stacks of sweet-smelling dried hay onto the wagon for Carl's precise arranging, while Mindy drove the horses and watched a silver half moon dangle among the darkening pines. Sometimes they sang, Carl leading out in "Sweetheart of the Rockies" or "The Old Rugged Cross," whichever suited his fancy. He liked the old familiar hymns. She often wondered what he felt, if anything, about that Young Man on the cross.

When the load was heaped high on the wagon, Stephen swung up beside her and took the reins, for it was no easy task to guide the horses home over the side hills. Carl and Ned leaned on their forks behind, swaying to the rhythm of the creaking wagon and watching the load with practiced eyes.

But now the fields were twice shorn, the barns full, the house bereft of boyish banter, the days quiet and orderly.

Mindy staked the mare in a grassy plot behind the school and turned the key in the lock of the schoolhouse with anticipation. It would be a half hour before the first student straggled in. She had previously settled the room and sorted textbooks; so all was in readiness. She sat down at her desk, facing the empty rows in the quiet room. A little world of her own in which to exercise all her creativity. She bowed her head in prayer. "Dear God, they're all in their homes now, rushing around to find pencils and notebooks, having their hair braided and their cowlicks slicked down. It's a big day, the first day of school. Some have worked so hard this summer that they are more adult than child. Life's not easy for any of them. Let this place be a haven of joy and wonder for them. Let me teach them to know the world beyond these mountains but never to underestimate their heritage."

The door opened a crack. "Come in," Mindy said. "You're early. I like early birds. I'm one, too, you see."

A tiny girl in a faded dress eased fearfully into the room. The lovely, long-awaited event had dissolved into panic.

"Come here." Mindy motioned the child to her desk. "What is your name?" she asked, putting her arm about the child's waist and marveling at the fragility of little girls.

"Lucy," she replied in little more than a whisper.

"Did you see anything interesting on the way to school this morning, Lucy?"

The child thought a moment and then shook her head without looking up.

"What did you see that was pretty?"

Lucy wound one thin leg about the other uneasily. "Nothin'."

"Would you like to see what I found on my way to school?" Mindy asked, opening the drawer of her desk.

The child looked up then, curiosity showing in her great brown eyes. Mindy took the girl's hand and upon the palm placed a half-opened milkweed pod. The white down, soft as angel's hair, tumbled over the tiny thumb, and the child stroked it shyly. Mindy peeled back the rough pod and pointed out satiny scales lying tightly one upon another.

There was laughter in the hall and scuffling of feet. The day was on, but for a second longer, Mindy and the girl shared the moment. "You may have the pod," Mindy said, smiling, "to remind you of your first day at school; and every morning when you walk along the road, look for something lovely to show me or tell me about. Will you do that?"

The brown eyes lifted, shining and eager. "Yes'm,

115

and I'm going to keep the milkweed pod forever and ever."

Mindy opened the window facing on the playground. Leaning, chin in cupped hands, she watched the children racing about in a game of tag. She breathed deeply of the fresh air, its summer softness still lingering. The girls, seeing her there, clustered beneath the window, a bouquet of gingham and braids.

"See my new dress, Miss Matthews. I made it myself."

"I got a surprise for you in my lunch box, Teacher."

"I practiced my tables all summer, Mrs. Matthews. I know 'em good."

"We got a new baby, Teacher. Just another boy."

She chuckled. Little girls, so eager to please. So ready with news. So hungry for recognition. The boys went on playing tag with little more than a friendly wave or a "Morning, Miss Matthews" as they raced past the window. What did it say about men and women? So many things she didn't know. So many questions. She wished she were a student herself.

She rang the bell and watched the playground empty into her classroom. Rowdiness settled into disciplined anticipation as the children sought out their desks and looked to her expectantly.

"How many of you took a trip during your summer vacation?" she asked.

Not a hand was raised. "Well, never mind. Neither did I," Mindy said, laughing. "But before we start school officially, I think we all deserve a holiday." She moved from desk to desk, placing back copies of *National Geographic* before each of the older children. "I want you to choose a country you would like to visit from the magazine you have just received. Read all about it. Use your geography book and the encyclopedias, too, if you like. Then write me a letter about your trip, telling me how you traveled, what you ate, what you enjoyed, and all about the people you met. Write the letter in proper form, for

116

remember I am a teacher, and I will notice your errors more than others might. You may cut out pictures to illustrate your letter and show me the sights of your travels too.

"I am taking grades one through four with me to Switzerland," she added, leading the younger children to a circle of chairs at the front of the room. They were soon snipping, gluing, and listening to her description of a land of mountains, not so unlike their own.

Thus she led them day by day to an exploration of the world about them and the world beyond their journeyings until her classroom was a tumble of experiments, projects, and happy, painless learning.

*　　*　　*　　*　　*

The Sabbath had become for Mindy, as the years passed, a time of rare delight. Now with the boys gone and Carl working away from home, she hitched Star to the buggy and drove alone through the hills to the small, white church six miles away. There she worshiped with her fellow Christians, loving them but never forming close relationships. Carl, her sons, her students, and her God—these were enough. It was the afternoon which she anticipated most, for it was then she packed a sandwich, tucked her Bible under her arm, and set off through the pasture for her rendezvous with God. Once when searching for a lost calf, she had stumbled onto a hidden spot of breathtaking beauty. It had become for her a sacred place.

Now on this September Sabbath she set out through the pasture, savoring the penetrating warmth of a late summer sun. She stooped at the stream to crush a leaf of mint between her fingers and then sat down on a rock beside the water. Unpinning her hair, she let it fall glistening over her back and shoulders as she bowed her head upon her arms. She was part of the earth, as much as any stone or flower. She did not dream or hope or

117

worry. She was neither old nor young. Only a whimsy in God's plan, like a buttercup. It was a marvelously irresponsible way to feel for a moment. Relaxed, warmed, lulled with the sound of water whispering in and out among stones.

But she had not come to nod beside the brook, and so she rose and moved upward into the woods. She never liked the transition. Woods were dark and stirred some deep uneasiness within her, but her goal lay ahead; so she sang hymns and picked her way through underbrush and over fallen logs.

At last she parted a few scrub evergreens and stepped into a tiny clearing high on a cliff. Bands of sunlight falling through towering pines lay in strips across the lushness of pale green wild grasses. It was as though it had been prepared by God for some special purpose . . . a miniature Eden in the forest. Startled into reverence, as always, she lifted her face to the sky and prayed. In this place she rarely prayed in specifics about the ordinary problems of life. She could find only praise for her Creator upon her lips and then a great hunger that His presence might fill the mysterious longing within her. She had never brought anyone here. To her knowledge no other human foot had ever walked here. She entered and sat down with her back against a pine. For two hours she read her Bible and pondered the things she found there. Only the turning of an occasional page broke the stillness. Birds and chipmunks came and went. Shafts of sunlight edged across the clearing, and the heart of Mindy Matthews came ever closer to its God.

* * * * *

That evening as she laid the table for supper, Mindy hummed softly to herself. She chatted eagerly to Carl, attempting to draw from him the small happenings of his day. Noting he was quiet and not in a mood to share his thoughts, she silenced her own tongue. He was often

118

taciturn, and sometimes she tried teasing him into companionship, but this night she did not. They ate silently, silverware clinking nervously against their plates. When he finished, Carl pushed his chair away from the table and remarked, too carelessly, "After the chores I'm going to the dance in town."

Mindy made no attempt to hide her amazement. "Carl, you haven't been to a dance in years. Whatever has gotten into you?" It was not uncommon for men of Carl's age to attend the Saturday night dances. They were lively, noisy affairs which attracted a wide age range, but she had not dreamed her sober, hardworking Carl retained any tendencies for that kind of entertainment.

"I'm weary of all work and no play," he said defensively.

"Well, I guess you're old enough to go where you please." Mindy tried to smile and say it lightly, but she knew in this decision Carl had spelled out a new answer to their old problem of differing life-styles.

"I'd be glad to take you with me, but I know how you feel about it."

"Carl, surely you don't believe all that close dancing between mixed partners is good. And you know how noisy and smoky it all gets. You've said yourself you're glad the boys don't go there. Somehow one loses his best self in such an atmosphere. It becomes so very easy to look lightly on sin."

"You make the most innocent things sound like a dime novel, Mindy. It would do you good to whirl around in a bit of square dancing, and if some neighbor happened to ask you for a waltz, I doubt you'd be soiled for life." Carl's voice was cold, and it birthed an unfamiliar anger in Mindy.

"Why did you marry me if I'm so odd? You knew then I didn't dance. What has happened to you? Are you afraid life is slipping through your fingers and hope to recapture it in some cheap flirtation on a shoddy

119

dance floor?" She was taunting and hard on the outside, crumbling chaos on the inside.

Without a word he went to the barn. She left the dishes and headed down the hillside to walk along the brook which split the valley. She saw him return and then come out again, dressed for town. She scrambled up onto a ledge so he wouldn't see her and sat there watching him drive away. She then tumbled onto the bed of pine needles beneath her and sobbed.

She had rarely spent a Saturday night without him. Sometimes they drove to one of the surrounding towns and shopped, sometimes they just made popcorn and read or played games with the boys. The valley, the house, seemed desolate. She could not even think of his dancing some young thing about. He could be so appealing when he chose.

But worst of all had been her anger. She had not known herself capable of such ugliness. So, following Christ was more than sitting against a pine tree and reading one's Bible. Would she ever learn it all? When her tears were spent and fog had begun to settle uncomfortably about her, she got up and walked with purpose back toward the house.

For nineteen years Carl had fitted himself around her way of life. If he now chose to reverse the pattern, it was his right. She would apologize in the morning for her anger, and never again would he drive away with her shrewish words ringing in his ears. The fog's chill seemed to follow her into the dark house. She fumbled for a match and lit the lamps, then set about to make some fudge for mailing to the boys.

When she went to bed, her left arm ached right down to her fingertips. It occurred to her it did that often lately.

120

Chapter 13

Mindy lay rigid in the darkness, straining her ears. Something had awakened her, a muffled thud in the kitchen below. Her first instinct was to awaken Carl, but his spring road and farm work demanded grueling days, and she could not bear to disturb his rest. Lying almost without breathing, she heard a cough, then a retching. Her heart slowed to its normal pace. She moved carefully away from Carl and slipped into her robe. Feeling her way down the stairs, she entered the kitchen and lit a lamp. She was sickened by the sight before her. Seth lay sprawled in the doorway, the stench of vomit and alcohol heavy upon him. Since Martha's death some months before, he had, at Carl's invitation, made his home with them. Occasionally on Saturday nights a friend stopped by to take him out for the evening, and this was not the first time he had arrived home to tumble across the threshold in a drunken stupor. Usually Carl cared for him, but Mindy well knew the exhaustion which had shut out all sound to her husband this night. Everything in her recoiled from the form at her feet. His sharp tongue slashed away day by day at the brittle peace within their home. His influence upon Ned strengthened with the years. Martha's death seemed to have left him shorn of any shreds of tenderness. She found respite only in the classroom.

The house was cold. She could not leave him here. She refused to call Carl. Yet she could not bring herself to touch him. She was filled with emotions she dared not label. *Christ would have had pity upon this lonely, troubled man.* The thought urged itself upon her, but she found herself unable to submit. Sometimes it demanded too much, this discipleship. She put her hands under the old man's shoulders and tugged his sturdy frame through the doorway until she could close the door against the sleety rain that soaked his legs and her kitchen floor. Removing his soiled clothing, she dipped warm water into a basin from the reservoir at the end of the wood stove and bathed the vomit from his face. She could not get him into bed, so bringing blankets and pillow from his bedroom off the kitchen, she wrapped him snugly and proceeded to give herself a thorough scrubbing at the iron sink. Before blowing out the lamp and climbing the stairs, she stood looking down at him for a moment. Even in age his face was haughtily handsome. She had seen in him every evidence of a quick and clever mind. His hands turned with skill to almost any task. What quirk of fate had led such a man to this condition?

As she fumbled her way up the stairs and slipped into bed, chilled and weary, she wondered what Carl would think when he found his father there in the morning. Sleep enticed her as she curled, snug and secure, against Carl in the warmth of the old brass bed.

Pouring cream over his apple pie at the breakfast table next morning, Carl said, "You should have called me last night. Father isn't your responsibility."

"No, but you are, and you needed your rest." Mindy buttered toast carefully. "Why must he come home in such condition anyway?"

"He's not been himself since Mother died. It's tough to be alone."

"Why do you always make excuses for him, Carl? Your mother put up with this sort of thing for years. Do you love him so much?"

Carl did not even look at her. "He is my father."

Mindy rose from the table and refilled his coffee cup. "And that answers everything, I suppose. Would you love *me* if you found me lying in filth on your doorstep?"

"I'd care for you," he told her.

She gave him a wry little smile. "You would at that, Carl. You really would."

When he had gone about his work, Mindy said into the silence, "It's no fair that he was born good, Lord, and that I have to struggle so hard. I wish I knew how to get you two together. He'd bring you a lot more satisfaction than I do."

There was no time for daydreaming this morning, however. Ned and Stephen were coming for the weekend, and both were bringing girls. Over his three years at the academy, Ned had brought home several. Always the same type—light, laughing, and frivolous. And never the same one twice. He seldom appeared to take any of them very seriously, but sometimes Mindy worried that on the spur of the moment he'd marry some irresponsible little thing with a pretty face. For they were always pretty, Ned's girls.

She had been surprised at Stephen's request. He'd never mentioned a girl. He was only sixteen, and she wished he'd wait a bit. Knowing he was steady and sensible, she refrained from counseling. She was wildly curious. What kind of girl would interest Stephen? She had tried to talk to Carl about it, but often he barely answered her these days. He spent long hours at his desk keeping the books connected with his position as road commissioner. Sometimes when he was gone, she opened them and marveled at the neat, precise figures and his amazing accuracy. Never an erasure. At such times she was saddened at the thought of what he might have been.

The freshness of April poured into the guest room, ruffling white curtains, as she opened the windows. Deftly she made up the wide old bed where the girls would sleep. She wished there were a rug for the floor instead of the worn linoleum, but at least it was clean and welcoming. There might even be a daffodil or two for the dresser by the time they arrived.

Then to the baking. Never let it be said that Mindy Matthews failed to set a good table. Carl insisted on that. For all his thriftiness, they had fresh fruit at every season, and she never lacked the essentials for cooking.

On Friday when the four young people stepped down from the train, Mindy stood on the station platform to meet them, her dark coat whipping about her in the spring wind. She wore her graying hair in smooth puffs about her face as was the fashion of the day. Her softly rounded figure bespoke approaching middle age, but the joy in her eyes at sight of her sons was youth itself. The soft-eyed girl with golden hair floating along on Ned's arm was a pleasing replica of all that had gone before. Once they were home, Ned would leave her to Mindy while he went off to the woods with Seth. Well, never mind, they were always rather sweet, these bits of fluff her eldest attracted. And she'd never had a daughter.

Stephen's voice broke through her appraisal of Rose. "Mother, I'd like you to meet Grace."

She looked then into one of the loveliest faces she'd ever seen. There was in it such compassion and depth of character that then and there she found herself frightened that this girl would somehow slip away from her younger son. She saw laughter in Stephen's eyes. He counted it a little joke that he had taken his mother by surprise. She noted he helped Grace into the back seat of the buggy with unusual care.

Ned and Rose climbed into the front seat beside Mindy. "I haven't ridden in a buggy since I was twelve," the girl bubbled. "This horse seems pretty lively. Is she safe?"

124

"Perfectly," Mindy said, wrapping the reins firmly about her hands, "but she doesn't believe in dawdling along."

"If you'd only learn to drive the car, Mother," Ned needled, impatiently. "I feel silly trundling along in a buggy in this day and age."

"Well, you'll meet more wagons than cars along this road, Ned. Cars are still luxuries. Be thankful we have one at all."

Mindy eavesdropped shamelessly on Stephen's conversation with his little friend in the back seat.

"This *is* beautiful country, Stephen. No wonder you love to come home. Just smell the evergreens."

"I know *every* twig in this valley," Stephen answered, "and I can't wait to take you on a tour; but someday I'm going to leave and see the rest of the world. I wish I could go tomorrow."

Loneliness settled over Mindy like the fine dust of the dirt road. It was as though he were already gone, for Stephen spoke no idle words.

"Where do you want to go?" the girl asked softly.

"Everywhere. I want to see the Rockies and hang over the Grand Canyon, then I want to settle some place where the land is big and beautiful and difficult."

"How will you do all that and still become a doctor?"

"There are years and years ahead, Grace. Time enough for everything."

"That's what your father thought," Mindy mused. "Time enough for everything, and he's still milking cows."

Later, as she went about supper preparations she glanced at her reflection in the mirror over the sink. A streak of chalk dust blurred across one cheek like some ghostly rouge. Well, it matched her graying hair. She was not sure she liked getting old, especially with these glowing young creatures flitting about in her kitchen. Ned, as she had expected, set off for the woods with Seth, with only some teasing apology to Rose. Stephen, changing

125

at once into work clothes, headed for the barn. He would have the chores done and surprise his father. He had invited Grace to join him, but she chose to help with the meal.

Tying each girl into a starchy apron, she assigned them small easy tasks, not knowing their abilities. She was serving what Stephen called gold dust toast. It was one of his favorites. Slices of toast in a creamy gravy with a dusting of finely chopped hard-boiled eggs over the top. There would be a platter of fried chicken, home-canned limas, and one of the new gelatin salads everyone was making. For dessert she had baked Ned's favorite raspberry pies.

She could barely take her eyes from the graceful girl arranging lettuce and squares of gelatin on small plates. Rose, stirring cream sauce at the stove, chattered on about their train trip, but Mindy found herself hardly listening.

"Grace," she said, finally squeezing into a brief gap in Rose's monologue, "what are your interests? What do you hope to become?"

The girl turned from her task, and Mindy was startled once again at the innocent beauty of her.

"Music is my life, ma'am," she replied. "I plan to go just as far as I can in that field. I spend every spare moment at the piano."

"And how about you, Rose?" Mindy turned to the pretty, flushed face at the stove.

"I don't know yet. I guess I just want a home and children, but my mother says I should have at least two years of college."

"You should *finish* college, Rose," Grace told her firmly. "There's plenty of time for marriage after that. Don't you agree, Mrs. Matthews?"

Mindy laughed wryly. "I'm in no position to comment. I married right out of high school."

"But you teach," Grace protested. "Stephen says you are an excellent teacher."

126

"Only because I limp from year to year on summer school sessions. I would give a great deal to have gone to college."

"There, Rose. You see, even though Mrs. Matthews is doing her work well, she still wishes she'd had more education."

"Why didn't you skip Mr. Matthews and go on to college," Rose asked soberly, "if it was really that important to you?"

Mindy hesitated and then answered shyly, "Because I loved him very much, and I wasn't sure he'd wait that long."

"There would have been someone else," Grace said quietly.

For a moment Mindy was back on the sunny hillside twenty years before, Carl lifting her onto Belle, his arms strong and sure about her. She could almost smell the sweet pungence of late summer grasses.

"Not for me, Grace," she said, placing a bowl of pussy willows in the center of the table. "I'm afraid I'm a one-man woman."

"There's no such thing," the girl replied, "but it's marvelous you still feel that way."

Mindy, watching her place salads precisely in the proper spot, thought to herself, "You're so sure of everything, little girl, but life's not like laying the table, a proper spot for each item. Sometimes it's just a desert where there's only the heart to lead."

As they sat about the table Mindy decided everything was perfect. The table, the food, her handsome sons, and the sparkling girls beside them. Carl, tanned and lean in a clean denim shirt which matched his eyes, was his best self, witty and teasing, glad to have his sons about him, and not displeased at their choice of companions. Seth sat erect and still at the head of the table, a striking figure.

"We are so lovely," she thought, "except that Ned already smells of cigarettes after two hours at home.

127

And Carl talks to everyone but me. And I'm so weary of Seth I can hardly bear to look at him. Don't peek behind the pretty picture, girls. It's ugly on the other side."

The sun had slipped behind the mountains by the time Carl pushed back his chair and rose to leave the table. "Don't go, Mr. Matthews," Grace said in her soft voice. "Let's sing some hymns to welcome the Sabbath. You pick the first one."

"In the Garden," Carl chose after a moment's thought. And he sang, to Mindy's delighted surprise, with pleasure and enthusiasm. Grace led them in a clear soprano. If only Stephen might have met this girl five years later! They were both so young. Seth moved to his rocker, lit up his pipe, and watched dusk sift over the valley. Smoke curled in silvery wisps about his white head, and it occurred to Mindy that he must be very lonely. Perhaps she was wrong to begrudge him Ned's love, but she feared him so—his caustic tongue, his power over her son. She rose to light the lamp. Soft pink roses, clambering over the globe, glowed in the flickering light.

"Let's all join hands, and Stephen will lead our sun-down prayer." Grace looked up at Stephen with assurance, and he smiled his agreement.

"It's as though they've known each other all their lives," Mindy thought. As the circle of hands formed round the table, she realized Seth would be left out—alone with his bitterness and his memories. Impulsively, she moved her chair a bit and reached out to him. He looked at her for a moment, then with an impatient gesture took her hand. Had she only made him angry? Would she never understand this man?

Stephen prayed, his voice sure and confident, and when he had finished, while their heads were still bowed, Grace sang "Day Is Dying in the West," the sweetness of her voice falling like a benediction over the room.

* * * * *

Mindy, high on a ladder, was supposed to be washing windows, but the valley was bursting with life, and she found it hard to concentrate upon her task. School had been out a week, and she was savoring the joy of days to herself. Housecleaning, long overdue, had filled most of them, but she took pleasure in bringing the house to shining perfection. It did not take long, for there was a Spartan simplicity about all the rooms. Carl had never believed in anything but the barest essentials in furnishings. At first Mindy had longed for pretty things, but as she grew older, it no longer mattered. She rather liked the freedom it gave her to garden, sew, study, and roam the woods and fields.

She liked this high perch on the ladder. It gave her a whole new view of the valley. She polished the windows with three different cloths. She wanted them to sparkle for every traveler who rounded the bend. In four days Carl and she would leave for Ned's graduation. She was as excited as a child. She had seen the school only once. They rarely went more than a dozen miles from home. Her eyes were hungry for new sights. She had sewn herself a suit and two dresses, an unheard-of thing.

Finishing at last, she turned backward on the ladder to rest and feast her eyes upon the varied greens of early June. There was someone on foot rounding the bend. She watched the figure idly. It was rare to see anyone walking the valley road. There was something familiar about the easy stride of the tall figure. Her heart suddenly swung into a faster rhythm. It was Ned. But it couldn't be. He was 150 miles away. But there was no mistaking the blue sweater and coppery hair. She was hidden from his view by the trees; so she just watched him as he made his way quickly along the road. Then he turned back, searched out a shallow spot in the stream, and leaped across on a few large stones. It was only moments before he was at the top of the hill and almost at her feet. He did not notice her there on the top of the

129

ladder and started to go around to the back door.

"Welcome home, my son," she called from her perch and had to laugh, in spite of her concern, at his startled face. "Would it be rude of me to ask what you are doing here?"

"Come down, and I'll tell you. You make me nervous up there in the treetops."

When she faced him on the ground, she knew he was neither ill nor in trouble. There was a confidence about him that she had not seen before. At eighteen he looked much as Carl had in his youth.

"I decided not to graduate, Mother."

Mindy gasped. "After four years of hard——"

"Let me explain first. Then if you want to preach, I'll listen, but it won't change my mind. I have no intentions of going to college. Graduation costs more than one hundred dollars. You and Father could well use that money for many things. Besides, you know what I think of parading down the aisle in one of those silly outfits."

"But, Ned, you've been an honor student. You could go so far. It's such a waste."

"I promised you I'd study, and I did. I promised you I wouldn't smoke at school, and I haven't. I'll still get a diploma—for whatever that's worth—but I'm going to be a mechanic. It's all I've ever wanted to do. If that isn't fancy enough for you, I'm sorry. Maybe Stephen will put the family on the map, if that's what matters to you."

Her eyes filled with tears. And then she was crying and hugging him all at once. "I love you just the way you are, Ned. Don't ever forget that. I'm probably crying because I won't get to wear my new suit. But when Stephen comes home, we'll all go out to dinner, and I'll wear it then. Where will you learn to be a mechanic?"

"I was born one," Ned replied, grinning. He was relieved that she was not angry. "I can hear what's wrong with a motor when a car is going down the road."

"You're so modest!" Mindy shook her head.

130

"Come, I'll fix you some lunch. You must be starved."

"Where's Grandfather?"

"He's mending a wagon in the back part of the barn. But first you eat."

"Where's Father working?"

"I don't know. It seems to irritate him when I ask; so I keep still."

"Why should that irritate him?" Ned looked at her sharply. "You *should* know where he is. Sometimes people call, looking for him."

"True"—Mindy shrugged—"but your father hates being questioned about anything, and more so as he grows older."

"Or perhaps it's just *my* questions he resents," she thought to herself.

"Does he still go to dances in town on Saturday nights?"

"Whenever the spirit moves him," Mindy replied, buttering thick slices of homemade bread. "Often he's too tired when he does both road work and farming."

Ned took the sandwich and went whistling to the barn. She heard Seth's whoop of pleasure and the two of them laughing.

She did not allow herself to think more of Ned's decision that evening. Carl accepted it without a word, only giving his son a long look and then going to the barn.

"Is he angry?" Ned asked.

"No. I imagine he's only thinking how much he'd have enjoyed what you have cast aside. He was never given any choice about education. It's a topsy-turvy world, Ned, but your father loves you too much to force you into his dream for your life. Work hard at whatever you do, and he'll be proud of you. You know the password in the Matthews family is *work*. Already I hear him bragging to others about your ability with engines."

That night, finally shielded by darkness, she let the tears escape. Carl slept beside her. He had spoken no word of disappointment, nor had he even mentioned Ned for that matter. She had longed to turn into his arms and be comforted, but somehow his very silence restrained her.

When there were no more tears, she slipped out of bed and stood at her window looking down the valley. Stars hung high and bright in the black sky. She longed to leap, as had Ned across the stones of the brook, from star to star, until she reached the throne of God. But what would a poor farm woman do there amid all the splendors of heaven?

"I would search out Christ," she thought. "His mother was a peasant too. I know He would listen. I would tell Him all my fears for Ned and just let Him take it from there."

Then her sensible New England spirit chided her. "You don't have to hopscotch off to heaven to do that. He's as near as your thoughts." So she attempted to commit Ned to the Young Galilean and tried to ignore the ache that squeezed along her left arm and into her hand.

Hours later she awoke to frightening pain deep within her chest. She tried to breathe in shallow little gasps, but it did no good. She bit her lip hard against any sound. Surely it would go away. But it became instead an impossible thing for which she was no match. Pain and fear intermingled and drove from her mouth a frantic little cry which awakened Carl.

"Are you sick, Min?"

"I can't breathe, and it hurts so bad. Hold me, Carl. I'm scared."

"I'm getting a doctor," he determined, moving away from her.

"It would be an hour before any doctor could get here, Carl. I'll be dead or better before then. Just put your arms around me. I think it will go away."

He held her then, and she felt his fear, but even so she could not refrain from crying out when the pain

132

bored into her chest unmercifully. At last she felt it receding like a weary animal which would rest but return.

"It's better now," she told him, relaxing. "I'm sorry to mess up your night. I was so frightened. And when I'm frightened, I still need you," she said softly.

He touched her face lightly with his hand, but said only, "Tomorrow you go to the doctor . . . and no more housecleaning."

Chapter 14

"What would you like for supper, Seth?" Mindy asked.

He didn't look up from the *Saturday Evening Post* which he was reading, but said after a moment's thought, "Boiled potatoes with codfish gravy, corn on the cob, and lettuce with vinegar and sugar."

Mindy had to smile. Nothing wrong with his appetite. "Anything else?"

"I'd love to set my teeth into one of those deep-fried apple turnovers Martha used to make, but there's no sense in your tryin' 'em. She's the only woman I ever knew could make 'em decent."

Mindy knew better than to attempt those turnovers. They were held so sacred in both Seth's and Carl's memory that she would not think of exposing herself to their comments.

"I made blueberry pies this morning. That will have to do." Mindy drew water to soak the cod and brought potatoes from the cellar.

She wasn't humoring Seth because of any mellowing between them—only on principle alone. She had no idea whether there was any virtue in that or not. There were times when it was difficult to be civil to the man.

Her Christianity was ever at the test. She had noted of late he sat in the rocker more and moved with slow, unsteady step about the yard when he did venture out. She did not let him know she saw these things, for it was shameful somehow to watch age stalk such a one as Seth.

Her men would soon be home. Both boys were working on the town roads for Carl this summer—Stephen to put away money for college and Ned because he couldn't, in his youth and inexperience, find the garage job for which he yearned.

As she laid Stephen's place at the table she placed upon his plate an envelope addressed in Grace's flowing script. Her letters came every two or three weeks, and Stephen saved them until the evening work was done, then read them on the porch step, squinting against the dwindling light. He placed them afterward in his shirt pocket and sat thinking quietly awhile in the darkness.

Supper preparations completed, Mindy sat in a chair at the living room window reading. Flies buzzed against the screens, and oppressive August heat hung over the room. Yet there was something good about summer at its ripe peak. A cloud of dust rounded the bend of their curving drive, and Carl's truck rumbled toward the garage, Ned at the wheel. When they stepped down from the cab, Carl's shirt was black with sweat. The boys' bare backs gleamed, tanned and muscular. They would bring the cows from pasture to barn, line up at the kitchen sink for a scrubbing, then circle her table hungrily.

She went about arranging ruffled garden lettuce in green glass bowls, dropping ears of early corn into boiling water, and lifting small new boiled potatoes in their pale, curled skins onto a platter.

Ned came first, having avoided any contact with the cattle or stable. "What a scorcher," he said, pouring hot water from the stove reservoir into the washbasin.

135

"The roads are so dry. I feel as if I'd eaten half the county today."

Mindy reached around him for a dipper of water, and the strong odor of whiskey rose to her nostrils.

She spoke to her son's back as he bent face and curly head to the pan of water. "When did you take up drinking, Ned?"

He did not reply, burying his face instead in the sudsy water, then proceeding to thoroughly scrub his arms, back, and chest. "Off and on for a few months," his answer came at last.

"Another little gift from your grandfather, I suppose," she said bitterly, pouring codfish gravy into a silver bowl.

"He doesn't look at these things the same way we do, Mother. They're just harmless amusements to him. He says a little snort after a hard day's work puts you back on your feet. It *does* have a way of making the world look great. Is there something wrong with that?"

"Ned, you well know it becomes a crutch with which we escape reality. God never meant us to hide out in some rosy, artificial world. If we have problems, He wants us to bring them to Him. He has *real* solutions, minus the hangover. Besides, Ned, you are young and strong and dearly loved. Why do you feel the *need* of drink?"

"I didn't in the beginning. I just did it to please Grandfather. Now I *do* look forward to a drink when I get home from work. It's not a problem, Mother, unless you let it get out of hand."

"Could you look God straight in the eye and say that?" Mindy reached out and stopped her older son as he attempted to pass her.

"I can't even look you straight in the eye and say it," he answered, a cockiness in his voice that masked the soberness in his eyes. "I know all the reasons why you don't want me to drink, Mother, and they all make sense. I may never be able to admit that to you again; so

136

put it on record. But it's too late now, and I'm sick of trying to hide things from you. From now on I'm going to smoke and drink in the open. It's not what you want for me, or even what I want for myself, but it's what I am; so why pretend?"

"You mean it's what Seth has made you. Can you never deny him anything, Ned? Does God's love for you, or mine, mean nothing? Drinking is a dead-end street. Seth is a good example. There's still time to turn back."

"I'm afraid there isn't. Just leave me alone, Mother." He moved away from her impatiently, but she heard the break in his voice, and such hatred for Seth filled her that she knew she could not sit at the table with him.

As she served them all but did not sit down, Carl asked testily, looking up, "Aren't you eating, Min? Are you sick?"

"No, I am not eating, and no, I am not sick."

"Well, you couldn't be sulking. Your religion doesn't allow that." He smiled without warmth and went on eating.

"Leave her alone, Dad. We all have bad days," Ned said, quietly.

"Not all, Ned." Seth chuckled. "Only us heathens."

"You two have been too long at the wine," Carl reprimanded sharply.

So he knew. All this time he had known Ned was drinking and done nothing about it. If just once Carl would speak to his father or even to Ned. He could yet solve the problem by laying down some ground rules for Seth. But he would never do it. He was still Seth's little boy—afraid. Peace at any price. Well, the price was too high this time. She would take matters into her own hands. When Carl and the boys left for the milking, Seth still sat at the table nursing a last cup of coffee. Mindy sat down in a chair beside him.

"Seth, if you intend to stay here, you are going to have to make some changes. You have no right to pro-

137

vide Ned with drink and urge him to follow in your steps. Carl has been a good son to you. How can you destroy Ned in return? I don't ask anything from you for myself, but surely for Carl you could leave Ned alone."

"If Carl is concerned, let it be between him and me," Seth said.

"Carl will never speak to you." There was pleading in Mindy's voice.

"Then let's hear no more about it." Seth rose from his chair as indifferent as if she had ceased to exist. Filling his pipe, he limped off toward the barn. Mindy bowed her head but could find no words. She just pleaded, "God help me" over and over softly like a confused child.

That night the pain came again, but this time she knew what to do. She crept noiselessly down the stairs and lay on the living-room couch. Now if she couldn't control the sounds, it would bother no one. The doctor had said whenever she felt pain or aching to stop whatever she was doing, as it was a warning that she was overexerting. And above all, she was not to become upset or to worry. Mindy had laughed at that. "How does one take part in life without ever becoming upset?"

The old doctor had been quick in his reply. "Let the good Lord do the worrying. He doesn't have angina."

It was good advice, she thought now, fighting off her fear and trying to relax as the pain strengthened its attack. The medicine was in her purse. Where had she left it? Why was everything so much more frightening at night? She longed to call Carl, but she could not bring herself to beg for his love and concern.

There were footsteps on the stairs. He was coming after all. She felt tears of relief running down the sides of her cheeks. But it wasn't Carl. Stephen's voice gentled the darkness.

"Is everything all right, Mother?"

"Oh, Stephen, I'm so glad you came! I'm not very

138

good at this business yet. Perhaps you could light a lamp and look around for my purse. My pills are in it. On the shelf in the kitchen, maybe." She could speak no more. The pain moved in and left her fighting for control.

He was back in a moment, with the pills in one hand, a lamp in the other. Oh, the comfort of light and companionship! He brought pillows and propped her into a half-sitting position which enabled her to breathe more easily. Then he sat beside her and took her hand. She knew by his bowed head that he prayed, and in his quietness she found strength for the ordeal.

When at last the medicine held the enemy at bay, she said, "You're going to be a marvelous doctor, Stephen. You can't know how you helped me. The doctor says this may happen now and then until I learn to live within my limitations. I'm not sure I want to spend the rest of my life tiptoeing along, but perhaps a few sessions like this will change my mind."

"Mother"—Stephen was sober—"it's not hard work which is doing this to you. Don't you realize it keeps happening after some problem with Ned or Grandfather?"

"Really, Dr. Matthews?" she said, teasing.

"Don't be funny, Mother. I want my children to have a grandmother. You must learn there are some things you can't change. You have to accept what Grandfather has done to Ned, no matter how heart-breaking it is. Father doesn't follow Christ, and you don't get upset over that. Why do you fight so hard for Ned?"

"You are wrong, Stephen, if you think I don't sorrow over your father. It is the worst sorrow of my life, but I knew when I married him that I must walk alone as a Christian. So I suppose I am resigned to that. But Ned. Stephen, what can you know of love for a child until you are a parent? I raised him so tenderly and taught him so carefully of God. I saw the weakness in him when he was

139

very small, and I tried the harder for it—and prayed fiercely for him. And if it weren't for Seth, he'd have been all right. Tell me, Stephen, not as my son but as a Christian, how do I forgive your grandfather? I can forgive him easily for every hateful word or act to me, but for destroying Ned's character, how do I forgive him that?"

"Maybe you're too pessimistic," Stephen told her wistfully. "I can't stand what's happening to Ned either, but his story isn't finished yet. I know from what he says to me that he's not satisfied with life as he's living it. Perhaps when Grandfather is gone, he'll be able to get things sorted out."

"No matter how badly he wants to stop smoking or drinking, he'll not make it, Stephen. Ned is not strong like the rest of us. The spirit is willing, but the flesh is weak."

"You are leaving God out. You are trying to save Ned with your own fierce desire for his good. Let go of the battle. Just go on loving him and praying, but quit worrying and let God run things for a change. You are so sure Ned is weak, and we are strong. We are all weak, Mother, in some area or another. His weakness just happens to be in an area that shows. Ned is generous and warmhearted. He never holds a grudge."

"And I can't forgive Seth," Mindy said softly. "Go on, Stephen, you're making your point."

"I don't imagine forgiveness is something we can conjure up within ourselves. Probably it has to come from God as a gift. Why don't you ask Him for it, instead of carrying such a load of guilt around?"

"I will," Mindy determined humbly.

"Do it right now. You'll sleep better." Stephen bowed his head and waited. Mindy felt a shy reluctance. She had never prayed a personal prayer in front of anyone before, but her son's bent head spoke with an eloquence she could not deny.

"Dear Lord"—the words came slowly—"I have a

terrible anger in my heart toward Seth. I have tried to will it away, but it's strongly rooted. I turn it over to You and ask You to remove it from me."

She raised her head, but Stephen urged quietly, "You need to pray about Ned, too, Mother."

She was still a long time. She knew the prayer Stephen asked of her but was not sure she could trust God to such an extent.

"Do you doubt God's concern for Ned?" Stephen asked, his dark head still bowed.

"No."

"Do you doubt His ability to overcome all the exterior circumstances in Ned's life over which you've had no control?"

"No, I guess not, when you put it that way."

He waited then, saying no more.

"I turn Ned over to You, Lord. Work out his salvation when and as You will, and teach me to trust You."

Stephen stood up then. Her heart moved with gratitude for this son who at sixteen was already more man than boy. She noted weariness on his young face and realized he was working too hard for his years. He badly needed the hours of rest he was sharing with her.

"You must get some sleep, Stephen. Four o'clock will be upon us all too soon, and you work so hard. Instead of fretting over Ned's problems, I should be praising God for the joy you are to us."

"Mothers are dumb that way," he said, grinning and tucking her snugly round with blankets. "Don't get up in the morning. I'll tell Father you had a bad night, and Ned will be glad to get breakfast. It'll spare him the milking."

She slept then, a deep untroubled sleep, and woke hours later to a quiet house and a sinkful of dishes.

Their lives fell that autumn into a rhythm which, in spite of its seasonal patterns, changed little for nearly two years. Mindy found hours of satisfaction in the classroom, Ned lumbered with his father winters and joined

141

Stephen in working on the roads with Carl summers. Seth, slowed in pace but caustic as ever, stoutly refused any concessions to his years. Carl took pride in his work as road commissioner and on rare occasions took Mindy on Sunday excursions to show her new or repaired roads on which he and the boys were working. He was genial with the outer world but taciturn, even sharp, at home. At first, in the face of his edgy silences, Mindy had chattered and teased, but over the years she had grown weary of hearing her own laughter tinkle into nothingness. Now at the end of day, she spoke to him gently, briefly, sharing what small happenings had come her way, and then left the quiet between them alone.

She watched the growing relationship between Stephen and Grace with interest. Twice over his last two years at the academy he had brought her home, and it was with satisfaction that Mindy observed the girl's developing personality. She was so perfect in every way. If there were times when she seemed too mature for her years, they were dispelled within moments by a girlish giggle or a silly game of hide-and-seek with Stephen in the front yard. They would head off through the pasture, hand in hand, to find the cows at milking time, innocent as children, yet Mindy was well aware of the strong feeling each bore for the other.

Once she had asked Stephen teasingly if he meant to lock Grace away from all her admirers through his long years at medical school. He had said soberly, "We just live one day at a time," and she had known it was not a teasing matter.

And now, at last, he was to graduate. This time instead of sewing a new suit she planned simply to wear the old one she had prepared for Ned's graduation. Ned volunteered to stay with Seth, and Mindy and Carl set out in their black Buick which Ned had polished to a mirror-finish and put in perfect running order. Carl had said at first he could not spare the time to go, but Mindy had exploded in a rare outburst, "Carl Matthews,

142

what kind of a man is too busy to attend his son's graduation?"

Ned had backed her. "It really is important, Father. Everyone's parents will be there, and Stephen would be badly disappointed if only Mother came, even though he'd never let on. Besides, you and Mother have never had a vacation of any kind. I'll tend to things here at home for the weekend—and that's a noble offer on my part, considering how I feel about cows."

Seth chuckled from his corner. " 'Twon't be all work and no play, boy."

"See that you keep a clear mind for business, Ned," Carl warned sharply, and Mindy felt the twisting of an old sorrow with which she had learned to live, but not without pain.

As they drove through the apple-blossomed countryside, Mindy looked at the dark-suited stranger beside her and fell in love.

"You are very handsome," she said, placing her hand over his on the steering wheel.

"All the Matthews men are good-looking," he replied, not taking his eyes from the road.

"And modest too." Mindy moved to sit beside him. He only smiled, but the silence was warmer than the ones at home.

"We don't even look like poor hill people. Ned has made the car so splendid, and no one would ever know from our clothing that we fight our living from rocky old Vermont soil. Let's pretend we're wealthy Bostonians heading for our summer home in Maine."

"Grow up," Carl said, but he turned and looked at her—*really* looked at her—and Mindy felt an old familiar sensation travel over her which she'd have sworn was reserved for lovers only.

Stephen welcomed them with such delight that she knew at once Carl was glad he had listened to Ned. Grace, too, hugged them both and insisted on a tour of the campus before the evening meal. Stephen seemed

143

different, somehow, here. Not her little boy anymore but a person in his own right. She saw the affection with which he was greeted by student and faculty alike. And that night she said to Carl in the privacy of their bedroom, "Stephen is someone special. I felt it everywhere we went today. It sort of takes my breath away."

"The principal told me as much in his office this afternoon—that they hate to see him go, yet expect big things of him. If only we had money to help him. How can he hope to get through medicine on what little we can do for him?"

"He is determined and full of optimism. With that combination, one can do anything," Mindy said.

"Reminds me of a girl I once knew who licked tuberculosis with sheer stubbornness." Carl held out his arms, and she walked into them with great joy.

The Sabbath was a day of pure pleasure for Mindy. Well-trained singing groups and excellent speakers filled some thirsting deep within. There was so much to be seen and heard beyond the valley. She didn't blame Stephen for wanting to roam the earth. Grace sang a solo at the sundown service, and Mindy noted that her eyes came back to Stephen over and over again; in them was a haunting sadness which made her yet more beautiful.

As the graduates marched from the auditorium next morning, their diplomas in hand, and lined the front walk to receive congratulations, Mindy said to Carl, "Now and then in a lifetime there are perfect moments. This is one of them. The sun is shining, the world is a garden, you and I are free and lazy like other people for a change, our son is everything we could hope for, and beside him stands the loveliest girl on the campus, with stars in her eyes."

"They look more like tears to me," Carl commented. "Neither of them is happy in spite of their big day."

"Well, I noticed Grace has seemed unusually quiet this weekend, but girls are sentimental about school days and saying good-bye."

144

Later, when the festivities were over and Carl was helping Stephen pack his belongings in the car, Grace stood by watching but taking no part in the conversation. When they had finished, Stephen came and stood beside her.

"Sure you don't want to come home with us, Grace?" Carl tilted her chin and gave her his most winning smile, but she did not return it.

"Grace and I won't be seeing each other anymore," Stephen said stiffly. "So this is sort of a final good-bye for all of us."

"Do you want us to ask why?" Mindy questioned gently, fighting down such disappointment that she wondered at the calmness in her voice.

"We both have years of school ahead of us," the girl informed them, her control matching Mindy's. "It's unfortunate we met so young, but it would be a disaster for us to marry now. Sometimes you have to be practical."

"Can't you talk her out of all this good sense?" Carl said to Stephen, impatiently.

Stephen's eyes shone black with the tears he refused to shed. "I agree with her, Father. There's no solution. If we tie ourselves down to a lot of vows and promises, one or the other of us will get hurt in the end, for we'll be miles apart for years, and even if we weren't, you can only go together so long."

"I don't think you should make a hasty decision," Carl growled at both of them.

"It's not a hasty decision, Mr. Matthews," Grace said, tears running down her cheeks now. "We've talked and talked and plotted and planned, but we both know what we want in life, and marriage would be the end of all our dreams."

"Or the beginning," Mindy thought sadly.

Grace kissed Stephen swiftly, hugged Mindy and Carl, and fled across the campus toward the girls' dorm and her waiting parents. Stephen watched until her long blue dress and shining hair were only a blur.

"Are you *sure,* Stephen?" Mindy asked softly.

"Absolutely sure," he replied. "There will be someone else."

"Sometimes you should listen to your heart more and your head less, Son." Carl started the car abruptly, and Stephen requested, "Drive slowly once around the campus, Dad. I want to see everything one more time and then go on to whatever lies ahead. I'll probably never come back."

"So the perfect moment hadn't really been perfect after all," Mindy thought. "Perhaps there's no such thing."

They had not been home a week when Seth became ill. Mindy had noticed he coughed badly upon their return, but she had learned that to inquire about his health was to invite a sharp retort. When he failed to appear for breakfast, Carl went to his room to investigate. Often of late he came to the morning table pale and shaky, but always on time. Something was wrong.

"His breathing is very poor, and he's just too weak to stand up. He must have felt a lot worse these past few days than he's let on," Carl said as he returned to the kitchen. "I'll get the car. Ned, you help him get some clothes on, and we'll get him to the hospital."

"Will he go?" Mindy asked.

"Not willingly, but he'll never make it if he stays here. I think he knows that."

Within ten minutes Ned and Seth came out of the bedroom. Mindy caught her breath at the suffering on the old man's face, the agony with which he fought for each breath. She herself knew a bit about the struggle for breath. She moved quickly to his other side and understood when he leaned heavily upon her how sick he really was. When she had wrapped him in blankets and made him as comfortable as possible, she squeezed his hand, saying, "We Matthews are a hardy lot, Seth. You'll soon be home, and we'll celebrate with a lemon meringue pie."

146

When Carl returned, Mindy knew before he spoke that the news was not good. "He has pneumonia and less than a fifty-fifty chance."

"Let Stephen stay home from work today and drive me to the hospital this afternoon. Then you and Ned can go tonight. That way we can be with him most of the day. Did you let your sisters know?"

"I called them both," he said tersely. "Do as you like about this afternoon."

When she stood at Seth's bedside later that day, having freed Sally to go to lunch, she knew he would not come home. He was barely conscious, and the strong, proud spirit was broken. She sat by his bed, holding his hand and thinking down the years. Stephen read by an open window. How could death invade this room when forsythia brushed the sill, sunshine lay in squares across the starchy sheets, and chickadees celebrated summer among the evergreens outside?

"I'm here, Seth. Is there anything I can do for you?"

He made no reply but shook his head feebly.

"I wish I knew how to tell him of Christ or offer him hope of something beyond," she thought. "Has my life said anything to him, I wonder?" She took a small Bible from her purse and read softly for a time from the Psalms, but he made no indication that he heard.

The hands of the clock in the hall stood at four when Stephen said, "We'd better go and get the chores done, Mother, so that Ned and Father can come early tonight."

She rose and spoke quietly to the still figure on the bed. "We must go, but Sally and Carrie are here, and Carl and Ned will be here soon."

He groped for her hand. Through his raspy breathing, the words came faintly: "I've brought you a heap of heartbreak, Mindy. Can you forgive an old man?"

She felt Stephen's eyes upon her. She heard Ned saying, "He doesn't look at things the way we do, Mother." She saw the mended eggbeater left upon her kitchen shelf, the bushel of peas picked and ready for

147

canning, a laughing boy holding a tiny car made from a walnut shell.

She bent and kissed his forehead, placing her cool hands on his feverish face. "We all stand in need of forgiveness, Seth. You have mine. Now rest and get well."

"Tell Ned——" he faltered and had no strength to go on.

She waited, and he tried again.

"Tell Ned I said to listen to his ma and to think of me when deer huntin' comes around."

*　*　*　*　*

Before the cows were stabled, the phone rang, its bell jangling the end of a life. Stephen looked at Seth's empty rocker by the kitchen window.

"If that powerful personality could have been submitted to the will of God, what a man he would have been!"

"He was quite a man as it was," Mindy said.

Chapter 15

It was a bleak summer. If Mindy thought the brief trip to Maine had tokened a new era in her marriage, she was mistaken. Carl withdrew yet further into his private world. A world of mourning? Mindy did not know. She wondered sometimes if life for him had lost its purpose at his father's death. Had he lived only to prove his worth in that stern paternal sight?

Ned found himself adrift upon an unfamiliar sea. There was no longer anyone to say, "Eat, drink, and be merry. Let the long-faced ones fret if they will." He dated a succession of girls, bought a motorcycle, and drank with increasing regularity. Mindy watched, prayed, and refrained from mothering. He was no longer a child. Sometimes when he came home, unsteady on his feet and too easy with his words, she saw the pain in Carl's eyes. She did not suffer alone.

Stephen worked from dawn till dark, was cheerful and considerate, but joined in no small talk. No letters awaited him at day's end, nor did he write any. Only when the college bulletin arrived did his interest flicker temporarily. But it was enough. It told his mother he would mend, that he would substitute learning for love after a time.

Mindy did not try to put all the pieces back in place. She understood at last that it was not her task to solve the problems of everyone about her but only to rise up each morning and minister in love and quietness to their needs. She attended college most of that summer; so the family members each went his own way, fumbling for roles, seeking purpose, doing necessary things in joyless ways.

September moved down across the valley, bringing tangy air, snow on the mountaintops, and change. Stephen swung onto the train, heading for college, with something of his old eagerness. He had stoutly refused to be taken, insisting that he was perfectly capable of finding his way about a new and larger campus. They sensed he was hungry for adventure and let him go, though Mindy longed to prepare his room.

Mindy herself entered the schoolroom with new ideas and a heavy sense of responsibility. She must live frugally and put away every penny for Stephen's expenses. She could not possibly handle them, even though Carl had promised to help when he could. But she would pay her tithe and trust God to make a way. Had He not promised to open the windows of heaven for those who were faithful? Stephen had worked for three summers, and that would help a great deal. She refused to worry.

Something new was going on with Ned these autumn days. He was gone a great deal in the evening, his motorcycle roiling the peace of the valley road. His drinking lessened, and his laughter fell about the house as it had not in years. He no longer brought home the pretty village girls on Sunday for Mindy's chicken dinners. Finally she could control her curiosity no longer. "What has happened to you, Ned? When you walk into the house, I feel the happiness ricocheting off the walls. It even makes *me* feel good."

He grinned sheepishly. "May I bring someone for Sunday dinner?"

"Of course. Do I know her?"

"Yes, but I'm not going to tell you who it is. You'll be surprised."

"And pleased?"

"I hope so." His words told Mindy this girl mattered, and she was suddenly afraid.

That night, after Ned left, Mindy said to Carl, "He's bringing a girl for dinner Sunday, but he wouldn't tell me who. I have a feeling he's serious this time."

"Well, he's twenty-one. What do you expect? He has to settle down sooner or later."

"He needs a very special person."

Carl, his newspaper spread in the circle of lamplight, made no reply. Mindy took from her schoolbag a stack of papers for correcting and settled into the evening routine. The clock beat a steady rhythm against the quiet. "Almost as though it's embarrassed at our strange silence," Mindy thought, methodically moving her red pencil up and down the columns of figures. Precisely at 9:30 Carl folded his paper, got a drink, and climbed the stairs. Sometimes he commented on the weather, but this time he spoke no word.

Tonight Mindy *wanted* to speak and to listen. She was weary of silence and curt answers. She blew out the lamp and found the kitchen flooded with moonlight. Impulsively throwing on a sweater, she went outside and knelt in the dew-moistened grass beneath the balm of Gileads. Turning her face toward the moon, riding pale gold across the sky, she watched wandering bands of white clouds move over its surface and then on into the loneliness of space.

She felt tears streaming down her face, partly because the night was so vast and lovely and partly for her own desperate need. Somewhere out there beyond the clouds was God, and she sought Him this night, not for child or mate but for herself alone.

"I am Mindy Matthews, God," she said. "Just a farmer's wife tucked in here among the mountains. Do

151

You know me? Do You know that You are all I have? I love Carl, but we cannot pray together, we cannot speak of You together, we do not share the same goals, and he often finds me a mystery because I am more Yours than his. Thus we are ever separated by that which should draw us closer together. I hardly know the silent stranger with whom I live. The boys are growing up. I have done for them about all I ever can. I commit myself and my remaining years to You. I believe in the principles of Your kingdom and long to be as pure as the angels who serve about Your throne, but I'm very much of this earth. I'm often filled with anger or self-pity or impatience. But You have promised to ready Your followers for heaven, even ordinary folk like me, so take my humanity and make of it something good."

She would not have been surprised had God written a reply across the serene expanse of moon-washed sky, but in all of earth and heaven only the white clouds moved. She knelt there a long time, loath to go in, but when she heard the hum of Ned's motorcycle far down the valley, she rose and moved quietly through the darkened house toward the bedroom and her sleeping husband.

Mindy laid the table with great care on Sunday, using her best linen cloth and her green glass dishes. There were few flowers left in the garden, but she arranged the last of the white chrysanthemums with some sprigs of evergreen in a milk-glass bowl and was satisfied with the results. When Ned drove in, she realized her knees were wobbly and her palms moist.

"They're here," she called nervously to Carl, who sat in Seth's rocker reading the Sunday paper.

"Should we have hired a band?" He picked up the scattering of papers he had tossed about. "Good heavens, Mindy, he's been bringing girls home for years. What are you so flustered about?"

"This is different. I feel it in my bones," she said.

When they entered the kitchen, Ned and the girl, she

had all she could do not to gasp. Sara Houghton! If she had guessed for a month, she would never have considered this one. Suddenly she wanted to laugh and cry all at once. The Houghtons had moved into town a few years before, and Sara had completed the eighth grade under Mindy's guidance. She had loved the tall, plain, graceful girl from the first day. But how had Ned, who never saw beyond a pretty face and flirting eye, recognized her worth? She chuckled inwardly at Carl's puzzled face. *Now* who was flustered?

"Sara"—Mindy took the girl's hands in hers—"welcome, welcome! This is the nicest surprise! Ned wouldn't tell us who it was he was bringing."

"I told him that was a dreadful thing to do." The girl's wide smile included Carl, and she reached out a hand to him. "Hello, Mr. Matthews. I remember you from our eighth-grade graduation three years ago. Ned looks so much like you."

There it was, the same warm, steady maturity she had seen in the girl at fourteen. "Are you going to high school?" Mindy asked, bringing food to the table.

"I went for two years, but there was a little school on South Hill which was going to close because they couldn't find a teacher; so I applied and was hired. I would like to have finished school, but my parents have had a struggle raising our big family, and I felt I should be on my own as soon as possible."

"How did you ever know where to start? I had only had a few months of teacher's training when I started out, but it helped a great deal."

"I just remembered the way you ran your school, Mrs. Matthews, and tried to do things the same way. You were the best teacher I ever had."

"I remember now," Mindy replied thoughtfully. "You always had your work done before everyone else, and I often let you take over some classes for the little ones. That was your student teaching, only we didn't know it."

153

At dinner Sara debated local politics with Carl, and Mindy noted with amusement that her grasp of the subject left Carl scrambling for solid ground. "Next time you bring home a woman with a mind, give me some warning," he said to Ned, smiling ruefully.

"It's good for you," Ned declared. "She does it to me all the time."

By then Sara was discussing the pattern for the lace insert in the tablecloth with Mindy. It was as though she had been born to the house.

When the dishes were finished, Ned suggested to Sara that they go hunting.

"Hunting!" Mindy exclaimed in amazement. "What makes you think Sara wants to go hunting?"

"He really means, 'Let's go for a walk.' Carrying a gun just makes it seem more logical," the girl said, laughing. "The woods are lovely now, but I can't. It's too awkward clambering around in a dress."

"Try a pair of Stephen's pants," Ned suggested. "He's pretty skinny." Mindy rummaged around in Stephen's dresser until she found a pair of outgrown Levis. When they set off for the woods, the girl wore the pants with a bright blue jacket of Mindy's and a pair of Stephen's old hiking boots. Her fine brown hair was short and shaped to her head, unlike the fashion of the day, soft bangs reaching nearly to her eyebrows. The jacket deepened the blue of her eyes. "She's not pretty, but there's something about her," Mindy thought as she watched them wandering hand in hand along the pasture path.

"Well?" she placed herself squarely in front of Carl. "What do you think?"

"I think Ned has a lot more sense than we've given him credit for. She'll be the making of him."

"Do you think this is it for Ned?"

"If she'll have him."

"Oh, she'll have him," Mindy replied with confidence. "It's impossible to refuse Ned anything."

154

And she was right. They were married in January in a simple service at the local minister's home. Afterward Mindy prepared a small feast for both families and a few friends. Stephen was still home for the Christmas holiday, and it was a time of rejoicing. Ned could rarely be induced into dress clothes, but this day he wore a dark suit, and it was difficult for Mindy to take her eyes from his tall figure as he moved about among the guests. He was a handsome man who spent his happiness recklessly as he went along, never hoarding for tomorrow. It took courage to live thus among the valley folk who moved cautiously into each new morning.

Sara, in a soft apricot dress, sat quietly, chatting with Stephen on the couch. Mindy joined them.

"I have never seen Ned quite like this," Stephen was saying. "It's as though all the pieces of his life have finally fallen into place and he can hardly contain the joy. Are you responsible, Sara?"

"I hope so," she said simply. "I love him very much."

"Why?" Stephen laughed. "I never noticed he was so beyond the ordinary."

"He's lighthearted and loving. Those are rare qualities in our sober world. Whenever I see him coming, my heart sings."

"Spoken like a true bride. I'll ask you again in five years." Stephen was teasing, but Mindy wondered if there was a warning in his words.

"It will always be that way," the girl said, her eyes resting lovingly upon Ned as he made his way toward them.

Watching them over the following months, Mindy dared to believe Sara was right. They took a small apartment in a neighboring town, and Ned went on lumbering with Carl. Often they came to the farm on Sundays, Mindy and Sara working together on school projects, Carl and Ned hovering over the engine of car or truck, father learning from son. It was an interlude of joy.

Mindy couldn't remember when she had known such peace.

One late afternoon as Ned and Carl were done with the lumbering for the day, Ned stopped in Mindy's kitchen to warm up a moment before driving home. Mindy, having just returned from school and stabling Star, was chilled, too, and urged him to join her in a cup of cocoa.

"Where's your cigarette?" she asked, noting he didn't light up as usual.

"Can't afford them," he said, not unhappily.

"Are you and Sara having financial troubles?" Mindy asked, startled.

"No, actually we're getting along pretty well with both of us working, but Sara gives me only a bit of allowance, and it doesn't provide for much smoking."

"You mean *she* handles the money?" Mindy, who had no idea of hers and Carl's finances, struggled to grasp such an arrangement.

"You know I never could make it between paydays; so I dump the whole thing into her lap, and she's tighter than you could ever imagine."

"Do you mind?" Mindy asked, smiling in spite of herself.

"Best thing that ever happened to me. We even have a savings account. Fancy that."

"You were so wise the day you chose that girl."

"I couldn't have helped myself." The blue-green eyes, so often crinkled in laughter, were sober. "She's everything I've ever wanted."

"She's very dear to me too," Mindy said, rising to rinse their cups, "but tell me what *you* think is so special about her."

"Well, she likes to go hunting with me," he replied thoughtfully. "She knows all my weaknesses and what to do about them, and she's more fun to be with than anyone else in the world." When he went out, he stuck his head back in the door and added, "Besides, she thinks I'm wonderful."

156

Mindy made a face at him and went about her supper preparations with a light heart.

Stephen's letters of late had been sparse, and something in them left her uneasy, yet knowing his studies were difficult, she convinced herself that he had little time or inclination for letter writing. When he was due for spring vacation, she aired and straightened his room with eagerness. It seemed a long time since his Christmas holiday. He would arrive around six in the evening; so Carl had asked Ned and Sara to meet his train in the village and join them at the farm for supper. When Ned's horn sounded in the backyard, Mindy came from the pantry, dusted lightly with flour and anticipation. Carl rose from the harness he had been mending and moved toward the door. Both of them came to a startled halt as Stephen stood hesitantly in the doorway, his arm about a pretty wisp of a girl.

"Well, Stephen, you didn't tell us you were bringing a guest, but welcome anyway," Mindy said, turning to the girl with a smile, her natural hospitality asserting itself.

"She's not a guest exactly," Stephen explained steadily. "This is my wife, Rita."

Mindy would always remember the crackling of fire filling the stillness as cheerfully as if the world had not stopped turning. She saw Ned's eyes with a hint of laughter over Stephen's shoulder. There was an asking in Stephen's eyes that broke her heart, yet behind the asking a firmness with which she had learned never to tamper. The girl—what was her name?—looked both frightened and defensive. She could not be more than fifteen or sixteen. Mindy glanced at Sara and saw something in that steady gaze which said, "This is part of your life. There is no running away," but before she could speak a word, Carl had moved toward the girl, his hand outstretched, his voice warm. "Welcome home, Rita."

Only the routine of familiar tasks took Mindy through the next hour. She went on cooking automatically and heard Stephen's voice saying calmly, "There's no sensible explanation for our marriage. I suppose it was an impulse thing, but we haven't had any regrets," and he turned to the girl with a smile so radiant that Mindy wanted to cuff him.

"How are you surviving?" Carl asked.

"Rita's grandmother is providing the rest of this year's tuition for her. Rita is a sophomore in academy. I have a night job, and we only rent a couple of rooms. So far we haven't starved."

"Do you live with your grandmother?" Sara asked, turning toward the girl, "or *did you* before Stephen talked you into this whirlwind marriage?"

"My parents died in the flu epidemic. Since then I've lived with my grandparents." There was a clipped preciseness about her speech. She was as fragile as a seashell and as lovely, but Mindy sensed there was more to this girl than met the eye. "There will be someone else," Stephen had told them less than a year before, and this was the "someone else." What had happened to all that noble dedication to career?

After supper the young ones wandered outside in the April dusk. Mindy stood at the living room window watching them go down the winding drive. Sara, in knickers and sturdy boots, moved beside Ned with easy grace. Mindy didn't really approve of girls in pants, but even as she watched, Ned challenged Sara to a scramble up a cliff, and laughing, they fought for footholds until they reached the top where they stood hand in hand against the sky like young conquerors. Stephen looked up at them but made no move to follow, for Rita's feet were clad only in a few patent straps which were already providing too little protection against the muddy road. She said something to Stephen, and he picked her up, as easily as he would a child, and carried her across the puddles, kissing her thoroughly before he put her down.

"Ned has a buddy, and Stephen has a project," Carl said wryly from behind Mindy where he also watched.

158

"Why, why?" Mindy asked.

"Maybe he likes someone to look after. Grace didn't really need a man, you know."

"Well, I'm not going to cry about it." Mindy sat down and took up her knitting. "Stephen has made his own decision without consulting anyone, and he will have to live with the consequences." And as she said the words her tears dropped onto the creamy sweater she was making for Sara.

"What makes you think it's anything to cry about? She seems like a nice enough little thing."

"And how will Stephen get through medicine with that pretty little creature mincing along beside him?"

"Perhaps it's more important that he be happy."

"He won't be happy if he has to give up all his dreams. Stephen has known what he's wanted for years. At this moment he might think she's all that matters. Five years from now he'll be miserable."

"You may be right, but he will not give up easily. Not Stephen."

Later while Ned was warming the car, Sara drew Mindy into the kitchen. "Don't worry, Mother," she consoled. "Rita's known a lot of sorrow in her sixteen years, and undoubtedly her grandparents have spoiled her a bit, but I rather like her already. She has a good mind. Stephen says she's a straight A student."

"I'm a stubborn old woman who wants everything my own way," Mindy said wearily. "It will take time for me to get used to this. At least I'm hoping time will solve it."

"Surely your God will help you," the tall girl said, giving Mindy a quick hug and running toward the waiting car.

"Surely your God will help you!" Was there any helping such a one as she? It seemed she daily found new ugliness within herself. It had all seemed so easy in years past, sitting in church every week, the boys docile and attentive beside her. She had thought herself then

159

quite fit for the kingdom of heaven. God must have chuckled. Mindy Matthews all proper in her pew, her heart full of undiscovered potential for selfishness. The old familiar ache crept along her left arm, and her throat was tight with disciplined emotion.

Taking a flashlight she went outside to the back of the wagon shed where the pussy willows grew fat on a clump of bushes. In a protected corner at the back step, she knew there were five or six daffodils in bloom. These she added to the pussy willows, arranging them in a copper teakettle. By lamplight on the dresser in the guest room they looked just right. Then from a drawer in which she kept her handiwork, she took sheets and pillowcases with wide inserts of fine lace. These she wrapped in tissue and laid on the bed with a little card which said, "For Stephen and Rita from Mother." She tried to put, "Love, Mother," but couldn't bring herself to that. Later maybe, when God had done His work. Tonight she was all humanity—bitter, disappointed humanity.

She went down to say good night, told Stephen and Rita she had prepared the guest room for them, and climbed the steep stairs to her room. When she had made her bedtime preparations and brushed out her hair, she sat in the rocker by her window waiting for Carl and idly turning the pages of her Bible.

In the fifth chapter of 1 Thessalonians her eye was caught by two ridiculously tiny verses. Verse 16: "Rejoice evermore."

She smiled at that one. Rejoice that Stephen had traded everything for a pretty face? Ha!

Verse 17: "Pray without ceasing."

Maybe that was God's message to her for the day. Surely she'd have to if she ever learned to accept this new situation.

She went on to verse 18: "In every thing give thanks: for this is the will of God in Christ Jesus concerning you."

160

An utter impossibility. She put her head back, *eyes* closed, and rocked quietly. So that's what God wanted from her. Submission. A willingness to accept *anything* that came along. She just wasn't made that way. Things *mattered* to her, especially concerning those she loved.

"All right, God," she said, "thank You for Rita. Now You must help me to love her and not blame her for problems which their marriage creates. And thank You, Lord, for carrying the burdens. If only I were better at letting You do it."

Voices in the hall bidding good night told her Carl would soon come, and she realized with relief her arm no longer ached. She was weary but at peace.

Chapter 16

Small trickles of perspiration escaped Mindy's hair, which she had piled into a bun at the back of her head. She felt as seared as the fields which hugged, in vain, the nearly dry riverbed. Every car which rounded the bend sent dust drifting over the choking roadside weeds and on up the hillside until it seemed she had looked through a shifting film for days.

Stephen and Rita had spent the summer with them, and Mindy's resolutions to thank God in everything had at times worn thin. Stephen worked on the roads with Carl and often helped neighboring farmers with haying after supper. Not yet twenty, he had become a man, though Mindy had to admit he didn't go at it with grim determination. There was yet about him an eagerness for life which made everything seem possible, and he loved the girl. There was no doubt about that. It was written on his face when he came through the door at night, swinging her off the kitchen floor with such delight at sight of her.

And there *was* something about her. She could be so very alive and appealing; at other times, petulant and bored.

"What can you expect?" Carl asked. "Our quiet life

here is hardly what she bargained for when she married Stephen. It's probably been a long summer."

Mindy could agree to that. Now she arranged kindling in the wood stove and wondered how they would endure the heat of a fire, but the meal must be prepared. At least they would eat on the porch, and perhaps by then it would be cooler.

"May I help?" Rita, managing to look wilted in a flowerlike way, came from the living room where she had been reading. But however delicate she might appear, she was strong and quick. Maybe that's what had been most trying. With amazing efficiency this child had set the house to rights day after day, leaving Mindy feeling slow and old. She sewed well, and though she had known little of cooking upon her arrival, she had watched and learned.

"You could peel some potatoes," Mindy suggested. "It's too hot for anything very fancy tonight, but Sara and Ned are coming, so we'll have to put something together."

"How about potatoes, some of that good egg gravy you make, and just a huge platter of fresh things from the garden? With homemade bread that will be plenty on such a night."

"I'll get the vegetables from the garden," Mindy said, finding herself, as so often of late, simply following directions. When she returned, her pan heaped high with lettuce, cucumbers, and tomatoes, Rita stood at the sink peeling the last of the potatoes. She had a curious way of chopping at them rather than letting the skin curl off in a long thin peel as Mindy did.

"You waste a lot of potato that way," the older woman admonished impatiently. "We can't afford to waste in this house."

She heard her own voice in wonder. When had she become so niggardly? The girls lips tightened, but she said nothing.

"Here, like this." Mindy struggled for a kinder tone,

163

and her fingers moved rapidly about the potato, the resulting spiral of skin now paper thin.

"I've tried to do it that way, but I just don't get the knack of it."

Mindy felt the girl was close to tears, but she was not the crying kind. It occurred to Mindy that Carl's sharp tongue had often reduced her to the same feelings of defeat.

"I'm sorry, Rita," she apologized quickly. "I guess all this heat has made me irritable. You've been a wonderful help to me this summer. It's not really important how one peels potatoes."

"It's all right," the girl said, but something in her voice told Mindy the hurt was beyond erasing with a few words.

Later when the meal was cleared away and the chores done, they took kitchen chairs out under the trees in the front yard. The sun, red and round, eased behind the pines and out of sight. Dew fell scantily over the parched land. Even Carl sat passively without looking about him for some uncompleted task.

"Ned and I have an announcement," Sara said, "so please ignore your discomfort and listen. You tell them, Ned."

"You're going to have a baby," Rita sang out impulsively, her thin face alight with sincere joy.

"You have just spared me the announcement," Ned commented, tipping his sister-in-law's chair back at an alarming angle.

"It's truly today's news." Sara looked pleased and shy. "Only this morning I went to the doctor and found out for sure. It won't be born until March, but we decided we didn't want any secrets from the rest of you."

Mindy could find no words. It seemed she hardly adjusted to one change when another charged and left her reeling.

"This has been the year of surprises, Mother," Stephen said, almost as though he read her thoughts.

164

"We've brought you daughters and now a grandchild. I think it demands a speech."

Mindy looked at the loved forms about her, softened with night, and realized the truth of Stephen's words. "For years we have been four, and now we are six with the promise of another. God has been good. I hope we are all worthy of the little new one. It is indeed a grand announcement, Sara. Ned, you must not challenge her to races and drag her up and down mountains anymore."

"The doctor says I'm in perfect condition, and lots of exercise is good for me."

"He means doing your housework and taking a walk once in a while, not clambering around behind that mountain goat you live with," Carl warned.

"I don't intend to be careless with her," Ned assured them soberly. "There'll be plenty of time for mountain climbing later on."

"And I'll tend the baby," Mindy said, finding herself suddenly excited at the thought of a toddler in her kitchen once more.

"Let's make some lemonade to celebrate." Rita jumped up and started for the kitchen.

"There are those sugar cookies we baked this morning too," Mindy remembered, rising.

Sara started to join them, but Rita motioned her back. "Tonight, Sara, you are the guest of honor. Sit down with the men and play the lady."

It was a good night, with the cool sharp tang of lemonade, ice tinkling frostily against glasses, and a strong sense of family knitting them all together.

*　　*　　*　　*　　*

September brought rains for the greening of the earth and routine once more to their lives. Stephen and Rita went back to school, their old car laden with the canning Rita had done over the summer. Sara began

165

filling a small chest with baby things, and Mindy stood once more before a roomful of students. She liked the rhythm of fall days. When October's bright leaves scuttled along the roadside, lifting and dancing about her black mare's hooves, she felt a youthful delight in all the earth. November's somber skies and gray mornings were to her a sweet, sad poetry out of the past. And the days when a few hesitant snowflakes tumbled lazily from dark clouds she felt the same excitement which rippled over the youngsters in her classroom.

They awoke one morning, Carl and Mindy, to a steady rain. "Seems like we've had enough of this already," Carl said. "It's time it should be snowing."

Mindy did not mind the trip to school. Snug in raincoat and hood, blanket over her knees, she exulted in the drops which stung her face. The mare moved at a fast clip, sending the buggy jolting from side to side along the dirt road. All day, rain streamed down the schoolhouse windows, and the playground turned to mud. The room buzzed with the accumulated energies of twenty-six children denied the out-of-doors.

"You shall have your recess time now," Mindy announced at the end of the day, excusing them a half hour early. "There may be some minor flooding in some areas, and I want to be sure you all get home safely."

As the black mare splashed her way through puddles on the way back to the farm, Mindy observed the streams which usually bubbled spiritedly down hillsides to the river on the other side of the road. Today they foamed, wild and muddy, beyond their boundaries. Overflowing culverts, they cut their own courses across the road, leaving deep ruts.

"I'm glad we're both safe at home and high above the river," Mindy said to Carl that night as they sat down to eat.

"It's not the right time of year for a flood," Carl replied, "but it *does* sound like it has settled in for a wet night."

166

"If it keeps up, many of the children will never get to school in the morning."

"You may not yourself," Carl said. "The river was coming over the falls tonight like when the ice goes out in April. It's going to tear the roads all up, and I'll be hard put to get them repaired before snowfall."

At bedtime they stood on the porch with a lantern, straining their eyes for a glimpse of the river's course through their lower meadow, but darkness only mocked the small, flickering flame. Steady drumming of rain, however, and the faraway roar of angry waters told them that all was not well in the valley.

Carl had already gone to the barn when Mindy rose the next morning. Fire crackled a welcome as she entered the kitchen, but when her eyes moved to the window, she gasped in dismay. The river had swallowed road and meadow, leaving only barren trees and sprawling fences as familiar landmarks. The valley was a long lake, swirling and churning with its cargo of debris. She had seen it like this before in spring breakup. One could expect it then, the great chunks of ice cracking and grinding against one another. One knew it would snarl itself out in a couple of days, leaving the roads gutted and the fields sodden with mud. But this was another matter. The rains showed no signs of slowing, and grayness hung over the land.

"Could it ever climb the hill?" Mindy asked uneasily when Carl entered, milk pails clanking.

"You know better than that," he said sharply. "We're perfectly safe, but I wish I could be sure that Ned and Sara were."

The same thought had been knocking at the door of Mindy's mind, but she had refused it entrance. Now she bit her lip with worry. "Do you think the villages around are in any danger?"

"The ones along the river can't help but be, but Ned's not one to sit around and wonder what to do. They'll be all right."

167

After breakfast they walked down their winding drive to see if the bridge still held. The strong side rails Carl had built rose out of the water, but the main force of the brook broke wildly over the floor of the bridge as though to tear it from its foundations.

"We are trapped here," Mindy gasped in wonder. "We could not leave no matter how urgent our need."

"If that bridge goes, we'll be here all winter." Carl's forehead furrowed in concern.

Mindy cleaned house methodically all day, and Carl repaired machinery, as if in their doing ordinary things Nature's out-of-the-ordinary antics might be shamed away. But Nature, once launched upon her insane course, knew no turning. The rain came down in torrents, soaking Carl between house and barn.

They spoke no more of Ned and Sara, each knowing the other's fear. Mindy found herself muttering small, jumbled prayers for them, keeping tight rein over the knot of panic coiled within her. Telephone service had long since vanished. One could only wait and try not to watch the water's stealthy ascent up the hillside. Carl was right. It would never reach them, but what was it doing to villages along the river's edge?

They slept once more, wrapped in foreboding, the enemy hurling itself wetly against Mindy's slanting window.

"I am going to walk to the village," Carl announced next morning, cleaning the last of the French toast and syrup from his plate.

Mindy looked at him in astonishment. "Have you lost your mind? Only a fool would go into those waters."

"I'm not a fool. I shall keep to the ridges. If I see what the village is like, I'll know better how Ned and Sara are faring in Canton."

"It will not be an easy hike," Mindy said. "I'll fix you a lunch."

Half an hour later Carl climbed the hill behind the house, angling toward the village two miles away. Mindy

168

had always enjoyed solitude, but in this new gray, frightening world, the quietness followed her about like a witless child asking questions. Would Ned and Sara underestimate the seriousness of the storm? Would Ned have been home or away working? Would God still watch over this son who no longer offered Him recognition? Her eyes swept the hills nervously for Carl's return all through the day, but it was growing dark when he finally removed his boots on the back step and came wearily into the lamplit kitchen. Mindy helped him from his dripping outer clothes and put a chair before the open oven door. Handing him a cup of steaming tea, she inquired, "Well, what did you see?"

"You will never believe it," he answered, his voice strained. "The water in the village is at second-story windows. Everyone has gone. Only a couple of boats paddling about among the rooftops."

"Where have they gone—the people?" Mindy asked.

"Most are staying with those who live on higher ground outside of town. Some have tents on the hillside."

"Is everyone safe?" Mindy's thoughts turned to her school children.

"Two drowned," he said dully. "Paul Wheeler and Norman Jones. Paul was helping someone out a second-story window into his boat. There's so much confusion. One hardly hears the same story twice."

"It may be days before we have word of Ned and Sara. Do you think Canton is under water too?"

"I believe the entire valley is a raging flood," Carl told her. "It wouldn't surprise me if a good share of the state were having problems. We can only trust that Ned exercised good sense. I assume you've been in contact with your God. Have you no faith?"

"Sometimes God asks us to bear heavy sorrows for good reasons. We must pray, 'Thy will be done.' I've been almost afraid to do that."

169

Carl looked up at her quickly. "Suppose we lost them both. How would you feel about your God then?"

She was quiet a time, facing the question honestly. "My heart would break, but I would not doubt His wisdom."

"I hope you are not put to the test," Carl said, taking the plate of hot food she placed in his hands and moving closer to the stove.

They woke next morning to silence. The rains had ended, but dark clouds still frowned over the earth and angry waters churned between confining hills. "I shall always read the story of Noah with more understanding after this," Mindy said from her dishpan at the sink. "I feel as though you and I are alone on the face of the earth."

"And too old to repopulate it," Carl remarked dryly from his town bookwork which he had brought to the kitchen table.

"Oh, I wouldn't say that." Mindy flipped her dish towel at him in a playful gesture. "But I think I'll pass up the assignment."

They both sat quietly at the table—Carl with his ledgers, Mindy writing to Stephen and Rita—when they heard a faint, familiar whistling.

"Well, we are not alone on the earth after all," Carl said, rising with such eagerness that Mindy realized how tense they had both become.

"That's Ned. And if he's whistling, all is well. Oh, Carl!" She flung herself into his arms, laughing and crying in relief. They stood on the back steps and watched the tall figure coming down the hillside, his music falling like sunlight over the gray land.

"Thank God," Mindy breathed reverently.

"That comes from both of us," Carl added, lifting his eyes for a moment toward the dark skies. Mindy looked at him in surprise but said nothing.

"How in the world did you get here, Ned?" Carl asked. "I had trouble enough going to the village and back."

170

"I didn't wander these woods with Grandfather all my life for nothing," Ned said, as unconcerned as if he had just walked up from the corner.

While he ate toast and eggs before the fire, they took out their fears, one by one, and wrapped them in words. Where was Sara? What was it like in Canton? How had he found his way through miles of forest?

"When it got up to our knees in the streets," Ned reported, "I made up my mind it was no place for Sara; so we got into boots and warm clothes and set out for some friends of Sara's family, the Campbells, who live on high ground beyond the village. Since Sara wouldn't leave without the baby's things, I carried the chest on my shoulders, and we hiked three or four miles. It was hard, sloshing along on the lowland, but once we began to climb, it was okay."

"Sara shouldn't have had to do that," Mindy worried. "Was she exhausted?"

"No, she thought it was a great adventure. Mrs. Campbell made a fuss over her and insisted she go right to bed. Sara's more likely to die of loving care than anything else," Ned chuckled. "I couldn't stand another minute of being cooped up in the house, and knowing you'd be worried, I decided to follow the ridges and head this way."

"Did it worry Sara to have you come?"

"No, she would have come along if I'd have given her a word of encouragement. When I left yesterday morning, I felt sure I'd be here by nightfall, but all those pretty little streams had turned into torrents, and I had to make a dozen detours."

"What did you do when it got dark?" Carl asked.

"Made a lean-to out of spruce boughs and holed up like an animal, but I don't recommend it. Got pretty soggy by morning."

"What about your things in the apartment?" Mindy's thoughts turned to the cozy rooms Sara had created with such joy.

171

"They're gone," he said simply. "But that's one advantage of being poor and newly married. We didn't have much to lose."

The next morning he started back, confident he'd be with Sara by evening, now that he knew better how to chart his course. They waved him a last good-bye as he moved over the hilltop and out of view.

"He made it seem a small thing," Carl said, "but there are few who would have attempted such a journey. Perhaps we can help them a bit in getting some furniture together again." He turned toward the barn, and Mindy noted he walked tall and easy like a man who felt good about something.

*   *   *   *   *

By Christmas, snow covered the scarred earth and the villagers had scoured the mud from their homes. They would still show visitors the waterline in their upstairs bedrooms with a sort of awe at what they had survived. Ned had taken a good-paying lumbering job some distance from home, and Sara was staying with her parents until spring so that she would not be alone. But for Christmas they all gathered at the farm. Carl had cautioned Stephen it was dangerous to travel over the winter roads from Massachusetts in his old car, but they arrived the day before the holiday, nearly penniless and perfectly happy.

"We worried so when we were young and poor," Mindy said that night, as she and Carl readied for bed. "I'm glad the boys aren't that way."

"They inherited all that optimism from you," Carl stated matter-of-factly. "Might be better if they had a few grains of fear."

Christmas afternoon found them grouped about the tree opening gifts. Stephen had made a box of his famous peanut butter fudge for each one. A bright pillow for Mindy and a red hunting jacket for Sara ("so

you'll come back alive") had been born of Rita's skill-
ful needle. Mindy held Sara's gift on her lap, running
her fingers idly over the design. Around a pine-framed
mirror, Sara had painted a border of wild flowers.

"I had no idea you could do this," Mindy told her.
"You are a real artist."

The younger woman smiled her pleasure in Mindy's
praise. "Mother's the artist in our family, but I do like
to dab around a bit."

"She not only paints, she writes," Carl chuckled.
He had just opened woolen gloves and found enclosed
an original poem entitled "To My Feathery Pop," the
nickname with which Sara had affectionately endowed
him because of his thick unruly eyebrows. Carl read the
clever lines to much laughter and handclapping. Snow
fell softly over the old farmhouse. Red and green tissue
lay in drifts upon the pine floor. The tree shed its woodsy
aroma over the room, and the six were knit in a circle
of love and sharing. They had become a family. They
little dreamed it would never be that way again.

Chapter 17

When Mindy arrived at the schoolhouse on the morning of St. Patrick's Day, she found Ned sitting on the front steps and knew without asking why he was there.

"Boy or girl?" she called from the buggy seat, looking fondly down upon her firstborn son.

"Girl," he said. "Born at four this morning. Sara's fine, and she insisted I come down here and tell you in person."

"Bless her. Did she have a hard time?" Mindy's thoughts turned back to her own struggles to give birth.

"She went into the hospital at midnight; so I guess she did pretty well for the first time."

"I had planned to be so brave when you were born," Mindy said, remembering, "and then made a lot of noise and took forever. I'm glad it wasn't long for her."

"I could hear her crying out softlike, and I knew it would take a lot to force a sound out of Sara. It's strange, frightening business, isn't it?"

Mindy looked down into the weary young face. "Indeed it is, but very rewarding when it's all over. Women soon forget the pain."

"I must go." Ned turned toward the car. "The foreman only gave me two days, and I want to spend it all with Sara. I hate to leave her and go back to camp, but she'll be in good hands in her mother's home."

"You haven't told me half enough. Who does the baby look like? What did you name her?" For once Mindy longed to play hooky from her beloved schoolroom.

"She looks like every other baby I've ever seen, and her name's Katherine Jean," he answered, starting up the car. "Sara said to tell you she has her mother's eyes and her father's dimples."

"We'll be there tonight to see for ourselves. I can hardly wait. Tell Sara I'm really proud to be a grandmother."

Ned gave his mother a quick amused glance. "I never thought about that. How does it feel?"

"It's all so new I hardly know, but I think I shall be very good at it."

He grinned and drove away. Entering the classroom, Mindy sat down at her desk, oblivious to all the green construction-paper shamrocks she had prepared to decorate the room.

A girl. She had never considered a girl. She was disappointed. How shameful! But little girls giggled and pouted and whined. They chattered too—everlastingly. She even liked the boys in her classroom better. She'd never admitted that before, even to herself. Well, she'd just be still about it, and perhaps it would at least be a sensible girl like Sara.

They didn't get to see the baby that night after all, for it stormed—a real old March blizzard that blotted out roads and had no concern for new grandparents. But Sara wrote them every few days telling of the baby's progress, of a shower which had been given her, and how annoyed she was at not being able to tend the child herself. "I have a sharp pain in my right side," she wrote, "so the doctor's keeping me in bed. Seems ridiculous. I feel so well otherwise and long to care for little Kate myself instead of leaving it to Mother. But I shall be patient, for Ned is coming this weekend, and the doctor has promised I may get up a bit then."

"Let's drive to Greensboro Saturday night ourselves," Mindy said to Carl eagerly. "I can't wait much longer to see this baby, and we'll get to chat with Ned a bit too."

"If there's no more snow between now and then," Carl promised, heading wearily for the bedroom after days and nights of plowing on mountain roads.

But they did not go to Greensboro Saturday night. For when Mindy returned from church, her red cutter bright against the snow, she found Ned's car in the yard.

The moment she saw him at the kitchen table, head in hands, she knew something was wrong.

"What is it, Ned?" she asked softly. "Is the baby ill?"

He looked at her then, and she was startled, for the openness about him had vanished. It was as though a door had closed upon the old Ned. "Sara is dead," he said flatly.

There was a tiny three-cornered tear in the blue-checked tablecloth, and it seemed to Mindy that if she did not take her eyes away from it, perhaps Ned's words would drift into the distance, growing fainter and fainter until they were no longer true. But his voice went on dully, forcing her to believe.

"I got to her mother's late last night. The doctor had told her she could get up for breakfast if she was back in bed in half an hour. I helped her down the stairs this morning. It was the first time she'd been on her feet in the two weeks since Kate was born, and she was laughing and happy." He stopped then as if he himself could not believe the tale he bore. Mindy had not taken a step.

"The baby was in a basket by the window," he went on, "and we stopped a minute to look at her. Then I took Sara to her chair, and just as she was going to sit down, she cried, 'Ned,' in such a strangled, frightened

176

way, like she was calling for help, and fell onto the floor. The doctor said a blood clot went to her heart."

"Nineteen years old. All that talent and ability. What a waste!" Mindy was talking to herself, avoiding the moment when she must talk to Ned. She felt tears streaming down her face. She placed her hand then on the curly head bowed before her.

"You had her more than a year. Perhaps some marriages do not know that much happiness in a lifetime. We can thank God for that."

He made no answer.

"Your father and I loved her very much. She was a blessing to us all. And she will live on in the little one." Empty, empty words! Mindy could sense their futile falling on her son. Then she spoke the truth. "You will suffer, Ned, and something of you will die with her. You will never be quite the same person again, but Sara would not want you to become bitter. She loved you for your glad heart and your laughter."

His silence frightened her. She had no more words. She could only put her arms around him and hold him like a child in the quiet room.

"There are a dozen things I'm supposed to be doing," he said finally, rising. "I don't know much about funerals."

"Who would at twenty-two?" Mindy thought. "Let me go with you," she urged. "You'll need help."

"Sara's father is waiting for me. I'll let them make the decisions. None of it matters to me."

"Do you want to bring the baby here?" Mindy asked.

"I think it's good for Mother Houghton to keep busy. Let's leave her there for now."

Mindy looked long at him as he stood, hand upon the doorknob. "Are you all right, my son?" He seemed so defenseless, so vulnerable. "Can you handle everything?" She didn't mean the funeral. She meant could he go on living, doing all the ordinary things, without being consumed by sorrow.

177

"I have no choice," he said abruptly, the door closing behind him.

How would she endure the afternoon? She wished he had asked something of her. She had no idea how to find Carl, who could be anywhere among the mountains freeing small back roads with his plow. Going to the woodbox in the back room, her eyes fell on Sara's hiking boots sitting neatly by the door as she had left them. Suddenly the enormity of Ned's loss swept over her and seemed beyond bearing. Never would there be another girl who walked the sunlit woods at his side. She held the boots tightly against her and cried as she had never cried before. It was worse than losing Father or Mother, this agony for one's child.

Carl found her spent and quiet, reading her Bible in the living room some hours later. When she told him, gently as she could, he bowed his head against the tears. How had the girl crept so securely into their hearts in so short a time? Mindy felt strangely adrift. She realized Sara had been strength not only for Ned but for them all.

Carl stood at the window watching long, mauve shadows finger the snowy hills. "She had so much undeveloped talent," he mused. "I'd hoped somehow we could help her get more education."

Mindy made no reply. One could say, "What a waste" for a hundred years, and it would not bring her back.

"Was Ned all right?" Carl asked, as though almost afraid to phrase the words.

"Well, he was perfectly calm," Mindy said, "if that's what you mean. He was *too* calm. It didn't seem normal somehow."

And that's what everyone said. He sat erect and dry of eye throughout the funeral, and the townsfolk murmured, "Who'd have thought Ned Matthews was so cold? Must have a heart of stone."

Mindy and Carl watched him with concern. Once she said, "It's healing to cry, Ned" and met such a look

178

in his eyes that she mentioned it no more.

The night after the funeral he came holding the baby awkwardly in his arms. "Will you take her?" he asked simply.

For a night?

For a week?

Forever?

What was he asking? It had been twenty years since Mindy had met the needs of a baby. She knew nothing of girls. She had once said, "It's impossible to refuse Ned anything," and now looking into the empty bewilderment of her son's face, she met her own words coming home. In reply she held out her arms for the child.

"I have her things in the car." He brought them into the kitchen, one by one. A lacy bassinet, the chest of clothes lovingly sewn and carried on a young father's shoulders through a flood, cans of Pet milk, and bottles.

They said little. It was the wrong ending. No one knew his lines.

When everything rested in a pile on the kitchen table, Mindy urged, "Now stay awhile, Ned, and relax. You've been running for three days. Sit down and enjoy your little one while I try to think what one does with a baby."

"No, thanks, I'm on my way back to camp," he muttered, his words slurring. Her heart lurched with an old fear.

When she had given him over uneasily to the winter night, Carl said wearily, "I knew where he'd turn."

The baby whimpered softly in her basket. Mindy searched through the pile of supplies for some instructions relating to formula, and she found it at last, written neatly on a card in Sara's familiar hand. Somehow it steadied her. Something of the girl's calm spirit clung to the card, and she set about warming milk with more confidence.

Going to the bassinet, she picked up the crying

child and took it to Carl. "Maybe all she needs is a little love."

In his arms the baby lay quietly, looking up at them with questioning eyes.

"We're all she's got," Carl said.

"Why, she has Ned. What a strange thing to say!"

"He's hurt too deep." Carl touched the baby's cheek curiously. "He'll never be much good to her."

"Why, Carl Matthews!" Mindy found herself speechless.

"He didn't give her so much as a second glance when he left."

"Well, he's not himself. It's been a terrible ordeal. The child will be everything to him once he gets righted around." Mindy poured milk into a bottle. "Here, this will do for now. I must make a good supply for the night. We didn't fuss so when the boys were babies."

Watching Carl, it occurred to her that he'd never given a bottle to either of his sons. Probably she'd never asked him. He had always been so weary and so busy. Now his eyes, lingering on the baby's face, wore a faint smile. Kate's tiny fist curled around his little finger.

"You'd better phone a substitute to teach for you tomorrow. In fact, you'll need a week or so to find someone to look after the baby while you're gone."

For a long moment Mindy surveyed the messy kitchen and realized the complications of her new role. What had Ned expected her to do? He knew she had responsibilities away from home. "I'm not sure I'm equal to all this," she said, panic moving in. "Do you suppose Ned ever thought this through?"

"What did you expect him to do—take the baby to the lumber camp or drop her in a snowdrift?"

"No, of course not. He did the logical thing to bring her here. It's just that I can't see the solutions to all the problems, and I feel very unsure of myself as a mother."

"Grow up," he snapped, laying the sleeping baby in its basket. "You don't have to solve everything tonight."

180

When a plaintive wail dragged Mindy from sleep, she rose with effort. How long did babies demand attention in the night? She couldn't remember. Heating the bottle in the cold kitchen, she knew once again a good sharp jab of distaste for the task at hand. She was too old. The cycles of her life had moved out and beyond this role. Where would she find the strength?

Settling into Seth's old rocker, she pulled a quilt about herself and the child. Putting her head back, she rested as the baby drank. When the bottle was finished, the baby slept, her face lit softly with moonlight. The woman was moved with the utter defenselessness of the child. So new in the world, and so alone. With sudden insight, she realized God had handed her an assignment. He had assumed her mature enough to handle it, and she'd been whimpering like a child. This warmth cradled in her arms was a life, a human being who would one day hurt and laugh, think and act, create and destroy. It was up to her, Mindy Matthews, to nurture in the girl Sara's gentle strength, Ned's joy, and a healthy loneliness for her Creator.

She held the babe before her on her knees and smiled as the tiny face puckered at the disturbance. "Sleep on, little one," she whispered softly. "All is well."

Chapter 18

One month later Ned walked in unexpectedly on Friday evening. Mindy warmed food for him and could not contain her joy at his presence. "It's so good to have you here." She touched his head lightly in passing. "You'll never believe how Kate has grown."

She went to the basket and brought the baby to the table. Ned took a tiny fist in his hand and looked long into the little face. The faintest flicker of a smile danced from the baby's eyes to her lips. But Ned said only, "I knew she'd thrive here, Mother," and went on talking to Carl about his plans for the summer.

"Well, the Matthews men always have been awkward with babies," Mindy said to herself in his defense. She put the baby to bed in her own room and slipped outside, leaving father and son talking. The Sabbath hour drew near, and she loved to welcome it high on a pasture ridge overlooking the valley. April had tiptoed across the winter-weary land, leaving pussy willows and wild little streams flinging themselves helter-skelter down mountain sides. She was weary. Her heart often ached for Ned. She missed Sara. Finding the right help to care for Kate had proved to be a problem. She worried about Stephen and Rita's finances. It wasn't easy teaching and playing mother at forty-three. But she was also content. Out of adversity had come a new strength. Some days she could honestly "give thanks in everything." She sang softly the old song she'd taught the boys so long ago, "Day Is Dying in the West." It was a fitting song with which to greet the holy hours. A hymn of praise. Once in her girlhood she'd found her father sitting on the hill behind their home singing hymns on the Sabbath. She'd questioned, "How can you love the Sabbath? It's a long day, full of things one can't do."

And Hiram had replied, "It's a day when God comes very near to His people if we'll but cease our busyness and meet Him. It's hard for human nature to be still, and especially difficult for little ones, but someday, Mindy, if you guard the sacredness of the Sabbath carefully and learn to be alone, you'll find a little bit of heaven right here on earth."

She'd sought it carefully, the Sabbath blessing, and knew its mysterious joy. Would either of her sons ever find it, or the babe that slept beneath her roof? Thinking of the child brought her to her feet. She should not be so long away.

Far down the valley Carl collected debris left along the riverbank by spring flooding.

Mindy entered the kitchen and tiptoed up the stairs to check on the baby. A sound alerted her. In the half-darkened room she saw Ned in her rocking chair by the window holding the baby tightly against him. As he rocked, his tears fell onto Kate's face and hands. The sound of his crying broke harshly the quiet of the old house. Mindy stumbled through her own tears back down the stairs. "He mourns at last. Now he can heal," she thought to herself as she laid out the baby's clothes for church upon the morrow.

*   *   *   *   *

When Stephen and Rita came home from college

in June, Rita big with child, they did not celebrate. The family feared to rejoice lest tragedy pursue them once more, but they went instead about their preparations quietly.

"Nothing seems right without Sara," Rita said one morning, bathing small Kate. "It breaks my heart to be doing all the things with her baby she would have so loved to do herself. What do you suppose God had in mind when He let her die?"

Mindy, shelling peas for canning, did not answer at once. Rita had not been a Seventh-day Adventist when Stephen married her, but she had made a serious attempt to fit herself into his life-style. Mindy had loved her for that, and she did not wish now to shatter a faith so fragile and new. "I have no good answer for that question," she at last admitted honestly. "Only that I believe God always knows what He's doing. Sometimes it looks all wrong to us, but if our faith is worth anything, we must assume there is a purpose in His actions."

"So no matter what life dishes out, one must just bow the head and say, 'Thy will be done'?" Rita soaped the baby's head and shaped the hair into a curl on top.

"It makes all the difference in the world how you say it, Rita," Mindy replied. "You can say it willingly, trusting in God's all-wise love, or you can say it bitterly, denying that He even exists. I guess you don't ever quite know how you feel about God until sorrow comes along."

"Did you not feel angry with God when Sara died?"

"Not angry," the older woman answered sadly, "but puzzled. I asked Him *why* over and over again. Ned needed her so much."

"Ned will mend. He's young. Already he seems to have forgotten. He never mentions her. Doesn't that seem strange?"

"It's not good," Mindy said. "He's not forgotten. Something terrible happened to Ned when Sara died. Once I found him with the baby, crying, and I thought he would be better then, but it didn't help. All that was

184

best in Ned is locked away. He's cynical, and he drinks too much."

"Some girl will come along and fix all that. Ned has such a way about him," Rita assured Mindy, in the confidence of her youth.

"Carl says he'll never be the same again." Mindy put a teaspoon of salt into each quart of peas as she talked, and there was such sorrow in her words that the girl placed the towel-wrapped baby into her arms for comfort.

Rita bore, in mid-July, a dark-eyed beauty. They named her Ellen, and now there were two babies in the old house. Sometimes, bathing and bottling alongside her daughter-in-law, Mindy felt young again. Other times she felt old, *too* old for coping with teething, fevers, and bouts of fussing in the August heat.

Stephen worked with increased frenzy. Upon his shoulders rested a new responsibility. Never for a moment did he give up his dream. "When we go to Loma Linda" * was a phrase intertwined throughout any mention of their future. Mindy could not bear the words. It had once been her dream for Stephen, too, but she feared for his health. How long could he hope to work night and day? There wasn't a spare pound on his lean, young body, and she could not face the time when he would grow grim and silent as Carl had under overwork.

When they headed back to college in late August, Carl tucked a $50 bill in Stephen's shirt pocket. Mindy felt a terrible helplessness that they could do so little, but she was comforted briefly by the jars of canned goods packed into the back seat alongside the baby's basket. At least they would eat. How Stephen kept his grades up she could not imagine, for Rita had told her she often found him asleep over his books after long hours of work.

---

*Loma Linda is a Seventh-day Adventist medical school in California.

185

"He's making it," Carl exulted, his voice edged with wonder and pride, as the car rounded the bend and disappeared from their sight. "He's clicking off the years one by one against all the odds."

"They didn't really need that baby right now," Mindy sighed, "but one couldn't wish her away, she's so precious. If only Stephen's health doesn't break."

"You forget how much abuse the body can take at twenty, Min."

"Or even at forty," Mindy replied, thinking of her own long days and Carl's. Once Seth had said only work mattered. Perhaps his clan was doomed to his declaration. She turned back toward the house, pushing aside her concern for Stephen, to cope with the decisions awaiting her.

A new girl was coming in a couple of hours to apply for the task of looking after Kate. Mindy did not look forward to the interview. They were all the same, these teenage girls, anxious for some spending money but totally indifferent to the needs of a baby. They never liked the isolation of the farm either. She often came home to find the girl at the door, coat in hand, the baby whimpering and soiled in her crib. She wished she could afford to stay at home and tend the child herself.

Gloria Miller was a pretty young woman, too pretty in Mindy's opinion to be of any real value. Great gray-green eyes sparkled in a heart-shaped face. When she smiled, it caught Mindy off guard. There was something impish and merry about her dimpled grin that made the older woman laugh in spite of herself.

"Have you ever cared for a child before?" Mindy asked, determined not to be influenced by dimples and big eyes.

"No, but I like babies," Gloria said shyly.

"We're a long way from town, you know, and you'd be alone here with the baby all day."

"I'm nineteen," the girl stated simply as though that fact erased all need for further discussion.

186

"Suppose one's as good as another," Mindy sighed to herself, resignedly. "Well, come on the fourth of September. That will give me a couple of days before school begins to help you get started."

A month later Mindy could hardly believe her good fortune. She came home from the schoolroom day after day to find Kate clean and happy. The young woman had spoken the truth when she said she liked babies. It showed in her affectionate handling and gentle words. "She's an answer to prayer," Mindy told Carl.

"And pretty to boot," he added.

On the rare occasions when Ned stopped by, he too found her pleasing. He had always enjoyed a pretty face, and in her lighthearted way she hopscotched into the deep woods of his sorrow, bringing sunlight with her. He came more often, and they dated occasionally. He laughed once more. But he was not the same. Carl was right. He never would be. Never so open, so vulnerable, so carefree again.

"Gloria's not right for him, even though she's a charmer," Mindy said one Sunday to Carl as the young folks drove away. "She doesn't understand his weaknesses or that she must be his strength."

"You ask too much of young women. Be thankful she loves the child." The sharpness edging Carl's voice had become so familiar, Mindy hardly heard it.

"I can't even think about that. They will take Kate away, and the house will be so empty without her."

Carl glanced down at the small figure playing on the floor at his feet, his face softening. "You don't really want the baby stuck with us, do you? What do we have to offer her?"

"Our love," Mindy declared firmly. "And a knowledge of God."

"Well, they're a long ways from married, so it's foolish to be fretting about what may never happen." Carl finished lacing his boots and stood up. He was graying at the temples, but it did not detract from his

187

appearance at all. Suddenly Mindy wanted to spend a whole day with him, to be idle, walking in the sun, holding his hand. There had to be something left, distilled from all the hard years. And if there were, he would respond to her need of him. Surely nothing as fragile and sweet as what they had shared could die. She reached out to him eagerly, lovingly. "Why don't we just declare it a holiday? We'll take a lunch and ride around looking at the fall colors—they're at their peak this weekend. We could stop somewhere and walk in the woods. Oh, please, Carl, let's."

He looked at her, unseeing, his mind already upon the work he had planned. "You know I have only one day for farming, Min. Why do you ask impossible things of me?" He turned toward the door and the tasks of the day.

When he had gone, she picked up the baby and sat down in a rocker on the long porch Carl had built across the front of the house. The valley had never been more beautiful, and it blurred through her tears into kaleidoscopes of red and gold and green.

"I have only one day for housework, too, Carl, but it could wait." . . . There was no one to answer. The baby patted the tears on her cheek and looked wonderingly into the usually cheerful face.

"These heartaches are not yours, child," Mindy insisted. "I will show *you* the autumn world. Six months is not too young to experience beauty." Going into the front yard she gathered leaves of every color. Then, taking Kate on her lap in the swing which hung from the balm of Gilead, she swung gently, letting the baby toss the bright leaves into the air. If she could not be a sweetheart, she would be a child. And so she played with the baby all the long morning. Carl, plowing on the hill, could surely see her frivolous waste of time, but she did not care. She would take her heavy heart to God and the out-of-doors. It was a lesson she had learned well.

That night the old enemy writhed and twisted within

188

her chest. Propping herself with pillows on the living-room couch, she waited for the pills to take effect. It was not the pain but the fighting for breath which frightened her. "O God, let me live as long as Kate needs me," she prayed, realizing there in the darkness that her life had purpose once more. "So I've come to love a *girl* after all," she thought, gripping her hands together tightly against the pain. She missed Stephen at these moments when she fought for life. His calm trust in God made death seem less to be feared when he sat beside her in the lamplight, his dark head bent in prayer. But more than Stephen, she wanted Carl. She wanted him to come down the stairs, hold her in his arms, and pray softly until she could breathe again. She coveted his concern. She longed to speak with him of God and things beyond the struggle of their present days. But it could never be. She no longer bothered even to wake him when she felt the pain creeping over her in the night. Why trouble his sleep? She was too proud to beg again for his love, and she knew the futility of her mentioning God.

She breathed a bit easier now, though the pain still seared in her chest. She was alone, yet not alone. The invisible God had become very real, and she relaxed into His love.

Chapter 19

Snow tucked the valley in snugly for the winter's long siege, then retreated before the green and sunny troops of May. Now Mindy knew Ned would marry Gloria, who asked nothing of him, loving him just as he came to her, witty, generous, kind, and weak. If his drinking bothered her, she showed no sign.

On the June morning when Ned left, dressed in his best, to bring his bride before a justice of the peace, Mindy sat in Seth's rocker with the baby in her arms, her eyes sad and unseeing as they looked out across the emerald valley. Carl came from the barn to find, for the first time ever, breakfast remains still upon the table and two flies buzzing above the milk pitcher.

"Min, you've faced plenty of tough things in your life. Are you going to mope over this all day?" His irritation hung in the air even after his words were out of sound. "He couldn't have found anyone to suit you no matter how long he looked, unless she was a member of your church, and he's left all that behind anyhow."

"I was well satisfied with Sara," Mindy said humbly. "She knew how to protect Ned from himself and keep him happy at the same time. Gloria loves him, but she'll never challenge him to any better way of life. I'm not mourning over Ned's marriage, anyhow. He's old enough to make his own decisions, and it's good to have him more like his old self again. But they'll take the baby, Carl, and I don't care how many trials I've faced, I can't face that." She buried her dark head—now well streaked with gray—in the child's soft neck, and her shoulders shook with noiseless sobs. Kate hugged her grandmother, crooning softly in a strange reversal of their conventional roles.

"If I remember right, you weren't too keen on taking on the job when Ned tossed her into your lap. Why all the tears now?"

Mindy lifted her head. "Carl Matthews, you can't care for a child without coming to love it. This house will be a tomb when she goes, and you know it."

He stood looking down at her, the sharp blue eyes momentarily tender. "Indeed it will, Min. Go ahead and cry. Shed some tears for me too. We were fools to become so attached to the child."

"It's never foolish to love, Carl."

"Even if it leads to hurt?"

"Often that's the price."

"Then isn't it better not to love at all?" Carl's eyes never left her face. She knew they were no longer talking about the baby.

"Sometimes we have no choice," she said softly.

"Or learn too late," he replied, his voice barbed with bitterness for her, or for himself—she knew not which.

Ned and Gloria took an apartment in the village, and every time they drove into the yard, Mindy felt fear trickle through her like tiny rivulets of ice water. She longed to grab up the baby and hide her away in a closet. She knew she was wrong. The baby deserved something better than two middle-aged parents who no longer laughed and loved together. She even made herself drop the right little comments.

"I'm getting Kate's things washed up so she'll be ready when you are settled."

"Plan to take the crib with you. The baby'll feel more at home in it than in a new one."

They nodded politely and chatted about other things. Mindy noted, puzzled, that Gloria no longer cuddled Kate or sang nonsense to her.

When the young couple had been comfortably settled into their apartment for more than a month, Carl told Mindy one night at the table, "I think you can breathe again. They aren't going to take Kate. They don't want her."

Mindy watched the child trying to find her mouth with a spoonful of mashed potatoes. Brown hair, soft and fine, framed a dimpled face with eyes as blue as Carl's.

"I'd already come to that conclusion," she replied, passing Carl a piece of apple pie afloat with thick yellow cream. "But how could that be? Ned is by nature an affectionate person, and Gloria was fond of Kate."

"Too many memories, perhaps. Kate represents everything Ned wants to forget." Carl was still a moment. "Or maybe Gloria has simply said nothing doing. Ned has never been one to take a firm stand."

"He ignores Kate, Carl. Sometimes I have the feeling he's being careful not to even glance in her direction. Is that guilt or sorrow?"

"Who knows?" Carl shrugged, finishing the last drops of his coffee and rising to leave the table.

"I've been thinking, Carl, these past few weeks. If Kate is going to be ours, I don't want to teach anymore. She deserves something better than an endless line of baby-sitters. Could we manage without my pay?" She held her breath. The fear of poverty had strengthened in him with the years. They'd both grown accustomed to the difference her paycheck made in their lives.

"I'd hoped you'd decide that." Carl's rough hand tousled Kate's hair. "I want her to have the best of everything, and for now that means a full-time mother."

Mindy looked up at him, surprised and pleased.

192

"Carl Matthews, I believe you've fair set out to spoil the child."

"We've little to spoil her with, Min. You needn't worry."

"She's ours—ours to love and train and enjoy. I can't believe it." Mindy picked Kate up, and Carl in a rare gesture encompassed them both in his arms.

Kate, basking in this uncommon shower of affection, placed a chubby arm about each of their necks and tugged their heads together.

Lightly, lingeringly, Carl kissed Mindy, and her eyes filled with tears. His lips were the lips of a stranger, but a delightful one. She would always love him. There was no escaping.

A month later Mindy stood in her empty classroom. The last child had gathered his papers, lingered at her desk, frolicked briefly on the playground, and gone home. The room smelled of chalk and children. Her own round, precise script still filled the boards, but her desk was clean. She felt stripped of that portion of herself in which she took most pride and pleasure, her ability to entice young minds ever onward into the green fields of knowledge. Was she making a mistake to center all her talents and attentions on one small girl who could not appreciate now, or perhaps ever, what it had cost her?

Maybe, but she knew she must do it. She could not allow the child to grow helter-skelter, her head crammed with whatever foolishness the hired girl of the moment might be dispensing. Already she'd seen glimpses of Ned in Kate—the quick, easy laughter, the open, vulnerable affection. She sighed, hoping those characteristics were linked to strengths, Sara's strengths. 'Twould be a good combination.

Putting on her sweater, she walked to the door and looked back at the orderly rows of seats. She would leave the day's assignments on the board for the cleaning crew to erase when they readied the school in September. A little bit of her could stay here all summer.

That way, until they washed down the boards, it would still be *her* classroom. An old jacket hung in the cloakroom. She'd leave that too. She shook herself impatiently. What an old fool she was! Life came in sections. One must not reject a new portion when it arrived, nor must he look wistfully back upon the old. There had always been something challenging in every assignment.

She hitched up the horse and buggy and drove smartly out of the school yard. Waving and smiling at the villagers, she nodded and called out a greeting to a woman here, a child there. She had their respect and their affection. She knew more about many of them than they dreamed, for innocent betrayals of family secrets often fell unsolicited from young lips. She had guarded those secrets with integrity, seldom sharing them even with Carl.

"I do not have a close friend in the village," she thought to herself, "yet I love these people. They have entrusted me with their children, and I have given them my best. I have taught their youngsters to think, to verbalize, to seek answers, to see wonder in the world about them. We have had a productive exchange and mutual respect. That is better than gossiping over the back fence." She had no regrets.

PART
III

Chapter 20

Kate ran ahead and, by standing on tiptoe, dragged the mail from the box. The child was tall for three, healthy and strong. Mindy watched her with pride. She had been right to give up teaching and focus her efforts upon the little one. She had seen a change in Kate almost at once, a shy but sure blossoming which delighted the older woman.

Now in the late June sunshine, carrying a bouquet of wild strawberries, Mindy felt pleasantly drugged with an uncomplicated earthy happiness. 'Twas a combination of the more leisurely pace of her life, her almost sensual delight in the earth, and her joy in the child. A letter would complete the moment. Preferably a letter from Stephen and Rita to read as she wandered back toward the house. And it was there, addressed in Rita's firm, decisive hand.

On the bridge which crossed the brook, Mindy sat Kate down beside the sturdy end post, transferred the strawberries to her lap, and gathered up some pebbles for tossing into the stream. Having bought herself a moment of quiet, she leaned upon the railing, enjoying the feel of the envelope in her hand, the warmth of the sun upon her back, and the anticipation of the moment.

The water beneath the bridge moved lazily through the lower meadow and on toward town, but behind her she could hear the splashing of its livelier course upstream and distantly the muted roaring of its descent over steep rocks. She loved the sound.

All her senses were satisfied, and she tore the envelope open, feeling almost wickedly content. It wasn't often Stephen had time for writing, but Rita's letters came regularly, not skimpy and dutiful, but filled with all the small happenings of their days, and sometimes with pictures of the child, Ellen, who had inherited her father's dark-eyed good looks and was destined to become the family beauty.

It did not seem possible they had been a year in California. Immediately upon Stephen's graduation, they had set out in their car—the same old car Carl had pronounced unfit to take them back and forth to Massachusetts—for medical school at Loma Linda. There were snapshots in the family album of Stephen on one knee peering into the Grand Canyon, tiny Ellen tucked into the crook of his arm; the repairing of a flat tire along some lonely road in Nevada; and finally, Ellen and Rita on the front step of the cottage they had rented close to the university. Stephen was seeing the world at last and working with a dogged determination toward his goals. It had been a difficult year. They had not complained, but Carl and Mindy read between the lines of their poverty and Stephen's valiant struggle to keep up with his studies while providing bread for the table.

Dear Mother and Dad,

The letter was short, only a few lines, and some warning deep within snatched away the serenity which had been Mindy's.

Stephen has not been well for several weeks but felt he could not give up until his studies were

*completed for the year. Now he has seen a doctor
and finds he has an abscess on the left kidney.
It will require surgery, which he should have done
here; but he is determined to come home. I think
he fears Ellen and I will want if his recuperation
should be long.*

*We are leaving in two days. Pray that we will
have a safe journey and that Stephen can handle
the trip. He is very ill. You will be shocked when
you see him, for beyond his sickness he is thin and
exhausted from much study and overwork. We
hope to see you on the fifth or sixth of July.*

> *Lovingly,*
> *Rita*

*PS: Ellen is fine and anxious to see Grandpa and
Grandma.*

Mindy realized she had practiced for this moment
many times over the years of Stephen's long struggle to
become a doctor, but she was not ready. She didn't want
the part. Already they were on their way, weaving across
the country once more in that terrible old car.

"O God, be with them," Mindy whispered. "Come,
Kate." She took the child by the hand and hurried toward the house. She must do something—cook, prepare
the guest room, or just pace on the front porch. Somehow, until they arrived, she must fill the days with anything besides thinking. It was cruel. They had tried so
hard, endured so much.

"Kate, your cousin Ellen is coming." Mindy looked
down at the brown head bobbing at her side. "She's just
your age, and you'll have a playmate."

"When?" Kate asked, hopping puddles and not
terribly interested.

"In a few days. We must prepare the little house."
The words passed her lips before they were well registered in her mind. The little house! Of course! Why had
she not thought of it before? Since Martha's death,

199

years before, it had sat with boarded windows beside the road. Driving by it on her way to the village, Mindy often thought she had no feeling for the place, but now it suddenly held great possibilities. It would give Stephen and Rita the privacy they needed, and at no expense during the summer months.

In the days that followed she worked far into the nights readying the house, sewing ruffled chintz curtains, and accumulating the essential furnishings from attic and secondhand stores. Kate, standing in the tiny kitchen on a Friday morning, observed, "Pretty house for Ellen," and Mindy, straightening from her floor polishing, had to agree. There was a scrubbed coziness about it that she hoped would spell home to her battered children until they were able to venture forth once more. And venture forth they would, for nothing would hold Stephen long in the valley. She well knew no illness could snuff out his lust for learning and adventure.

Mindy lifted a square in the kitchen floor to take some supplies to the small dirt cellar beneath the house. Kate lay on her tummy peering down into the dark opening. "I shall never go down into that place, Grandma," she said firmly.

Mindy laughed up at her from the foot of the ladder.

"And why not, young lady?"

"It's a very scary place. It must be full of rats and spiders. I hate black holes."

"Fiddlesticks." Mindy lined home-canned peaches on new shelves which Carl had built only the day before. "A country girl must not be afraid of rats and spiders. It would be a splendid place to hide."

"*With the lid down?*" Kate's blue eyes opened wide at the very thought.

Mindy chuckled. "Yes, with the lid down. But I'm not sure I would like that either. Now, let's take a tour through the house and be sure everything is in order."

"Will Ellen come today?" Kate asked as they climbed into the buggy and set out for home.

"I thought they would come yesterday," Mindy said. "We must be patient."

Later, as she brought the Friday night pan of beans to the table, she heard the sound of tires on the gravel drive and knew they had arrived. Carl's voice was warm and strong as he greeted them in the yard, but she could not move. All week she had been running from this moment. She didn't want to see Stephen ill and defeated. She depended somehow on his strength and his optimism—especially his optimism. There was so little of it about. Sometimes it seemed the valley folk took a perverse pleasure in anticipating trouble. Stephen had expected only good, but trouble had crept up on him anyhow.

"They are here, Grandma," Kate said quietly, pulling at Mindy's apron. Mindy reached for the small hand, finding comfort in its warmth. They stood that way as the rest filed into the kitchen.

Mindy's eyes fell first upon Ellen in Carl's arms. Her beauty always startled Mindy. There were handsome men in the family but no beautiful women. She felt Rita's fierce young embrace and saw tears in her eyes. This girl was not one to cry. It told Mindy much about the past weeks. "You're home," Mindy comforted. "Everything's going to be all right."

But when she looked at Stephen, she wondered if anything would ever be all right with him again. Rita had tried to prepare them, but Mindy could never have imagined him so thin, so frighteningly ill. How had he driven those endless miles? She could only take him in her arms and say his name brokenly over and over again, "Stephen, Stephen."

"Enough tears, Min," Carl advised, wiping his own eyes. "I'll help Stephen into bed, and you can get the eats onto the table. We're going to get some meat on this girl again so we'll be able to recognize her by something besides her voice." He gave Rita an affectionate hug and followed Stephen to the small bedroom off the kitchen.

Suddenly Mindy remembered the children and discovered them staring at each other with frank curiosity.

"Did you say hello to Ellen?" Mindy asked, kneeling down to their level and putting an arm about each of her granddaughters.

Kate shook her head shyly. "Will she sleep in the little house tonight?"

"No," Mindy replied. "They'll stay here tonight, and tomorrow maybe we'll show them the surprise."

"A surprise?" Rita said, coming from the pantry with a plate of freshly sliced brown bread.

"How efficiently she moves back into the pattern of our life," Mindy thought, marveling as always at the quick mind and capable hands of such a fragile creature.

"It's not really a surprise." Mindy sugared a milk-glass bowl of tiny wild strawberries. "We've just fixed up the little house down the road a bit so when Stephen is better you can move in there and have some privacy. You've had to spend so many summers under your mother-in-law's nose that we thought this would be a nice change."

"I wish we could move in tomorrow," Rita said, a flicker of anticipation dancing in her worried eyes. "I've always loved that little house. It looked so lonely all boarded up beside the road."

"You may move in whenever you wish. We thought you might not like to be alone while Stephen is in the hospital though."

"I've been alone so long that I don't know anything else. Ever since our marriage Stephen has been working, studying, or in school. To live with him in that little house, just an ordinary life, will be a bit of heaven."

"But his education, Rita. Stephen will never give up. You know how he is."

"He *has* to give up, for now at least. Neither of us could ever survive another year like the past one. There is no work. The depression may be just a news item here in the mountains, but it's very real in the cities. This table looks like a banquet. You can't believe how we've lived—and it's just as well—but if we don't eat soon, I'm going to attack this food like a wolf, and you'll disown me."

Mindy looked at her daughter-in-law with startled eyes. "You really mean you're that kind of hungry?"

"So hungry my knees wobble." Rita sat down at the table and buttered herself a piece of the dark, sweet brown bread.

"What a good, brave girl you've been," Mindy said quietly, filling a plate with food and putting it before her.

"Not so good or so brave as you think. Sometimes I was furious with Stephen for putting us through so much, but I never had money enough to get to the city limits, let alone cross the country." She grinned ruefully. "And besides, Stephen tried so hard, and I love the stubborn fool."

Mindy smiled, but her voice was serious. "He did indeed act foolishly. Determination can be carried to extremes, but he meant well. We knew things were hard for you, but we had no idea how hard. Has Ellen had proper food?"

"Always. Stephen insisted on that. Sometimes when we'd had only beans and bread, he would bring her an apple or an orange at night, always concerned that she have plenty of vitamins. You see she's rosy and strong."

When Carl and the children had joined Rita at the table, Mindy prepared a tray and took it to Stephen, but she knew at once that he could not eat. His face so gray and weary against the pillows broke her heart.

"You'll never know how good this bed feels, Mother. I don't usually like being waited on, but tonight it feels mighty good."

"I don't know how you ever did it, Stephen."

"I kept praying over and over, 'Lord, just help me get Rita and Ellen home,' for I realized many times on that trip that I had been wrong to put them in such a situation. Suppose I had keeled over out in the middle of the desert someplace and without a nickel to spare?"

"We would have come, Stephen. You know that."

"Yes, I did know it, Mother; without that knowledge I'd have never dared start out. Tomorrow I'll get myself into a hospital and have this bum kidney repaired. Then I'll be back in business. I'll have to borrow from Dad, but I'll pay every penny back."

"You always have." Mindy put tiny strawberries, one by one into his mouth.

"They grow huge, cultivated berries in California, but they taste like sawdust compared to these." Not a word of his disappointment, no sign of depression. What a son she had borne!

"We are proud of you," Mindy said softly. "It is just about sundown. Let us say the Sabbath commandment together, and then you must sleep."

With bands of the day's last sunlight rainbowing across the patchwork quilt, they spoke the ancient words in unison. " 'Remember the sabbath day, to keep it holy . . .' "

Mindy woke once in the night to find a strong breeze fluttering the curtains at her slanting window. For an instant her mind flew to the image of an old Ford tottering across the states, and she tensed. Then she remembered that Stephen and his dear ones slept within the walls of home, and peace filled her heart.

Chapter 21

Stephen's recuperation was neither quick nor easy. Both Rita and Mindy learned more about drainage tubes and the changing of dressings than they had ever cared to know. Stephen supervised their cautious efforts with detached efficiency. In mid-August, when he was able to be up and about, they moved eagerly into the little house. Rita was expecting their second child, and Mindy worried about the winter ahead. Stephen would need work, but not heavy work, for he was still far from well. She had, however, learned at last where to take her worries. She knew that Stephen, too, had left the matter in God's hands. He set about helping Rita with the canning as optimistically as if the depression had not smothered his every dream.

"I am concerned about the boys," Carl said one night as he and Mindy sat rocking in the summer darkness on the front porch.

"Why?" Mindy asked, thinking that moonlight spilled as wantonly over the valley as it had those first nights so long ago when their love was new.

"Well, they both seem to have been short-circuited in their dreams. Stephen's college degree is utterly useless to him at the moment, and Ned's garage work is so seasonal. Unless you have your own place, you're bound to get laid off in the winter. Now that Ned's got a child, he needs steady work."

"You can't remove every pebble from their path, Carl. No one worried about us that awful winter when we had to raise the house payment. Besides, I have some good news about Stephen. He told me this afternoon he had been asked to teach the Baker Mountain School this winter. That will take care of their needs, and by spring I predict they'll be off to some new adventure."

"That school's a good five miles from here, and you know most of the time Stephen's car doesn't run. How'll he get back and forth?" Carl wanted to know.

"He said he planned to walk, and I don't doubt but that he will."

"That's fine in September, but come February he may have second thoughts."

"He can always borrow our horse and sleigh if he wishes. I'm just grateful to God for providing work he's able to do. I think he'll make a good teacher."

Carl's thoughts had moved on to his first son. "I've decided to build Ned a garage right in the center of town. I've already put some money on the lot." His voice was edgily defensive.

Mindy looked at her husband in astonishment, thinking of the moment years before when he had announced the purchase of the little house for his parents.

"Carl, that is going to cost an enormous sum of money. Are you sure it's the right thing to do? It won't be good for Ned to have so much handed to him, and besides our savings were for our old age. I don't ever want to be a burden to the boys."

"I consider it an investment. I have no intentions of handing it over to Ned. He'll simply run it. It will provide him the place to prove himself. He's a skilled mechanic, and with his personality the garage ought to prosper."

Mindy laughed. "What a paradox you are, Carl Matthews! You can worry for days over a necessary twenty-five-dollar expenditure, yet empty your bank account and go into debt for someone you love with never a qualm."

"Oh, I have plenty of qualms," he said, "but I also have a responsibility to those in my care."

Mindy rose and turned toward the lighted kitchen. "In case I never told you, my dear, you are a good man."

He made no answer. She noted in the semidarkness that his shoulders were stooped and his hair nearly white.

"We are growing old," she thought, touching his shoulder lightly in passing, and told him, "I think God must be lonely for your friendship. You are so very much His man."

"I'm not agin Him," he said lightly.

The garage for Ned was up before snowfall, and Mindy could not believe the pleasure Carl took in the whole venture. He had built most of it with his own hands. It was no skimpy filling station but a large and sprawling building with ample room for Ned to ply his trade. Mindy realized in the end that it was an adventure for both Ned and Carl, with just enough risk involved to make it exciting. Carl spent every free moment there, putting the finishing touches on the small office, setting up the ledgers in his neat and accurate hand, or just talking with those who began to stop by for gas or service. She saw a strong bond growing between father and son.

One early November day she drove into town for groceries and stopped off at Ned's home to say hello to Gloria and to see her small grandson. At eighteen months Eric was a round-faced, golden-haired cherub. Mindy took a special pride in him, for he'd carry the Matthews name into the years ahead. She picked him up for a quick hug and asked Kate, who stood uncertainly in the doorway, "Isn't your little brother beautiful?"

Kate touched the baby's blond curls and made a funny face at him which sent both children into the giggles.

Mindy left a loaf of homemade bread on the kitchen shelf, bade Gloria good-bye, kissed the baby, and made her departure.

When she passed the garage, Ned took his head from under a hood long enough to wave a greasy hand at her, and she felt a deep gratitude that Carl had provided so well for this son.

At the corner where the valley road took its leave of the village, she spoke the horse to a halt. She had timed her afternoon, hoping to give Stephen a ride home from school. She waited now, chatting with Kate and watching the road for the thin, dark-haired figure she so loved. It was not ten minutes before he came into view, running in a leisurely fashion, with no jacket, no hat, though the day was harsh and gray. As he swung up into the seat beside her, she chided him. "Stephen, you are going to be ill again. You shouldn't be running, and you're not even properly dressed."

He laughed at her fears. "I can run effortlessly for miles, Mother. These two months have done wonders for me. You know I never did like jackets. By the time I've run five minutes, I'm perspiring in my shirt sleeves."

Mindy scrutinized him carefully and had to admit he looked healthier than in many a month.

"One can't stay sick long in this mountain air, Mother. I had to come home to be whole again, but now I'm ready for anything. Next spring we shall be leaving."

"For medical school?" Mindy asked.

"I hope so," he said, "but if I've learned anything, it's to let God make the plans."

"That's not an easy lesson, Stephen, and one we often have to repeat over and over again throughout life. What does Rita want to do?"

"She's content for the moment, just living a normal life with enough food on the table, but come spring she'll be ready to go too. There's a bit of the adventurer in Rita also, you know." There was a satisfied sound to his voice.

"You love her very much, don't you?" Mindy asked as they drove into the dooryard of the little house.

"There's probably no one else who'd put up with me," he told her lightly, but she'd had her answer.

*　　*　　*　　*　　*

In November Carl was elected as the town representative to the state legislature. He said little, but Mindy read his pleasure in the rare gaiety which crackled about him at the dinner she had prepared in celebration. She had had to put two extra leaves in the old kitchen table to accommodate their growing family, and she looked about her with gratitude. Her sons and daughters, well and prospering. Three beautiful grandchildren. What more could she ask?

With sadness, she admitted that deep within she *did* ask more. She asked that they each know God, not just bowing in a conventional way to His right to rule, but hungering for His presence as she did, loving Him. She wanted someone at this table to say, "Let's thank God for Stephen's health and for this new honor bestowed upon Carl." She glanced at Stephen, wondering if he'd lost the relationship with his Maker which had always set him apart. Their eyes met, and he smiled. She heard his voice, steady and quiet. "God's been pretty good to this family. Let's thank Him."

As Stephen prayed Mindy sent up her own petition. "O God, let him never change. Keep him close to You."

She felt Kate's small hand fumble for hers. "And this one, too, Lord. Show me how to keep this little heart tender toward You."

But that prayer was not large enough. What of Ned and Carl, Gloria and Rita and their little ones? "I'm greedy, Lord," she prayed. "I want them all for You. I want us to worship together, to pray together, to speak of You freely, gratefully, joyfully, together." Every instinct of her being told her that was His desire too.

209

On the morning Carl was to leave for Montpelier, wind and snow scuttled nervously around the house. Inside, Mindy admired red geraniums against the lacy frostwork of her kitchen windows. As she set about getting breakfast she realized she would no longer come downstairs to a warm kitchen. Tomorrow her ear would not be tuned to the clanking of milk pails at the back door. She and Kate would be alone. When storms swept down across the valley, cloistering the house in silence and snow, erasing roads and fences, Carl would not be there. But there was nothing to fret about. The cellar was full of food and the back shed stacked with wood. The child would be company.

After the chores and a leisurely breakfast, Carl came downstairs, dressed in his new navy suit.

"You look splendid, Gramp," Kate said from where she still dawdled over a bowl of oatmeal at the table.

Carl made a little bow in her direction and turned to Mindy. "I still don't feel right leaving you alone like this, Min."

"Nonsense!" Mindy kept her hands in the dishwater and her back to him. They had never said such a final good-bye in all their married lives. There was a strange feeling deep inside her, an unfamiliar sadness, heavy and numbing.

"Al will be here twice a day to do the chores, Stephen lives less than a mile away, and I have Kate. There is no need to feel guilty, Carl. Go with my blessing—and God's."

She turned then, wiping her hands on a towel. At sight of him, the unaccustomed foreboding engulfed her. He was not Carl the farmer, nor even Carl the road commissioner, but the Carl he was meant to be. Distinguished, handsome, about to take up a work which would utilize his keen and sober mind.

"Kate is right. You are indeed splendid," she whispered, her eyes filling with tears. "I am so proud of you."

"It is a very small honor." He shrugged, smiling.

"But I shall do my best to be worthy of it. I am privileged even to observe the process of government, to say nothing of having some small part in it."

"You will not be enticed away by any of those sophisticated ladies in the capital city?" Mindy asked as she felt suddenly very aware of her faded print dress and simple hairstyle.

"They will not be interested in this poor farmer," Carl chuckled. He held out his arms, and she realized, with his warmth enfolding her, that there would be no joy in the days without him. Sometimes she had thought there would be. When his sharp words stung her like hail, she had thought, "Let him go. I shall enjoy the solitude." But now she knew better. She did not understand the icy wall he erected between them, nor did she understand why now and then his tenderness melted through it like a lost ray of sun, but despite her hurt and confusion, she loved him and always would. She realized she hadn't verbalized that in a long time.

"I love you, Carl," she said, against the crisp white of his starchy shirt front.

"Of course, Min." His voice held a dear, cocky arrogance out of the far past. "I'm irresistible." But he did not say the words for which her heart hungered. Perhaps his stubborn lips could no longer form them, or perhaps he could not lie.

"And to you, my little slobber-face"—he smiled, kissing Kate gingerly amid the oatmeal—"I say, 'Farewell. I shall miss your useless chatter.' "

Mindy did not watch him drive away, but the sound of his car, mingling with the wind, grew fainter and fainter, and then there was only wind.

Chapter 22

It was a new thing to be cast completely upon her own resources. She had gone from her father's household to Carl's. Well, of course, she was still in Carl's care. He came home every second or third weekend. His income stocked the shelves and kept the flour barrel filled, his hands stacked the woodshed with the winter fuel. Oh, yes, she was very much within his care, but she experienced in this winter of his absence a new sense of self. When she woke in the morning, she did not *have* to get up. She could choose whether to brave the chilly house or doze until noon. Only once did she retreat into the snugness of sleep, however, and found then that when she woke hours later, she felt robbed. Life was too good to spend sleeping, and the early mornings were her special pleasure.

For the first time she did not have to rush about baking graham rolls and cooking oatmeal. After the fire was kindled, she sat close to the stove reading her Bible in stillness broken only by the crackling of flames feasting on new kindling.

The Word of God became alive and personal for her there in the wintry kitchen. Often she read on and on with no sense of urgency, memorizing now and then a verse which was especially meaningful. When the sun found its way into the valley, she stood at the window and prayed or composed a psalm of joy to her Lord. For those moments she was not wife of Carl, mother of sons, teacher of children, but Mindy Matthews, daughter of God.

When the kitchen was warm and breakfast prepared, she called Kate, and they ate in a leisurely companionship that was completely foreign to that household.

She kept her days structured and useful. The paths were shoveled whether or not anyone came. She sewed, made quilts, took walks with Kate, painted the living-room woodwork, and drove into town twice a week. Never let it be said that Mindy Matthews hibernated like a bear, with the snow piled up about her house, just because her husband was at the state capitol. But sometimes when dusk laid orchid shadows over the snow and all the day's activities had turned stale, she longed for the stamping of feet at the back door and the sound of his voice.

She had taken to letting the child sleep on the living-room couch until nine, when she locked the doors, banked the fires, and prepared for bed herself. The ticking of the clock and Kate's soft breathing made a background for her thoughts as she puckered small rounds of bright cloth into a rose-garden quilt for Gloria.

When spring winds blew over the valley, Carl came home, packed his blue suit away in mothballs, and took up his farming once again. Rita bore another girl, a frail child with but a slim grip on life. They named her Lois.

Stephen, his teaching assignment completed, was back at work on the town roads for Carl. Much as he longed to return to medical school, he realized that with two children and jobs nearly nonexistent his dreams must be laid aside.

Carl came home from the service station one night, tight-lipped and grim. "Ned just isn't working out in that situation," he admitted, his voice heavy with disap-

213

pointment. "He wasn't even there tonight. Had some young fellow filling in who didn't know a thing beyond pumping gas. People have come to depend on Ned for repair work, and he needs to be there."

"Is his work satisfactory otherwise?" Mindy asked.

"His work is flawless, and he's well liked by everyone. It could be the most successful business in town, but he's off somewhere drinking when he should be working, and his accounts are in bad shape. He's too generous and trusting. You can't run a business like that."

"Perhaps now that you're home to keep an eye on things, he'll do better."

"There's no fighting the alcohol problem, Min. You know that. I shall give him a while longer, but I'm not expecting any miracles."

"Maybe if you talked to him, Carl."

"Do you think I haven't? He is full of promises. Promises we both know he can't keep."

There was despair in Carl's voice. "I don't mind about the garage or the money lost. But I can't stand to watch Ned destroy himself."

"Sometimes one has to go right down to the bottom of the pit and realize his hopeless condition before God can help. Ned's story is not finished yet. God listens to a mother's prayers, Carl, and this mother has no intention of giving up."

"This mother had better brace herself for what lies ahead. I fear Ned is headed downhill, and all of us who love him will suffer along with him."

For a moment a terrible anger toward Seth burned in Mindy's heart, but it was smothered in the honesty which forced her to admit a weak man always finds a path to his vice. If it had not been Seth, likely it would have been someone else.

"Life seemed so simple," Mindy remembered, "when the boys were little, playing about the yard, helping you on the farm. Who could have dreamed that laughing little boy would come to this? And I fear for

214

Rita's baby. Her lips are blue, and it seems you can see right through her skin. Sometimes she almost stops breathing, yet the doctor is very vague when they question him. Stephen fears something is wrong with her heart."

"Does your God enjoy all this misery?" Carl asked.

"No, He hurts right along with us, but if we do not become bitter and are willing to accept and turn to Him for help, nothing can really harm us. The long struggle will be over eventually, and there will be harmony once more upon the earth."

"So what good are your prayers for Ned if every man must turn to God for himself?"

"I'm not sure just how prayer for others works, but I have the feeling that when Christ speaks to the heart of a sinner—say Ned, for instance—the devil says, 'Hey, leave this one alone. He doesn't even profess to follow You.' But because I have prayed, Christ can say to the devil, 'You are right. Ned *has* chosen your kind of life, but his mother's prayers come up before me night and day. At *her* request I am here.' "

"So then your God moves right into Ned's heart, whether He's wanted there or not," Carl needled.

"No," Mindy answered slowly, thinking. "He never barges into anyone's heart uninvited, but He knocks patiently and reminds the sinner over and over that help is just outside. Only Ned can open the door and let Him in. There is a point beyond which even a praying mother and a pleading God cannot help, but you'd be amazed, Carl, at the persistence and patience of both."

"You really believe all that, don't you?" Carl rose to wind the clock.

Mindy blew out the lamp and stood a moment at the front door, looking down the shadowed valley. "If I didn't, Carl, life would be without purpose. There has to be some reason for our existence."

"Not necessarily."

She followed him up the narrow stairway, feeling a

215

loneliness beyond that of winter solitude.

*   *   *   *   *

One hot evening in late July Stephen and Rita drove into the dooryard, and Mindy knew instantly that Stephen bore news. There was a tight-coiled excitement about him, evident in his every movement.

Carl, coming from the barn with a small tin pail of cream, saw it too. "Out with it, Stephen. What are you up to?"

Stephen grinned, even teeth flashing white in his deeply tanned face. "We're going to Alaska, Dad. Did you hear me? Alaska! What an opportunity! I still can't believe it." Behind him, Rita's blue eyes danced with approval.

Mindy stared at them both in disbelief. "Stephen, Alaska is nothing but wilderness. You can't take the girls there."

"And why not?" he asked, tossing Ellen into the air. "They'll make fine little Eskimos."

"Surely not this one," Mindy said softly to Rita, taking the baby from her arms. "She'd never survive."

"Do you think we'd leave Lois behind?" Stephen gave his mother a look she had long known and understood. There was no point in arguing with him. "She is doing much better. I will keep a careful eye on her. You know I would not make a decision I felt dangerous to Lois, Mother."

"Come sit on the porch and tell us what it's all about," Carl invited, leading the way.

Ellen and Kate chased each other about in a game of tag on the front lawn, Mindy rocked Lois, and Stephen told his story, delight sparkling off his every word.

"After I came home from Loma Linda, I filled out some applications for government work, expressing my willingness to go just about anywhere and do just about anything. I didn't really expect a thing from it but figured

216

I should try everything. Today, when I got home from work, there was a letter saying there was an opening in Blue Cove, Alaska. Would I consider it? Would I! It's the sort of thing I've always dreamed of."

"And what will you be doing there?" Carl asked. Mindy heard the controlled quietness in his voice and knew at once he didn't like the idea a bit better than she did, but he wouldn't meddle with Stephen's enthusiasm.

"It seems to be in a pretty isolated spot." Stephen eyed his mother warily, but she looked back at him calmly. If Carl could do it, so could she. "I will be there as a government representative to meet any needs that arise," Stephen went on. "As there are no medical personnel stationed there, they said it is sometimes necessary to pull teeth and sew up wounds among the villagers. I suppose the time I spent at Loma Linda was an asset. There is a school in the village, and Rita and I will both be teaching. And I'm supposed to settle disputes among the natives. Wish I had had a couple of years of law school."

"Hear this," Rita broke in. "All supplies come in once a year by boat. Can you imagine doing your grocery shopping for a year, to say nothing of buying clothing and household supplies?"

"Rita, you must not make a quick decision about this." Carl looked at his daughter-in-law almost fiercely under heavy brows. "Stephen thirsts for adventure and would drag you to the moon if there were any way to get there, but you have a right to keep him in civilization if you wish. Those two little ones should be your first consideration. Stephen's too."

"I would be terrified of the whole thing with most men, Dad, but with Stephen I can't wait to go. He seems"—she groped for words—"equal to anything. Even last year, riding across the country with him so sick, I knew he'd get us home."

"It was God who brought us home, Rita," Stephen acknowledged.

"Well, then"—Rita grinned at Carl—"there's your answer. With Stephen and his God, I'm perfectly safe."

Carl smiled wryly. "I hope you never have reason to doubt that, my dear."

The next weeks were a blur of planning and packing. Rita and Stephen sat late over the Sears catalog trying to anticipate their needs for the year ahead. Mindy kept Lois much with her, plying the tiny body with nourishing foods and daily walking her in the sunshine.

"I think Lois will live to be an old, old lady," Kate observed one day, lying on the floor and playing with the baby. "She likes to be alive. I can see it in her eyes."

Mindy laughed, strangely comforted by Kate's proclamation. There was, indeed, something beyond the physical which would not be easily snuffed out in this youngest of her grandchildren, a sort of hoyden gaiety shining from the frail frame.

On the Sunday in late August when they drove away, heading once more for the West Coast and the ship which would bear them to that bleak land, Mindy and Carl stood on the porch waving until they disappeared from sight around the bend. Carl turned without a word, shouldered his ax and headed for the woods. Mindy stood a long time, her heart like stone, remembering Stephen as a child running over the fields and hills. He who was her comfort and her strength was gone. Ned, who brought her only heartbreak, would stay. She loved them equally, but so differently.

As the morning mist lifted from the valley, she turned toward the kitchen, wondering if it were possible to function normally with such sadness dragging like a weight upon her. She found the kitchen tidied and Kate washing the breakfast dishes at the iron sink. Mindy stood watching her, seeing her suddenly as a lonely little figure going about the necessary things with a practical resignation too old for her years.

"Kate," she asked softly, "what would I do without you? I have an idea. Let's pack a lunch, and at noon

218

we'll go find Grandpa and have a picnic in the woods."

The child looked at her gravely. "Aren't you sad about Uncle Stephen anymore?"

"How can I be sad when I still have you?" Mindy touched her granddaughter's hair in a rare gesture of affection.

Kate smiled in relief, then, "How will we find Gramp?"

"We'll follow the sound of his ax," Mindy said, putting eggs on to boil. "I've done it many a time."

"Uncle Stephen would be proud of you." Kate polished a bowl and looked at Mindy thoughtfully.

"And just why do you think your Uncle Stephen would be proud of me?"

"Because you aren't crying. He told me that when you cried after he was gone, I was to try hard to make you smile again."

"Oh, he did, did he?" Mindy said, turning away with brimming eyes and a lump in her throat. "Well, I guess I fooled him, didn't I?"

*   *   *   *   *

Postcards arrived every few days, stamped Michigan, Illinois, Colorado, and finally Seattle. Silence. Then a letter with a blurry Alaskan cancellation.

Rita wrote:

> Dear Mother and Dad,
>   May you never know the tortures of seasickness. Stephen, of course, tromped about on deck while everyone else hung over the rail or suffered below. Ellen and I lay in our bunks longing for land or death—it didn't really matter much which—while Stephen cared for Lois, made himself useful to the ill, and conveyed unsolicited reports on the unbelievable scenery. Eventually I did find my

219

sea legs, and he was right. The Inside Passage is beyond description. It is so quiet and breathtaking with the mountains on either side. Only a little fishing village here and there along the shore.

The first night out they were going about the ship searching for someone who could milk a cow which was on board being transported to some Alaskan village. I guess it had seemed a simple matter to relieve her of her milk at the appropriate times, but it didn't work out that way. She definitely knew an amateur from an expert and had sent a couple of sailors and buckets flying. Quite a crowd had gathered by the time we arrived on the scene. Stephen volunteered, and everyone burst into applause when those first streams of milk hit the bottom of the pail. He sat there relaxed with his head against the cow's thigh, the bucket tight between his knees, just as I've seen him a hundred times at home. I wished you might have been there. It seemed so typical of Stephen to be prepared for any emergency, meeting it in his own cheerful way. That's why I think he'll do just fine in his new work. . . .

Carl chuckled. "The girl is right, Min. Stephen was born for adventure. It is inappropriate to worry about him. Let us be proud."

"Three cheers for Uncle Stephen!" Kate said, waving a milkweed pod above her head, its silvery down furling out like a tiny flag.

"And three more for Rita, who endures all things for the man she loves," Mindy added.

Chapter 23

"Kate, you really shouldn't read in that dark corner. Why on earth can't you sit by the lamp at the table with your grandfather?" Mindy peered into the small dim space between the iron cookstove and the wall where Kate lay stretched full-length, book in hand. The child had learned to read within a few weeks of her exposure to school, almost as if that first glimpse into a ragged primer had been a magic key for which she had long waited. Now she moved from book to book at a pace which left Mindy scrambling to meet the demand.

"I like it here," Kate said. "It's warm and cozy like a little cave. I can see okay."

"It's a strain on your eyes, cave or no cave." Mindy lighted a lamp and set it by Kate's head. "With your love for words, you're going to need your sight more than most people."

"Speaking of light," Carl said, peering over his newspaper, "did you notice anything unusual on the way home from school today, Kate?"

"I saw a truck; and some men digging holes."

"Those holes are going to change our life, Katrina." Carl looked at the child fondly.

Mindy glanced up from her crocheting. "What are

you telling us, Carl? You can't mean the power lines!"

"A month from now electricity will be available to everyone in the valley. You can sell these miserable, stinking lamps for the antiques they are."

"You mean you'll have the house wired?" Mindy looked at him in disbelief. "I hear it costs a fortune. Few can afford it."

Carl made no answer. So often these days he made no answer, leaving her to wonder; but a few weeks later two electricians prowled about the house, drilling holes and stringing cable between the partitions. On the late November afternoon when the last fixture was installed and they took their leave, Carl pulled the string dangling over the kitchen table and a circle of light fell bold and bright upon the red-checked cloth.

"No more reading behind the stove, young lady." Carl glanced at Kate in mock fierceness. "This foolishness cost me a fortune, and I expect you to use it."

As darkness fell Kate and Mindy went about the house pulling strings and marveling at the wonder of each room lighted to its dimmest corner. Finally they went outside and sat upon the damp lawn, staring, almost speechless, at the sight of light blazing from every window. Carl sat at the table reading. If he was himself a bit astonished at what his savings and Thomas Edison had accomplished, he did not comment upon it.

That night, as Mindy packed the lamps away for storage, she mused, "The valley will never be quite the same again, Carl. Somehow electricity seems the dividing line between an older and less complicated way of life and something that lies ahead."

"Like what?" Carl did not look up from the town books over which his pen moved in a sure and accurate manner.

"I can't name specifics"—Mindy held a sparkling shade up to the light, giving it a last wipe with her towel —"but such an invention must surely be only the beginning of a chain of new ideas. I predict Kate's world

222

will be very different from the one we have known. Someday she'll hardly remember she carried a lamp to her bedroom every night as a child." Thinking of Kate brought Ned to her mind. "Has it occurred to you that Ned treats her very strangely?"

"It has occurred to me that he no longer acknowledges her presence, if that's what you mean."

"Sometimes her eyes follow him about when he's here, and there's a look of bewilderment and hurt in them. Carl, it's so unlike Ned. He's an excellent father to Eric and Nettie. The other day I handed him some of Kate's school papers. She had done so well. He barely glanced at them and went right on talking about something else. Even if he doesn't love her, he could at least take pride in her."

Carl closed his books and made a long chain of penmanship O's on a scrap of paper. "I have told Ned to keep his eye out for work over the winter, for come spring I shall sell the garage or put it under new management."

"Then he's doing no better?"

"He's gradually drinking more and more. It isn't a matter of venting my displeasure. I simply can't afford the venture any longer. It long ago ceased to be profitable."

"Does Gloria realize what's happening to Ned, I wonder?"

"She sees him only as the handsome charmer she married. I don't suppose his drinking looms as any great threat to her at this point. He brings home a paycheck every week."

"But the real Ned is gone, Carl. He's still witty and clever and always teasing, but when I try to get beneath that surface, I can never find my son."

"Gloria never knew the old Ned, Mindy, so she doesn't miss him. He was tempered in his youth with your religion. When he walked away from that, something changed inside him. When he lost Sara, something changed again; and when he decided to put Kate out of his life, he changed a bit more. We are formed by our decisions. There's no point in spending your life, Min, looking for the Ned you planned him to be. Accept him as he is."

"I do," Mindy said, sighing, "but sometimes I'm so lonely for what he used to be."

* * * * *

When the first snow danced airily down from the mountains, whispering winter into the wind, Mindy decided to give the chicken house a thorough cleaning. It was a long way from the other buildings because Carl didn't like chickens—not the sight or the smell or the nuisance of them. But Mindy enjoyed the spending money, and there was something about the way they gathered around her at feeding time with their gentle, gossipy sounds which she found satisfying.

Though the December sun shone brightly, it was bitter cold, and Mindy bundled warmly in an old jacket of Carl's. If she started at noon and worked fast, surely she'd be finished in time to prepare supper.

It was four hours later that the refuse was shoveled away. She was spreading the light, aromatic shavings from the lumberyard when the pain rolled over her like a rock slide, crushing the breath out of her, sending her to her knees. She had shut the chickens outside while she worked, and now through her agony she could hear them fretting at the door. It was a comfortable, familiar sound, and she clung to it between the cries from her own lips.

Many times she'd trembled through the same ordeal, but never had the pain ripped and torn at her as now. Her body shook with chills, and she vomited into the clean, curled shavings. Carl would not be home for another hour, and he would not look for her here. She did not want to die. She *could not* die. Kate needed her.

224

Ten more years? Fifteen? She wept and moaned and screamed when the pain twisted without mercy even into her throat and arms. "Ten years, Lord, I need ten years! No child deserves to lose two mothers."

"Gram?" She heard through the blackness of her misery Kate's familiar voice embroidered with terror.

She could barely manage words. "Run! My purse. The pills. Hurry." She looked up into eyes so filled with fear that she attempted a smile.

When Kate had laid the small white pills upon her tongue, Mindy rested, spent and helpless, in the child's arms. The warmth of her small body and the steady beating of her heart were strength and comfort. They did not talk, and only later when Mindy felt tears dropping onto her face did she realize the child was weeping softly.

"We have gone through a hard thing together, Kate." Mindy spoke in little spurts between subsiding pains. "Death is forever nibbling at my heels, but do not be afraid of pain or death. When Jesus walked out of that tomb, death fell down, helpless. It can inconvenience us, but that is all. You are God's child, Kate, and He has a dozen ways of caring for you with me or without me."

"But I want *you,* not someone else." Kate rocked her grandmother gently in her arms.

"Well, as you can see, I don't die easy," Mindy said. "I think God knows you need me for a while. Now run and get your granddad. He must be here by now and wondering where we are. Tell him to bring the car and drive me home in style."

She listened to Kate's footsteps running toward the barn, young voice calling into the wind and softly falling snow. "Let her run into Your love like that, Lord," she breathed, "so she'll be strong and steady when the time comes to run alone."

*   *   *   *   *

225

When Carl left to fulfill the first year of his second term at the state legislature, he and Mindy moved into their assigned roles without comment. If Carl suffered any pangs of guilt at leaving Mindy alone through the brutal winters, he no longer verbalized them. It occurred to Mindy that with Carl away, Kate in school, and Stephen no longer close by, she could easily succumb to a heart attack; but she had long ago decided not to build her life around fearful possibilities.

One late winter afternoon she walked to meet Kate; and something about the sunlight, sifting like gold dust over the snowy fields, erased the years, and she was seventeen again, pacing the country roads, Death stalking patiently behind. Come to think of it, he'd always had an uncommon interest in her.

When Kate's slight figure appeared bundled and mittened against the cold, they ran to meet each other, laughing and eager to share the day's news. Mindy kept a careful eye upon Kate's learning and quizzed the small one thoroughly upon the areas she'd been studying.

At home Mindy prepared their meal, while Kate restocked the supply of doughnuts, raisins, and suet on the discarded Christmas tree by the front porch where the blue jays and chickadees gathered from dawn till dusk. When their supper had been cleared away, the evening stretched long before them.

"Do you have any homework tonight?" Mindy asked into the silence. It seemed they had been reading for hours, but the clock said only seven thirty.

"No, I finished everything at school." The child looked up, dragging herself from book-world back to reality.

"She reads too much," Mindy thought. "Her life is distorted. As if it's not bad enough that she's out here in the hills with two old people, but now Carl is gone all winter."

"Let's go sledding, Kate. I'll bet it's just the right temperature for a good icy base."

226

Kate looked at the older woman, a hesitant smile deepening her dimples. For a moment there was so much of Sara upon her face that a great loneliness settled over Mindy.

"Nobody goes sledding at night, Gram. What are you talking about?"

"Who made that rule?"

"Gram, you know perfectly well it's true. Only the big kids in the village slide at night."

"Well, I guess I shall have to go alone then." Mindy rose to change into a pair of Carl's warm woolen pants.

"Gramp said I was to look after you; so I suppose I shall have to come along to help you haul the sled up the hill." Kate kept a sober face, but there was delight in her every movement as she struggled into her snowsuit.

The valley glittered with moonlight and ice, shadows smudging the crystal snow where the forest met the fields. "Isn't it strange that people sit in houses around stoves when it's like this outside?" Kate scuffed the fluffy white stuff, and it rose in fountains of stardust ahead of her boots.

"It's always a temptation to stay beside the stove, Kate. We humans like things comfortable and easy, but if we are willing to break out of our ruts and routines, the world is full of marvelous things."

When they reached the top of the highest hill, Mindy suggested, "Let's lie down a minute first. Flat on our backs in the snow." As they stretched out side by side Kate made a strange little gasping sound. "Look at the sky, Gram. I never saw it like this before."

"We're always distracted by Earth objects when we're upright."

"What are they, Gram, the stars, when you get up close to them?"

"Planets—and suns."

"Planets like ours?"

"Who knows, child? God is filled with imagination. They may be like the snowflakes, each one different."

Mindy was quiet a moment, then went on. "You know, Kate, there are people—not uneducated people but scholars—who do not believe God created our planet and all we see in the heavens. Some of them do not even believe there is a God."

"Where do they think we came from?"

"Well, there are several theories. I do not know them all, but a common one is that life on our planet began with only very simple, single-celled creatures who over millions or billions of years developed into all that we see today. I do not know how those who reject God explain the heavens as we see them tonight."

"What do *you* think, Gram?" Kate's big question came very small into the vast night.

"You tell me first. What do *you* think?"

"I think God is out there keeping everything going with His magic mind," Kate told her softly.

Mindy laughed. "That's my opinion exactly, but I couldn't have said it half as well."

"How do they think those tiny, one-celled things turned into cats and birds and people?"

"According to their thinking it took millions of years. They seem to feel that if you wait long enough, anything can happen. Sort of like if you took all the letters in the dictionary and shook them in a container for years, they'd eventually end up as words and even in alphabetical order. Or maybe the parts of a watch, and they'd become a real ticking timepiece in two or three billion years."

"Even *I* know better than that, Gram."

"Maybe if the scientists lay down in the snow on a starry night once in a while, they'd know better too. Not only does God keep the whole thing going by the miracle of His power and mind, but He created it that way in the first place. Now let's have a go at the hill."

Mindy stretched flat out, stomach down, on the sled, and Kate lay on top. "Hang on, child. We'll cross the river and likely go right into the road."

"There can't be anything much more exhilarating than careening down a hillside at a hair-raising speed with a child's screams in one's ears," Mindy thought as she fought the steering bar over bumpy terrain and steep drops. When they came to a stop at last in the middle of the road, they rolled off the sled, overcome with laughter. "That's the scariest ride I've ever had," Kate gasped. "Let's do it again."

Mindy looked at the long steep ascent and knew she must not climb straight up. She would not bring the possibility of pain and fear into such a night. "Let's take the easy route up. It may take a bit longer, but we have all night."

Kate scrutinized her grandmother for a long moment. "Sit down on the sled, Gram. I'm going to pull you across the meadow." And because the runners slipped effortlessly over the frozen surface, Mindy let her.

Later that night when Kate slept on the living room couch and Mindy thawed her aching toes before the fire, she wrote Carl:

> *Dearest One,*
>
> *Tonight Kate and I went sledding in the moonlight. I had forgotten the thrill of racing downhill, too scared to go on but unable to get off. Kate sleeps now upon the couch, rosy and disheveled. She has in her the recklessness of Ned, for she went down twice alone while I trembled on the hill watching. I could not endure these lonely winters without her. How marvelously God arranges our days. . . .*

Chapter 24

Mindy brushed her hair appraisingly before the bedroom mirror. She had not taken a good look at herself in a long time. White hair, simply styled, framed a face severe in its bone structure but alight with a great eagerness for life. The tiny waist which Carl could encircle in his two hands at their marriage had thickened with the years, and she fastened her belt impatiently. Was it necessary for one to become lumpy with age?

The dark red dress she had chosen for the occasion highlighted the glow beneath sun-touched skin. Well, she'd done the best she could with herself. A family picture should portray the truth, not some wishful thinking on the part of the subject. She had insisted upon this picture. Who knew when the family would all be together again? Stephen and Rita were home from Alaska after six long years. The summer had slipped away, and now there were only days left before their departure. They had changed. There was about them a confidence born of dangers survived, problems solved, and hardships endured. However fragile Rita might appear, Mindy knew now there lay beneath the surface a strength equal to unbelievable tests. And in that far place where no church existed they had raised their children—her grandchildren—for God. When the girls sang the simple hymns of childhood for Mindy, she was humbly grateful to the young woman Stephen had chosen. Hiram's faith would live on in a future generation.

As she put her brushes away and tidied the dresser, she heard the sound of sobbing in the adjoining bedroom. Why would Kate be crying? Kate, who was never temperamental or difficult like other children. It must be one of the other grandchildren. She moved toward the door between the rooms, but before her hand touched the knob, she heard Rita's voice.

"What's the matter, Kate? You mustn't cry. You'll have a splotchy face for the picture."

"I don't want to be in the picture. Please, Aunt Rita, help me. I just can't be in it."

"Child, you are part of the family." There was a rare gentleness in Rita's voice. "The picture wouldn't be complete without you."

"I'm too ugly. I'll only spoil it. Take a good look at me." Mindy could not believe the despair in Kate's voice.

"Why you aren't——"

"Don't say it, Aunt Rita. Look at my hair hanging straight and limp. My clothes are funny and old-fashioned. Admit it. Ellen and I are both ten, and I look like an old lady beside her."

"Kate, it *is* true that Grandma Matthews doesn't always know the latest in little girls' hairstyles and dress fashions, but she's a very special lady, and she's given you a great deal beyond those superficial things."

"I love Gram," the girl sniffled, "and most of the time I don't mind being ugly, but I just *can't* be in that picture. For a hundred years, people will look at it and say, 'No wonder her father didn't want her. Who would?'"

"Hey, hey!"

The sobbing became muffled, and Mindy knew Rita had taken Kate into her arms. "It takes more than the wrong clothes to hide one's good points. You have your

231

mother's blue eyes and your dad's dimpled grin. There's nothing wrong with straight hair. Sometimes I think it's more becoming than all those ringlets I struggle with every night on Ellen and Lois. Besides, you're far too tall for ringlets. You've grown so much faster than Ellen."

"Don't try to comfort me, Aunt Rita. I'm not going to be in that picture. I'm all dumpy and horrid, and I just can't do it. You and Gloria are both so pretty."

"Speaking of Gloria"—Mindy heard a hint of a chuckle in Rita's voice—"you may not believe this, Kate, but I feel a bit uncomfortable about this picture too. I've been off in the wilderness so long that many of my clothes are out of date, and your stepmother is indeed a very pretty woman. I'm hoping I don't get put beside her in the picture. She'd leave me feeling a little dumpy too."

"You are always lovely, Aunt Rita. You could stand beside anyone." Then wistfully, "What was my mother like?"

There was a long silence while Rita thought. "She was a gentle, funny, talented girl who brought so much happiness to us all that even now, years later, we cannot talk about her because it makes our hearts ache. She would not want you to spoil this day for Grandma Matthews, you know. I think she would have said to you, 'This picture is only a small matter in a long lifetime.'

"Stephen and I will soon be leaving, and Gram has that burden to bear. She loves you so much, Kate, and you are richer every day from living with her. When you go away to boarding school, you'll learn how to do your hair and how to dress. In the meantime you are very special to me because you are all I have left of your mother, and we had such happy times together. Now hurry and splash some cold water on your face, and the whole business will be over in an hour. One can bear anything for an hour."

Mindy heard Rita's light steps descending the stairs.

There was no sound from Kate's bedroom for a few moments, then the pouring of water from the china pitcher into the bowl.

Mindy stood at the door, head bowed in sorrow. "How could I have been so blind? How could I have not known the dress patterns I cut so skillfully from old newspapers were all wrong? By looking at other children or even the catalog!" she chided herself impatiently.

She had seen only the child's quick mind, her delight in everything about her. She would go at once to comfort and apologize, but some inner caution held her on her own side of the door.

There was more to all this than lay on the surface. What had Kate said about Ned —"No wonder he didn't want her"? She had long wondered how the child had come to terms with Ned's rejection. Now she knew. Kate felt ugly and unlovable inside as well as out. It wasn't just clothes and hair, though Mindy herself had failed there. No, it would never do for Kate to know Mindy had overheard the bitter words, for between them there was a relationship beyond fashion and hairstyles. There were stability and healing to be had. The hours they had spent seeking to know God, discussing books, wandering in the out-of-doors—those were the important things. They would be with her forever. In the meantime, she would order future clothing from Sears Roebuck and let Kate choose ready-made patterns at the store.

When they all gathered at last in the photographer's studio, Mindy felt sure she would never look at the resulting photo without feeling the emotions of the day. She could not rest her eyes upon Stephen for the hurt of knowing he'd soon be leaving again.

Kate and Ellen, chatting quietly in a corner, confirmed the moment of eavesdropping. Kate's somber dark-blue dress looked positively matronly beside Ellen's starch and ruffles. Lois, thin and lively, was making

233

faces for the entertainment of her cousin Eric. Gloria struggled with Nettie's hair bow, while Stephen and Ned muttered comments about the punishment of dress suits on such a broiling day and the absurdity of family pictures.

The photographer, in his efforts to group them, began to sort out families. When everyone had been arranged to his satisfaction, Kate still lingered uncertainly on the sidelines.

"And whom do *you* belong to, young lady?" the photographer asked jovially. "How did we come out with one left over?"

No one said a word.

"She belongs to Ned," Mindy floundered finally, "but she lives with Carl and me."

That wasn't much help to the photographer. They were all staring at Kate as though she were a stranger who did not belong to any of them.

"Put her here between Carl and me," Mindy spoke from the chair to which she had been assigned.

"She's far too tall for that position," the photographer said, frowning. "The little one is perfect there as I have her."

"Stephen and I would be proud to have her stand by us," Rita told him. There was such compassion in her voice that Kate lifted her head for a moment and looked at her aunt gratefully.

There was no sound from Ned's lips, no invitation to his eldest child to take her place at his side. The photographer, frustrated with the indecision and delay, spoke sharply, "Nonsense. If she belongs to this family, that's where we'll put her," and he guided Kate to a position beside Eric, who grinned up at her mischievously. Kate had for him no answering smile, though she loved her younger brother dearly. She stood numbly, without a hint of emotion in her blue eyes. Mindy understood that she had willed herself away to some forest solitude where it did not matter whether or not you belonged to

234

anyone. Only her body, shapeless in the navy dress, stood obediently on the spot to which she had been assigned—beside her pretty stepmother.

*   *   *   *   *

Stephen stood on the long front porch overlooking the valley. It was the morning of his departure. At the far end, Mindy sat husking corn. She had planned a day of canning in anticipation of the depression which would overtake her at their leaving. Rita and the girls were flying about doing last-minute packing. Mother and son spoke no word to each other. He understood her sorrow. She, his need to seek far places.

"You are so lucky, Uncle Stephen, to live in Alaska. I would love to see the great snowy mountains and travel by dog team." Kate had appeared silently beside her uncle.

He put an arm about her shoulders, and Mindy thought how rarely her family touched one another.

"Alaska is a big, exciting land for sure, Kate, but I want you always to remember something. There is no spot on the earth more beautiful than this valley with the fog rising off the river. I've just been standing here storing it away. Sometimes when I've had too much of those great snowy mountains you're talking about, I think about this valley. I like to picture Dad mowing in the lower meadow. I can even smell the hay."

"Why do you go then?" Kate asked. Mindy chuckled to herself. She'd be interested in how he wiggled around that question.

Stephen looked down at his niece fondly. "I don't know how to explain it, Kate. I simply have to go places and try things, but it's very important for me that the valley and your grandmother are always here when I get ready to come home."

Mindy knew that was his farewell to her, and she cherished it.

Ellen called to Kate, and Stephen came to sit beside his mother. He removed husks from corn, and something told her that he did not know how to form the words he wished to speak.

"What is it, Stephen? You don't have to be careful. Just out with it."

He grinned sheepishly. "Rita and I would like to take Kate back with us this time, Mother. Rita feels Ned is destroying her with his indifference, but even with that aside, it would be something she'd never forget. She'd be company for Ellen. What do you say?"

"I say no." Mindy looked her younger son squarely in the eye. He knew it was useless but tried again, remembering the urgency in Rita's appeal the night before.

"Mother, do you have a right to deny her this?"

"It's part selfishness, I admit. Kate has become my excuse for hanging onto life. But there's more to it than that. This is her home. She needs to know that she's not just a stray to be passed about among the relatives. I know that Ned's visits are difficult for her, but Stephen, one must accept life as it comes. Perhaps she'll be the stronger and the kinder for what she's endured."

"OK." Stephen rose. "She's yours, and I accept your decision—but we'd still love to take her."

"I'm sorry"—Mindy stood to walk with him to the car—"but this old woman cannot lose all she holds dear in one day, my son. It is bad enough that we shall not see *you* for years."

She kissed the girls, longing to hug them fiercely, but reluctant to make a tragedy from what to them was only a normal event in their nomadic lives. She and Rita embraced with reserve, never really at ease, yet each respecting something in the other. Stephen held her tightly for a brief moment.

"I'm afraid," she said. "I may not be here when you come home."

"We have eternity, Mother." He spoke very gently into her hair. "Let's not fret over a few years, plus or

236

minus, here. Lay all your worries in God's lap. That's the best medicine for heart trouble. I love you."

Carl was relaxed, almost jovial, but she knew he hurt. He tucked packages of gum in the girls' pockets and hugged Rita with real affection. But as he shook hands with Stephen, the fierce blue eyes glittered with tears. When they were gone, Mindy put her head down on the kitchen table and sobbed. Kate stood beside her, awkwardly patting her shoulder, saying nothing. "I'm getting old," Mindy thought. "The first time he left I had more control." But it was something beyond his leaving for which she wept. It was the strange, sure knowledge she'd never see him again.

*　　*　　*　　*　　*

The wind had blown since morning, growing stronger as the day waned. Mindy found herself relieved when she saw Kate round the bend far down the valley. An eerie, early darkness was settling over the land, and she wanted her own gathered about light and fire. Carl would soon be in from the barn, and they would eat, converse, read, and sleep.

"I don't know when I've seen the sky so black," Carl said, milk pails jangling as the wind slammed the door violently behind him. Rain exploded against the kitchen windows, sluicing off in sheets of water, only to be replaced with a fresh avalanche.

"Is this another flood?" Mindy asked, recalling the nightmare of those other days so long ago.

"The wind bothers me more than the water," Carl worried, watching the kitchen curtains flutter as new gusts tore at the house.

Kate ate quietly, her brown head bent above her plate.

"This old house has stood through just about everything." Mindy spoke to reassure the child as she served small plates of berry pie.

"It sounds like a hurricane to me. We studied about them last year in school." Kate nibbled at her pie thoughtfully. "I wonder if the house has a hurricane in its past."

"Well, if it has, it's not talking," Carl answered, grinning at her.

"It's doing plenty of groaning," Mindy shouted above the noise, which was overpowering at the peak of each gust.

Suddenly the lights went out, and they sat for a moment, startled, in the darkness.

"See, it doesn't pay to be dependent upon new-fangled inventions," Carl said finally, and Kate laughed.

Mindy rose and felt her way about the familiar room, which didn't seem familiar at all with the wind screaming above the downpour. "I'll get a lamp. You two stay put so I don't fall over you."

When the dishes had been cleared away, they sat uneasily in the flickering lamplight. It was nearly impossible to talk above the noise. Mindy felt herself flinching as each new blast rolled over the house. Carl went to the basement, returned with hammer and nails, and began methodically nailing windows tightly into their frames.

"It *is* a hurricane, isn't it, Gram?" Kate asked as she watched her grandfather work.

"Yes, child, I believe it is. Let's ask God to be with us. Your granddad is right to do what he can, and the rest we must leave with the Almighty."

And so with Carl's hammer blows tattooing a background, Mindy and Kate prayed quietly. Even as they sat, heads bowed, a thundering crash drove them from their chairs and left Carl standing white and shaken, hammer suspended crazily. Kate and Mindy followed him into the summer kitchen where the limbs of one of the old trees protruded in an uninvited jungle.

"The front porch is full of tree," Kate voiced, wonderingly.

238

"A few feet to the right, and the *kitchen* would have been full of tree with us under it." Carl's voice was grim.

The night shrieked on. Carl prowled about nervously. Finally Kate leaned against her grandmother and slept. Mindy laid her on the couch and sat beside her, thinking and praying. It seemed impossible the house could survive.

"It's slowing down a bit," Carl said later, coming down the stairs. "We might as well turn in."

"Take Kate up then." Mindy lifted the lamp and led the way.

The first pale hint of morning edged the angry sky as they drifted off to sleep.

When they awoke a few hours later, wind still whipped smartly among the treetops, but the world glittered like a gem freshly cut and polished.

"Look, Gram. It's splendid out." Kate stood at Mindy's slanting window looking down the valley.

"Is the brook all over the meadow?" Mindy asked sleepily from the bed.

"It's wild and muddy right up to the road, with lots of limbs heading downstream. I'm going to be late for school if I don't hurry."

"School!" Mindy gasped. "Child, there will be no school for you today. I imagine the water is boiling over the bridge, if we're lucky enough to still own a bridge. There must be trees across the road everywhere."

"Oh, Gram, don't say I can't go. I never saw the world so beautiful. It's like God housecleaned it."

"He did, indeed, with a vengeance. We'll see what your grandfather says about going to school. I can't believe he'll be foolish enough to say yes."

Carl had no sooner appeared from the barn than Kate approached him, blue eyes beseeching beneath the straight brown bangs. "Please, may I go to school, Gramp? I have my lunch all packed, and it would be a shame to waste it."

"And there's no way you could possibly eat it here

239

at home, I suppose," he said, testing his coffee, not looking at her. "Do you realize there may be trees across the
road in a dozen places?"

"I will go around them if I can't get over. I'll be ever
so careful. Oh, I *do* want to see what the hurricane did,
Gramp."

He pushed his chair back from the table. "If I can get
you over the brook, you may go. The water's at least a
foot above the bridge and moving fast."

Mindy slipped into a sweater and walked with them.
Everywhere trees lay upon the ground, their roots ripped
ruthlessly from the tender soil. Above the shattered
earth, the sky sprawled bright blue and cloudless. It was
as though the morning denied the night's slaughter.

"Carl, surely you don't mean to cross that bridge,"
Mindy shouted as they neared the brook. The thunder
of the falls upstream drowned her voice, and Carl did
not even turn in her direction. He lifted Kate and moved
out onto the bridge, the waters swirling angrily about his
boot tops. Gingerly, feeling ahead with one foot, then
the other, Kate quiet and trusting in his arms, he inched
his way across. Mindy realized when he sloshed into
the shallows on the other side that she had been holding
her breath. Kate skipped away from them, turning once
to blow a kiss and smile.

"I still don't like her walking those two miles this
morning. Who knows what she'll come up against?"
Mindy reached out a hand to Carl as he waded back
across the torrent. "It's quite possible they won't even
hold school today."

They stood a moment watching the child walking
quickly down the road, lunch box swinging, head tilted
back as though drinking up the morning. Carl smiled.
"She'll be all right. She's perfectly tuned to the earth, as
Ned used to be. School or no school, she'll have an adventure and much to tell us when she returns."

As they turned back toward the house, his mood
changed, and he said, in a voice heavy with despair,

240

"Have you not lifted your eyes from the ground, Mindy? Did it never occur to you to look at the stand of pine?"

She knew then without looking. Those evergreens had been Carl's pride. He had refused to lumber that mountainside through even the sparest years. Reluctantly she lifted her eyes to the ascent above the pastureland upon her left. Where yesterday there had been towering pines, there now lay only a tangle of broken and splintered trunks as far as the eye could see.

"Oh, Carl!" She felt his pain in every corner of her being.

"They were Kate's education and our protection for our old age. Many times I've been tempted to cut them, but it gave me a real sense of security just knowing they were there. We were never poor as long as they stood."

"We are still not poor, my dear. God never failed us, even in those early years."

"'Twas the woods which saved us *then,* not God," he retorted sharply. "The woods and my own sweat."

"Who supplied your strength and put the miracle of growth in all those seedlings in the forest in the first place? We are dependent upon Him, Carl, in every act of life, whether we care to admit it or not."

He made no answer.

"What will we do with all that broken timber? Is there anything to be salvaged?"

"I don't know," he sighed. "I can't even bring myself to go and look at it." Could he have allowed himself the luxury, she knew he would have wept. They walked in silence toward the house through the cruel, shining morning.

Chapter 25

Only the crackling of Carl's newspaper when he turned a page broke the quiet of the kitchen. Mindy was reading *Patriarchs and Prophets,* a book Stephen had given her when he was home. She had read it twice before, but she never wearied of its pages. It was all she could do to keep from sharing a paragraph with Carl now and then, but since it irritated him, she kept her enthusiasm to herself.

Kate had gone sledding with the village young people. A tall boy with an engaging smile had called for her, and they had vanished into the starlit night. Watching them, Mindy realized it was time for Kate to go away to school. At thirteen, she was full grown and fast leaving childhood behind. The neighborhood sledding parties, once rowdy affairs with much shoving and snowballing, had now about them whispers of romance. The boy with the sweet smile would be very easy to love. She must talk to Carl about sending Kate to boarding school. It was important for a Seventh-day Adventist girl to marry one of her own kind. She looked at her husband a long, thoughtful moment as she closed the door and leaned against it. Indeed it was. Very, very important.

They had sat then in the silence, reading, each in his

separate world, not stopping now and then to laugh or speak or touch. Only five feet apart and absolutely alone.

The knock at the door startled them both. Carl called out a welcome, but half rose in his chair as the door opened. It was not the usual hour for callers. He smiled in relief as Ned stood tall in the doorway. Sharp winter air invaded the coziness of the kitchen, and with it came the penetrating smell of alcohol.

"Well, come in," Carl called warmly. "Don't just stand there like a stranger."

Ned tilted back in the captain's chair against the west wall, thumbs resting in his belt loops. He talked of his work. He was managing a service station in another town, operating a fleet of gas tankers, and prospering. He boasted that he would soon have more to show for his years than Stephen with his college degree. He was cocky, arrogant, and very handsome in the softly lighted room. There was something familiar about that arrogance. Mindy could almost hear Seth's scornful laughter filtering down through the years.

This man who stank of wine and empty words was not really Ned at all. *Her* Ned, the son she had raised with such care, was a gentle, tender, teasing man. Sometimes *that* Ned still came to her door, but rarely of late. She held the picture of him sitting there like that, still young, still possessed of dreams, for already she saw the lines of dissipation framing the vulnerable mouth, etching the high cheekbones of his Indian ancestors. "O God," she prayed, "save him yet from himself. He is generous and kind. There is much to be salvaged from his life."

When the laughter of Kate and her friends sounded at the back door, Ned moved uneasily in his chair.

"They won't be coming in," Mindy told him. "They've just walked her home from the sledding. It's a long hike back to the village."

He stood, and Mindy knew he wished himself well away, but before he could comfortably take his leave,

243

Kate opened the door. Tall and slim, there was about her the simplicity and dignity of Sara. Her face, which was rosy with cold and alight with laughter, changed in an instant to the cool reserve behind which she retreated in her father's presence.

"Good evening, Kate," Ned said awkwardly. "How was the sledding? I used to do a good bit of it on Billings hill myself." There was something almost gentle in his words.

Mindy thought for a moment Kate was going to cry, but the eyes the girl lifted to her father said nothing, and her answer was carefully courteous—words for a stranger. "Fine. The sledding was just fine, thank you, and now if you'll excuse me, I'm going to bed. I have school tomorrow." No staying for a cup of cocoa or a sharing of the evening's adventures *this* night.

Ned stood a moment, swaying slightly, then went out to his car without a word.

"He spoke to her," Mindy marveled softly. "That's the most he's ever said to her."

"He's drunk." Carl locked the door and put the night log on the fire.

"Maybe so." Mindy scrubbed her face before the small white framed mirror over the sink. "But I heard a pleading in his voice like he wanted her to understand."

"You heard what you wanted to hear. Don't be looking for miracles where none exist. I looked over Ned's books the other day at his station. He's giving customers way too much credit, just as he did here. You can't operate on good intentions. His prosperity will be short-lived."

Mindy thought of the boarded-up garage in town, Carl's dream for Ned's future. How many people he had hurt, this son who had never liked trouble!

When she went to bed, she stood for a moment in the doorway to Kate's room. Light from the hall spilled across the bed. The girl's hair lay tangled and wet about

244

her face, so like Sara's in sleep. "So you cried yourself to sleep, child," Mindy whispered. "Underneath the anger then, there is love. That is good."

"Good for what?" Carl asked, overhearing. "More hurt?"

"It is better to hurt than to have a heart of stone."

"Now, who said that? Moses or St. Paul?"

"Neither," Mindy replied, climbing into bed beside him. "I'm drawing from my own hard-won experience."

"If you think I'm going to lie awake all night puzzling about that statement, you're mistaken." He turned away from her and was soon asleep.

She lay long, sleepless, thinking and watching the stars creep across her slanting window.

*   *   *   *   *

Strangely, Carl did not object to Kate's going away to academy, though he had labeled Mindy a snob when she sent the boys. "I need to go to work," Mindy decided. "It is even more expensive now than when the boys went. I don't want to place that burden all on your shoulders, but my teaching certification has long run out, and what else could I do?"

"I don't think it will be necessary." Carl watched Kate raking the front yard. "The only problem will be this empty house when she has gone."

Mindy surveyed her husband wonderingly. He gave the girl little attention, had never disciplined her in his life. He took great pride in her ability as a student, though he never mentioned it in her presence. "Maybe he had always wanted a girl," Mindy thought, "or maybe we are both hoping this one will fulfill all our old dreams. Not very fair, but perhaps parents always hope that, right down to the final child."

In the last week of August they drove to the city to shop for Kate. It would be a scant wardrobe at best, but not as scant as Mindy's had been. Carl had given her

245

twenty-five dollars. Twenty-five dollars! What would that buy for a girl who had outgrown nearly everything she owned? The few remaining garments were homemade, and Mindy felt uneasy about them. She had not forgotten Kate's conversation with Rita. But they must make do with what they had, for Carl had never squarely faced the true cost of things, and Mindy could not gather her courage to inform him.

It was fresh and cool when they left the house, but by noon the city streets would be a furnace. Nevertheless Mindy and Kate were excited. Kate could count on one hand the times she had been to the city. She had determined to spend her money with a cautious hand.

"There's Ned," Carl said, turning sharply toward a parking lot beside a diner into which Ned had just disappeared. His big tanker sat in the lot. They all had a hot drink and took pleasure in their unexpected meeting. Smoke curled straight up from Ned's cigarette, but he hadn't been drinking. Mindy thought sadly what a special person he was, his eyes crinkling in laughter, the arrogance and boasting gone. She could feel the love between father and son. She had heard it in Carl's voice when he discovered Ned entering the diner. She understood that nothing Ned might ever do could change that. Carl simply loved the boy, all aside from his failures and successes. What a rare thing from a temperate man who had built his life around integrity and achievement. Rare and beautiful.

As they stood about the car, engaged in last-minute chatting, Ned drew his wallet from his pocket. He removed a ten-dollar bill and held it out to Kate. "This isn't much, but I want you to buy something pretty for school." She was as white as the blouse she wore, and she made no move to take the money. There was a tight look about her lips.

It seemed to Mindy that she was always having to choose between people she loved. She could have cuffed the child for her rejection of Ned's offering, yet an honest part of her had to admit Kate was justified. One couldn't hope to erase thirteen years of sorrow with a ten-dollar bill. The silence was painful and awkward. Kate looked at Mindy, her blue eyes filled with hurt and anger, but at last she reached for the money. Her thank-you was almost inaudible.

The day was ruined. Carl prowled the hardware stores while Mindy and Kate walked miles in the searing heat, comparing prices, not daring to spend lest the garment be all wrong, but at last trading the precious money for three or four items which seemed unbelievably splendid to both of them. Kate would learn soon enough that the cheap pink sweater stretched out of shape upon washing and the green dress would have been more appropriate for Mindy than for herself, but that knowledge could wait. She had handed the ten-dollar bill to her grandmother the moment her father was out of sight and made no mention of the incident, but for the first time ever there was a restraint between them.

That night, after they had eaten a lunch on their own cool porch, Kate had modeled her outfits for Carl and gone to bed.

"There's a lot of bitterness bottled up in the girl tonight," Carl noted. "You ought to talk to her."

"I know I ought, but Carl, I love them both. What can I say?"

"Maybe you could just listen."

"I'm not good at this sort of thing. You know we were all raised to pretend problems didn't exist, to just be polite. We weren't allowed the luxury of feelings."

"I often felt the need though, didn't you?" he said wistfully.

She didn't reply, rising instead to go to Kate. The girl's sobs shook the small birch bed as Mindy sat beside her. Mindy patted her back and said nothing.

"I hate him!" The words came muffled from the pillow, but Mindy had no trouble understanding them.

"He meant well."

"No, he didn't. His conscience hurt him. It ought to. You and Gramp spending so much money on me all these years while he pretends I never happened to him."

The girl sat up in bed, eyes flashing, her face red and swollen from crying. "The only reason I took his wretched money was to help you and Gramp. What he paid for, you didn't have to. I longed to throw it at him."

"I want to read something to you." Mindy rose and brought a book from her bedroom. "These words are from Volume 5 of the *Testimonies,* page 488. They were written by God's messenger to our people, and perhaps they are very especially for you at this hour:

" 'Circumstances have but little to do with the experiences of the soul. It is the spirit cherished which gives coloring to all our actions. A man at peace with God and his fellow men cannot be made miserable. Envy will not be in his heart . . .' "

Mindy hesitated. "Is it possible there is envy in your heart of the love your father gives his other children? It would be quite natural, Kate, in our human state, but the heart committed to Christ looks at things differently."

She went on reading, " '. . . evil surmising will find no room there.'

"Are you surmising about your father's motives when you say he's easing a guilty conscience? Listen to this next description of the Christian's heart: 'Hatred cannot exist. The heart in harmony with God is lifted above the annoyances and trials of this life.' "

Mindy put her arms around the girl and said gently, "It has been a long, hurting experience, but I think if you could look into your father's heart, you'd find it has hurt him too. And you, Kate, are close to God, who is a Father to us all. Ned no longer has that peace. Do not be too hard on him."

"I do not know how to let Jesus be the answer to everything the way you do," Kate blurted stormily. "Grandpa is so cross to you sometimes, and I don't see how you hold your temper."

248

"When I was your age, I felt just as you do, Kate. I used to hear my father pray, and it was like he and God had just had lunch together. I was filled with questions and bitter over my sickness, and sometimes Father's calm trust in God annoyed me."

"How did you get so chummy with God then?" Kate challenged.

"It came slowly after your gramp and I were married. It didn't take me long to realize there were going to be a lot of lonely spots in life, and I found the only way I could bear them was to spend time with Jesus. After a while, just like the book said, outside circumstances didn't really matter as long as I kept the channels clear between myself and God."

"I don't think that will ever happen to me," Kate said. "All I want to do is grow up to be somebody great and famous so that someday I can come home in a big car and beautiful clothes and drive up to his crummy gas station and say, 'Fill it up, please,' like he was no one I had ever seen before. Then maybe he'd have to at least admit I existed."

Mindy laughed in spite of herself. "That is absolutely evil, Kate. Bow your head." As Mindy held her, she prayed, "Dear Lord, give Kate a forgiving heart. Let her be so filled with Your love that she can afford to love Ned without any assurance of his concern for her. Let her experience the sweet joy I have known so long."

"I'm sorry I made a mess of the day, Gram." She hesitated. "I had an awful feeling I was going to cry right there in front of him. It hurts a lot to be mad and sad at the same time."

"Indeed it does," Mindy said, turning out the light and tucking the bedcovers in as tightly as if Kate were six instead of thirteen.

*   *   *   *   *

That moment when they left her, a week later, on the

249

steps of the girls' dorm in Massachusetts marked a turning point in Carl and Mindy's marriage. Silence fell between them. Oh, they talked about necessary things, but Carl rationed his words grudgingly while Mindy tasted the worst loneliness of her life. She missed Kate beside her in the pew of their small country church; she missed her playing hymns at the piano on Friday night; she missed the girl's wit and laughter, her company on walks about the farm; she missed the interplay of ideas, the girl's pleasure in the smallest details of living. One day she stood at the cherry desk in Kate's small room, running her fingers over the glossy wood, realizing a total lack of interest in the next day or even the next hour. The cherry desk was the only really good piece of furniture in the house. It was very old, handed down through her mother's family, and Mindy had felt it belonged in Kate's room, for the girl wrote hour after hour, sometimes long after Mindy and Carl had turned out their light for the night. She had Sara's talent, and God willing, perhaps she'd have time to do something with it.

Letters came, letters with no hint of homesickness. She had registered by herself, telling them there was no need to stay to help her when they were paying for help on the farm. A strong confidence had developed in this child who had been hidden away in the mountains all her life! She was discovering the academic demands heavier, the competition keener, but enjoying the challenge.

"She is launched," Mindy thought. "Tossed into the free-for-all of life, ready or not, and she's readier than I dreamed." It would never be quite the same again, even when she came home.

"O Lord"—Mindy dropped to her knees, placing her head against the cool wood of the desk—"I've always mothered or taught. I can't live with this emptiness. I would love to just be Carl's wife, to share his thoughts, and pour out all my love and attention on him, but he has grown hard and cold. I cannot reach him. Help me to be patient and loving. O God, give me a reason for my days."

Three weeks later, she received a letter inviting her to fill an emergency teaching situation for the year. Due to the war, which had brought about a manpower shortage, they were putting into circulation a few older teachers whose credentials were no longer up-to-date. Mindy walked back from the mailbox thoughtfully. The school was in another town. She would have to board away from home. The income would be a great blessing. Kate would need formal dresses occasionally, money for class dues, spending money. And, oh, the delicious independence of having money for offerings at church, a new pair of shoes, wallpaper for the living room— money for so many things.

But she must ask Carl. She would not take such a step without his consent, and surely he would never let her leave home. All that evening she tried to bring herself to speak to him about it. She trembled to force him to speak. His words came so reluctantly.

Finally, when he came in from hand-mowing about the buildings and sat on the porch, she simply put the letter in his lap. He read it slowly and laid it on the porch rail, saying nothing.

"What do you think?" Mindy stood beside him in the waning day, wondering where she had lost him, at what moment he had begun to steel his heart against her. And why.

She touched his shoulder lightly, needing something more from him than words.

"Whatever you like, Min."

"You couldn't stay here alone, Carl. You know nothing of cooking."

"I hear Old Widow Hoyt is looking for work. She always set a good table in her day."

Mindy realized then that even more than she had wanted him to say yes she had wanted him to say no. She had wanted him to grow angry and thunder that he

251

could not get along without her, that she must put such foolishness out of her head.

"We could use the money, I suppose," she said flatly. Then bending, she kissed him lightly, fleetingly, and ran upstairs to their room. She sat a long time before the window, unraveling the years, searching for the dropped stitch.

Chapter 26

It was a mountain school, far from the main highway. She stood in the small, poorly equipped classroom and wondered why she was there. The school had not opened in September for lack of a teacher, and now in the first week of October the golden leaves of an old oak in the front yard spiraled lazily past the window by her desk. She had no idea what to expect. There was hardly a house in sight. School would begin in forty-five minutes. Looking out across the rocky pastures and forests, it was hard to believe she'd have a single student.

Of course there'd be the LeMar children where she boarded, all eight of them. She didn't like to think of that household. It was the only home in sight now as she stood at the window watching for the first child to appear. Peeling paint and a cluttered yard only hinted at the confusion within. Mrs. LeMar, the victim of poverty and childbearing, wandered grimly through her days without any real hope of accomplishing more than setting food before her hungry throng and keeping some sort of clothing between them and the cold. There was not so much as a plant or flower in the home, only a haloed virgin Mary hanging crookedly above the tattered couch in the living room. Grimy clothing littered the floors.

The tiny room to which her hostess had led her contained only a dresser and a battered bed. Fortunately, Mindy had brought her own blankets, linens, a few plants and pictures, and a pair of ruffled curtains. When she had washed the windows inside and out, hung the curtains, and made up the bed with her best wedding-ring quilt, the children stood in the doorway with wondering eyes.

In response to her invitation to come in, they stood with dirty, calloused feet upon the soft ivory hooked rug which she had laid before her bed. Mindy had not the heart to chide them; instead she asked each one his name and tried to store away some identifying feature among the array of dark eyes and tangled manes.

On impulse she had said, "If you will all come here each evening when your supper chores are finished, I will read to you for a few moments before you begin your schoolwork." They had uttered not a word, but she saw a flash of unguarded joy in the eyes of one of the younger girls.

That had all been yesterday, and now she saw them, the LeMar children, straggling from their front door along the dirt road toward her classroom. From the crossroads a quarter mile away she noted others coming singly and in groups along the converging roads. Suddenly, as she watched them meet at the crossroads, boisterous in their excitement, pushing, shoving, laughing, snitching from their lunch boxes, she knew she belonged there, that they needed her—these mountain children—and she needed them, with their impish eyes and famished minds.

When they sat before her, they were a field of wild flowers. Saucy faces, shy faces, frightened faces, mischievous faces. Some as lovely as buttercups and daisies, some as plain as dandelions, but she loved them all. She had almost forgotten the challenge of facing a new classroom. She set about learning their names, their level of achievement, and their personalities. It

254

was the inner child she must find to teach efficiently.

By the time school was dismissed and the children had said their shy good-byes, she had all nineteen of them roughly sorted in her mind. There were the plodding readers who hated school because they were forever behind, the bullies who would make the others miserable and test the teacher to her limits, the thirsty minds who could not learn fast enough, and the steady, dependable ones who would still shoulder the responsibilities of life long after they had left the schoolroom behind.

She would teach the dull to read. Almost any child could learn to read if one knew how to teach the phonetic sounds of each letter. She would heap responsibility upon the bullies, keeping them too busy to cause trouble. She'd learned years before that bullies were only frightened youngsters who usually responded to any confidence placed in them. The room would soon be lively with projects. Already she was planning a Parents' Night. One must capture *their* interest and loyalty too. Yes, it was good to be a schoolmarm again. If only she didn't have to go back to that house at night—that cold, slovenly, uninviting house.

The aroma of roasting pork met her nostrils as she opened the door. She had told them she ate no pork, that it was contrary to her religious beliefs, and here it was on the table the first night. Mindy chuckled to herself. In all her fifty-nine years, she'd never really had to take a firm stand on any point. Carl had kept his promise to Hiram and left her free to worship as she chose. Now she ate her boiled potato, a piece of store bread, and a dab of tasteless, lumpy squash, leaving the pork roast to the others. They ate in an uneasy silence, not comfortable, she felt sure, with her at their table. She asked the children questions about their schoolmates and tried to draw her hosts into a conversation, but it was slow going.

When she was finished and had excused herself, she

255

looked at the children and said, "When you have finished your chores, you are invited to my room for a storytime. Don't forget."

They came, from the oldest boy down to the five-year-old who did not yet attend school. She read them the story of the Flood from the Bible, showing them illustrations as she went along and then teaching them a song with hand motions about Noah and his great adventure.

"Tomorrow night we'll start *Tom Sawyer*. Monday night will be Bible night, Tuesday night will be famous books night, Wednesday night will be travel night, and Thursday night we'll learn to knit or crochet." She looked at the three boys, puzzled as to what they might do on crafts night.

"I wish I knew you better," she told them. "Surely there is something you like especially to do or would like to learn to do."

"Ralph is daft about birds," the youngest girl said, grinning mischievously at her brother. "He's always snooping in the hedgerows looking for nests."

"Then, Ralph, each Thursday while we are learning to knit, you are to describe a particular bird to us. Tell us even what its nest and eggs are like. Describe it so well that we'll be able to identify it ourselves when we see one. I'll bring you a little notebook, and you keep a record of every bird you describe to us." She made a mental note to pick up a good guide to Northeastern birds when she was back in civilization.

"Now, Eddie, what about you?"

"He whittles." The same small girl spoke up quickly, and Mindy realized it was Mary, the one who had shown interest at her first mention of a story time. "He makes whistles and tiny canoes and everything."

Mindy looked at Eddie the whittler. He hung his head in embarrassment, but she noted the slim, long-fingered hands and could well believe they harbored talent. "Then bring your whittling on Thursday night and let

256

me have a look at what you can do." She would bring from home the beautiful sculptures in ivory which Stephen had brought her from Alaska, where some natives were skilled in the art of carving. Eddie the whittler would run his fingers over their satin surfaces with excitement, and he, too, might attempt the smooth contours of a baby seal or the intricate lacework of a reindeer's horns.

Joe, the youngest boy, decided he wanted to learn to knit with the girls.

"Now you must be about your homework, children," Mindy reminded them, rising to put her Bible away. The older ones left reluctantly, but small Mary stayed.

As Mindy took the day's papers for correcting and her plan book for the morrow, the child said, so softly that it seemed her lips moved without sound, "I hain't got no homework, ma'am. I be staying here."

Mindy flinched. "Mary, say this after me: 'I *do not have* any homework. May I stay here with you?' "

Obediently the child repeated the words after her.

"The English language is very beautiful, Mary. I will help you learn to use it correctly. Yes, you may stay here, but I do not think you will like it, for I must work and cannot chat with you."

"That don't matter, Miz Matthews. I just like to look at your pretty things." The thin, plain child, who looked like an elf, lay down upon the hooked rug and never said a word in the hour before her mother called her to bed.

When she rose, Mindy said, "Mary, one does not have many friends who can be silent for a whole hour. You may come any time, and perhaps some nights there will be time to talk a bit."

And that's the way the bright October days glittered into the gray of November. She learned to bring food from home, for there was little she could eat at the LeMar table, everything swimming in bacon grease as it was.

When Carl came on Fridays, she chattered eagerly on the drive home until she realized her words were tumbling into a canyon of silence, like foolish children who did not watch where they were going. Then *she* was quiet too. The weekends were familiar interludes in a strange new life. Sometimes it seemed the days at the hill school had more meaning than the ones at home. She was needed and loved in that mountain community as she had once been in the valley.

The awkward, untutored fingers of the LeMar children learned new skills; their minds wandered, awed and marveling through the Old Testament and the wonders of *Tom Sawyer* and *Little Women*. Mary embroidered a pillowcase with daisies and pink bows, laying claim at last to something pretty of her own. From a picture in the *National Geographic,* Eddie carved a sea gull, so light and graceful in its posture of flight that when Mindy hung it on a piece of fine thread from the ceiling in the school, the children could barely take their eyes from it.

But on that morning in December when the old pains tore into her chest as she struggled through waist-deep snow on the way to school, she knew that, much as she loved her work, it was eroding the time—that precious small bit of time—she had left.

She took the pills quickly with a mouthful of snow and simply made herself a little hollow in the drifts to get out of the wind. Sitting there, hidden from view, biting her lips against the pain, she thought it would be a strange place to die. Yet not so bad, really. Hidden and cradled by the pure whiteness of snow. Perhaps more natural than in one's bed or within the sterile indifference of a hospital. No, not a bad place at all to die.

She fought the nausea that seemed sometimes almost worse than the pain. Fought it with her mind. The stomach could often be made to obey the mind.

Was she ready to submit her life to God, writing "the end" in a steady, clear hand on this glistening morning with the black trees fingering the sky? How far had she come in her journeying? Was she any more like the Man Jesus Christ than she had been forty years ago when she first felt His presence in her life? She did not know. She was not sharp tongued and shrewish with Carl as some women she'd heard, but sometimes she felt a great pity for him, that he knew nothing of the joy that sustained her. Somehow she should have been able to bring *him* into its radiance with her. Carl, proud Carl, would despise her pity.

Had it been impossible or had she failed to find the way? Or had she been content to grasp it greedily to her own heart with no thought of sharing? She couldn't tell, and the pain was erasing thought, efficiently, coldly, like a machine. Vomit stained the snow. Mind became the slave of body. She hated that.

It was too hard to live. She relaxed into her snug blue-white cave and let pain consume her. It was the face that dragged her back to reality, a composite of Kate's and Mary LeMar's. Strange how she'd especially loved these two girls when she'd wanted only boys.

Mary was starting a sampler, and she'd need help with the French knots; and Kate would be coming home for Christmas, and Kate must never come home to a house where no fires burned and no tree twinkled a welcome. No, she wasn't free to die.

When the children came by on the way to school, Ralph and Eddie broke a path, then half carried her into the schoolroom. All day they tended her, taking care of the stove and reciting their lessons about her desk so she need not move. By taking her time at night, she made it home. After that, Joseph LeMar plowed a path with his team and stone boat on bad mornings.

On the Friday before Christmas it was dusk when Carl came for her. She was filled with excitement. Kate would be with him, and when the lights of his truck shone across the front yard, it was Kate who came to the door for her. Mindy drew her into the cluttered, dingy kitchen, into the circle of eager, curious faces, and sensed the girl's shock and distaste, realizing with a touch of humor her own feelings almost three months ago.

259

"Kate, I want you to meet my friends the LeMars."
Kate bobbed her head politely as Mindy called off the
names, and when she'd finished, Mary said in her innocent frankness, "She's right pretty, ma'am, Kate is."

Mindy looked at Kate. She'd never thought her any
beauty. Just a good sensible face. But something had
happened. Her hair was longer, soft and shining to her
shoulders, curled just enough to frame the sensible face
prettily. A light-blue scarf matched her eyes, and there
was a new confidence about the tilt of her chin. Rita had
said, "When you go away to school . . ."

Mindy hugged Mary. "She is, indeed, right pretty, my
little friend. I'm glad you pointed it out to me."

All vacation Mindy watched her granddaughter with
delight. The awkward, plain farm girl was gone. She
picked out patterns and material with confidence. With
her private income, Mindy was able to make her several
outfits. When Ned and Gloria came on Christmas afternoon, Mindy watched her son's reaction to Kate with
amusement. His eyes followed the girl with a puzzled
pride of which the girl was not unaware.

That night when the house was still and Mindy lay
beside Carl in the old brass bed, she commented, "Kate
has changed, Carl. For better or for worse, she's her
own person now. I guess I feel a little sad that she'll never
need me quite so much again."

She didn't really expect an answer, or at best a mocking one, but he said, roughly, as though each word
fought for its personal birth, "You should be proud. She
walked out into life from these backwoods and was
ready. In spite of Ned she was brave enough to risk
friendships and to assume the world was a good place.
You did pretty well for a woman who never wanted a
daughter."

"I didn't do it alone, my dear." She was touched and
humbled at his praise. "You have been a wonderful
source of security to her. Sometimes I've thought you
loved her more than you loved the boys."

"Not more," he said. "Just differently. But you're the one, Min, who has taught her to think and see and listen."

"You are painting a too-perfect picture. I tremble that she will find her new confidence pretty heady stuff. It would not surprise me if she wandered a bit off course before she finds who she really is and what she wants from life."

"I assume you can steer her long-distance by the sheer strength of your will," he said, "or by the magic of your prayers." His voice was taut with the old scorn, and the moment was gone.

Chapter 27

It was a strange summer. Kate moved back into her mountain world, almost eagerly, as though loath to let go of childhood. She wandered over the boulder-strewn pastures and into the forests, observing, savoring. She seldom mentioned school, though often when letters arrived from friends, she read them thirstily.

Her dresses were shorter, and she wore a soft rosy lipstick. Mindy wished she didn't. She had not sent her away to learn to paint her face. But the older woman said nothing. The child must find her own values in her own good time. She knew from bits of conversation between Kate and her best friend in the village that Kate's deportment at school had been less than perfect. But she did not chide her. For fifteen years she had taught this young woman to love God and obey Him. She dared to hope that training would hold when frivolous experimenting with lesser things had passed. Being a Seventh-day Adventist was not easy. It moved into all the corners of one's life, so readily becoming a proud discipline or a hated, but feared, collection of rules. Kate must find the Christ before any of it would be meaningful to her. She would not be one to whistle through her days, stepping in her grandmother's tracks just because they were there.

The girl would question, search, and think. "When she's ready, Lord, You make Yourself known to her," Mindy prayed all that summer.

With Kate around, the silence between Carl and Mindy was less noticeable. Mindy watched the waning August days with mixed emotions. She sensed Kate would be less child when summer came again. When they walked the dusty valley road together, they picked bouquets of black-eyed Susans as they'd always done, stopping on the way home to toss pebbles into the stream as it lapped lazily under the bridge and wandered on through the meadow. But there was a farewell feel about it as though they were doing these things for the last time.

"I'll never forget the valley, Gram," Kate said one day, twirling in the swing from the balm of Gilead in the front yard.

"Where are you going?" Mindy asked, smiling gently at the girl's serious face, "that you must remember the valley?"

"Well, I used to think I'd marry someone from the village and live here forever, but I know now that I won't."

"And how are you so sure of that?"

"It's different, Gram, after you've been away. There's so much to see and learn beyond the mountains. Yet I wouldn't have wanted to grow up anywhere else. Do you understand that?"

"I understand, Kate, and I want you to see and learn to your heart's content. You may decide in the end the simple life we've led here in the valley provides all one needs for happiness—or perhaps not. I have never been away, you know."

"Someday I shall take you away," the girl promised, her face lighting in anticipation. "You shall see the big cities and go to lectures and concerts. Won't that be fun?"

"There was a time I longed for all that. Now I'm not so sure. Sometimes here on these soft and peaceful days

263

I feel so close to God that the concerts of the birds are enough. There is wisdom in the Bible beyond the most scholarly lecture. Since I heard your Uncle Stephen say there's no place more beautiful than this valley, I've not yearned so much for far places." Mindy turned toward the house. "That's old age, I fear, child. It's normal for you to want a bit of something new and different. Youth has always been that way."

She looked forward to returning to her classroom more than she allowed herself to admit. Kate pleaded with her not to teach again, but Mindy laughed her fears away. "Kate, this house is a tomb with you gone. Your granddad lives in his own world, and I'm far happier with something to do."

"Gramp is cheerful and witty with others. Why is he so strange at home? He ridicules and belittles you. How do you keep from growing angry?"

"I love him," Mindy said softly. "I do not believe he means the things he says. Sometimes I feel he's very lonely for God. Your gramp is a good man, Kate. You would see a wondrous change in him if he'd give his heart to Christ."

"You set great store by that, don't you, Gram—making a commitment to Christ?"

"It is the entire point of our existence, Kate."

"I don't know"—the girl chose her words carefully —"I want to believe like you do, but sometimes I am afraid it will never be real for me like it is for you."

"It will if you want it. The Lord cannot resist my prayers and your desire. Be patient. It will come." She walked back to the swing and laid her hand for a moment upon the girl's shoulder. "You have been the joy of my old age, Kate. Thank you for all the happy days."

"I'm only going back to school, Gram. It will be years before I leave home. Don't sound so solemn."

"I just wanted you to know," Mindy told her gently.

*   *   *   *   *

264

Weeks later, Carl drove into the LeMar dooryard on a gray Friday afternoon. Mindy had moved into the pattern of her other life with ease this time. Now, gathering books and papers, she hurried toward the truck.

"I don't like it when you go home, Miz Matthews." Mary LeMar skipped beside her, Mindy's suitcase bumping against her knees.

"It's only a couple of days, Mary." Mindy took the suitcase, tilted the child's chin for an instant to smile into the dark, intelligent eyes, and then climbed onto the high seat of the truck. Mary stood waving, silhouetted against the house until she melted into the autumn dusk.

Mindy turned then to Carl. "I am glad to see you, my dear. How is everything at home? Was there a letter from Stephen?"

"I have news for you," he said, a smile tugging at the corners of his lips, "but it has nothing to do with Stephen."

"Well, tell me quickly. I am starved for news. All is well with Kate?"

"You have been elected as the town representative to the state legislature."

Mindy looked at him, her eyes wide with disbelief. "Carl, don't make jokes."

"It is no joke."

"I could not do that. I have committed myself to a teaching job for the year."

"They will have to find a replacement for you. I told them you would accept."

"Carl, I cannot believe this. Why me? You are laughing at me, aren't you, inside? You think it is foolish to send a woman to the legislature, especially this one."

His eyes did not leave the road. "On the contrary, I think they have made a wise choice. You are highly respected in the village."

Her eyes brimming with tears, she reached across the space between them to touch his hand. "Thank you, Carl. Only those words from you would have given me the courage to accept."

She spent the weekend in an uneasy state. She did not like leaving things half done, and the hill school had become very dear to her. Mary LeMar's thin, eager face haunted her. "I don't like you to go home, Miz Matthews." Well, perhaps she had given them a glimpse of something better. She would keep an eye on Mary through the years, maybe help her go on to school.

"I was wrong, Kate," she said to herself. "I have not outgrown my desire to try something new after all. I can hardly wait for this adventure to begin. Oh, Kate, how could this have happened to me?" She wanted to pour all her excitement into the girl's ears but had to be satisfied with a letter. And Kate would not understand. To her teenage mind it would seem a dull assignment indeed, but never mind, perhaps she would comprehend that it was important to Mindy and rejoice with her.

Thanksgiving brought Kate and a fine feathering of snow, which fell softly over the old farmhouse all day. Ned and his family joined them for dinner. Carl was always at his best with his older son. So unlike in character, they complemented each other in some mysterious way. This day Ned ate little, though Mindy had prepared a feast, and she scolded him that no one could live on coffee and cigarettes.

"And wine, Mother, you forget the wine," he reminded her, his eyes mocking, a sadness in his voice.

His business floundering, these were the last good days of his life. She wondered if he looked ahead to the blackness she and Carl foresaw for him. What were his thoughts when he woke in the night, this man who had once prayed at his mother's knees with a schoolboy's open love for God?

"Eat some of this fruit salad, Ned." She set a small dish before him. "Surely it would spark the most jaded appetite. You used to love it."

He picked at a few mouthfuls to please her but soon went outside to his car and returned with the heavy odor of cheap wine mingling with the clean smell of winter.

Kate watched him, but Mindy could not label the look in her eyes. Pity? Scorn? Love? She could not tell. The girl had long ceased to speak any word in his presence.

"Your mother has become a career woman," Carl said.

Ned looked at Mindy questioningly, mischief flickering on and off in his blue-green eyes, for a second so much the child she'd loved that she longed to take him in her arms and protect him from the world he could not handle.

She said nothing. The whole thing still seemed beyond belief to her.

"She's not used to her fame yet." Carl cast an amused glance in Mindy's direction. "She's going to state legislature." He could not hide the pride in his voice.

"Nothing will ever be the same again," Ned said in mock horror. "The state will sport a church at every crossroads."

Mindy scooped homemade ice cream onto apple pie. She only smiled at his teasing, knowing he was well pleased.

They talked then of other days and things that had happened long ago. The young folks listened and laughed at the frivolity of their elders. They spoke of Stephen and Rita, and wondered how they were celebrating their holiday. The past was much with them, but no one spoke Sara's name, and the girl, Kate, did not laugh with the others. She sat among them, but apart.

"She's like a young tree transplanted to a far land," Mindy thought, "flourishing, but somehow alien."

Snow softened the bleak November landscape, falling steadily upon the long green arms of the pines. When Ned and Gloria drove away, their tires etched parallel patterns down the drive. "All we have left of the day is tracks," Mindy said to Carl as they turned back toward the house.

"Tracks and me. I'm still here." Kate linked her arms in theirs, and they stood a moment together breathing the sharp, hurting cold.

The next day they drove to Montpelier so that Mindy could find rooms for the winter. She purchased a newspaper to check the advertisements, but though Carl drove her from place to place, he showed no interest in her search.

She crossed the first-floor apartments off the list at once, allowing herself no such luxuries. For hours she climbed stairs inspecting budget rooms—all afflicted with some flaw or another—finding at last a tiny apartment, cozy and well equipped within walking distance of her work. Well satisfied, she pronounced her search ended and suggested they have hot chocolate before the drive home. They made the return journey through the snowy forests in silence, Kate reading in the back seat, Carl encased in his familiar stillness, and Mindy resting her head against the back of the seat, eyes closed. She was weary.

After a light supper Kate sat down at the piano, and they welcomed the Sabbath with simple hymns. Though Carl took no notice of their other Sabbath observances, he sometimes joined in their singing with a kind of reluctant pleasure. Mindy thought, watching him, that she'd heard him singing everywhere—in the hayfield, over the roar of the truck, here in the living room at sundown, coming home from the woods, ax over his shoulder. It was a rare indulgence in an otherwise Spartan personality.

Tonight he asked Kate to play "Rock of Ages," and they sang it together. "It's a strange offering, Lord," Mindy thought. "Two old folks and the girl singing off here in the hills—is it pleasing to You?"

She awoke that night to her own screams, consumed with pain and choking on terror. The enemy had taken at least ten giant steps while her back was turned. She could feel his breath upon her neck. This was not the familiar sequence of pain, pills, relief. She could not move, and when Carl's face loomed over her, she could barely form the word, *Doctor*. She heard the racing of his footsteps toward the phone and pictured the good man on the other end twelve miles away rising from his bed at its ringing. Pain and nausea fought for supremacy, and she begged God to let her die. Biting her lips against screams for Kate's sake, she moaned softly in an agony of suffering such as she had never dreamed possible. Carl sat beside her, tight-lipped and helpless. She wished he would take her hand. She felt his fear, his distaste of illness, his aloofness, and it mingled with the physical pain searing through her.

"Carl"—she heard her own voice with wonder that she could still create sound—"is it all right if I go?"

"No more of that." His voice was sharp. "The doctor will be here any moment." Even as he spoke they heard his car in the dooryard. And when he stood above her, this good man who had cautioned her over the years to slow her pace, she wept. "Help me," she begged. "I can't stand the pain."

"You belong in the hospital, but I don't dare move you. This shot will help. You'll have relief within twenty minutes."

Twenty minutes was an eternity. She could not survive this nightmare another five. "Don't leave me."

"I won't," he consoled, pulling a chair up to her bedside. "Scream if it helps. You've never experienced it quite like this before, have you, Min? Makes having a baby look easy."

She wept and screamed when she could not hold it back, and she prayed. She had no bravery left for Kate. Sometimes she opened her eyes and saw Carl and the doctor sitting quietly. "Waiting for me to die," she thought, and then she drifted away into some land of horror where she ran down corridors of pain, crushed and strangling, fighting for breath.

At last she slept. When she awoke, the first pink of morning edged the darkness. The pain was gone. She could hear Carl and the doctor talking in the kitchen. Exhaustion weighted her to the bed. Fear, the stranger, sat beside her. She had never allowed him in her presence. She was not afraid to die but rather to live again through such agony.

Kate came into the room, her young face haggard. "The doctor says you are to rest, Gram. Not to move a muscle until you are strong enough to go to the hospital." She stretched out on the bed beside her grandmother. "It was a terrible night, wasn't it?"

"Yes, child, it was, but it is over. I am so tired. Will you stay here with me?"

"Of course, Gram. Don't try to talk."

She slept.

"Gram, wake up!" There was fear in Kate's voice. "You aren't breathing."

Mindy struggled back to consciousness. She had been dangerously close to some deep and comfortable sleep.

"Just squeeze my hand if I do that again, Kate. That will bring me around."

As dawn teased the valley into a new day, Mindy felt the quick, frightened tug three different times upon her hand. Each time she willed herself to force breath in and out of her weary body once again.

Carl stood beside her. "I'll not go to work today, Min. I'm going out to do the chores. Send Kate if you need me."

She opened her eyes and smiled. "I am so tired, Carl. I'm glad you'll be close by."

She roused a bit when he left, her mind clearing, her voice growing stronger. "Kate, you've had no breakfast. Go down and eat, tidy up the kitchen, and then rest awhile. I fear you've been awake most of the night."

"But what if you stop breathing again?"

"I feel stronger." She took Kate's hand. "You've been an excellent nurse, and I think your patient is on the mend. Now eat and rest, and a happy Sabbath to you."

When Kate had gone, Mindy lay watching the bright patch of blue sky framed by her slanting window. Would she ever see Stephen again? He had said it didn't matter.

There was all eternity. He was right, of course, but she longed for his quick bright smile, his assurance that she'd walk the earth again. "O Lord, take care of Ned. May Your stubborn love stalk him until he is Yours once more." She thought of Carl, of their sweet, young love, and the void which had come between them. Tears ran down her temples and onto the pillow. And finally her concern clustered about Kate. She could hear her in the kitchen below. Fifteen. Old enough to walk alone? She did not know. "I place her in Your hands, Lord." She realized suddenly she was not sure whether or not she trusted God with this task. Would He, there in His faroff kingdom, remember that one teenage girl walked alone down here and was yet unsure of whether or not she wished to pursue the ultimate relationship?

It was the test of a lifetime dedication to her faith. Either she trusted God to care for Kate, or she didn't. "Help me to believe. O God, take all my doubts away. Assure me that she is Your child. I give her to You."

With that commitment came a lovely peace, and she slept.

*　　*　　*　　*　　*

A half hour later the girl climbed the stairs and stood quietly in the doorway. She watched the white coverlet for a long moment. It did not rise or fall. Kate stood, head bowed, only the ticking of the clock breaking the stillness, then she ran for the barn.

"She is dead."

Carl turned, pitchfork in hand, at the sound of the girl's voice. "You are mistaken, Kate," he said firmly. They ran together through the bright November Sabbath toward her room.

He knelt at the bedside, touched Mindy's face, her hair, and groaned in an agony of his own.

"Too late!" he sobbed. "Too late!"

"Too late for what, Gramp?" the girl asked, her voice flat and strangely calm.

"To tell her I loved her. Oh, how *much* I loved her!"

The girl touched his white head with her fingertips but could find no words for his healing.